School begins with fire, chess, and girls—plenty of tinder for one year—but when Internet bullying morphs into a protection racket, the social order has just changed. What do you do when you discover the limits of your culture?

Devon parked his old junker car in front of the lake house then, and I was thinking how a jog around the lake would feel good. But Allen Mac, with his customary stranglehold on the obvious, had gotten bogged down in supplying an answer to Howie's non-question. If Howie says, "Any more bright ideas?" *you walk away.*

But this is what Allen Mac came up with. "Hey, Bessamer, you've got money. Hire a bodyguard."

Howie's jaw dropped. "I've got civil rights, same as you! Why should I have to buy protection when you've got civil rights to protect you?" *And then his fist came up. Fast and hard. Whacked Allen Mac in the head.* Thunk. *Howie literally dove for the door and ran off into the trees past the lake house.*

Also by Jean Stringam

The Cousin Cycle

How Not to Cry in Public & Other Victories – 2nd ed. launch!
Regrets Tree on Fire
Balance
The Hoarders

A Calgary Stampede Adventure

Riding on a Wish – Coming soon!
Solstice Magic

Christmas Far Away

Beyond the Polar Sea – Coming for the holidays!
Gathering the Wise Men

For your copy of **the original song**, "Regrets Tree on Fire," please go to
http://www.sheetmusicplus.com/title/19903943

For **exciting new updates**, visit the author's website at
http://JeanStringam.com

Please view the **publisher's website** at http://DollisonRoadBooks.com
for more information.

REGRETS TREE ON FIRE
The Cousin Cycle (Book 3)

Jean Stringam

Dollison Road Books

REGRETS TREE ON FIRE
The Cousin Cycle (Book 3)

Published by Dollison Road Books
www.DollisonRoadBooks.com

Cover image ©2013 Ben Hansen

Summary: When Internet bullying grows so big and ugly that a friend's life is on the line, loyalty demands more than chess, romance, and recreational fire can deliver.

ISBN 13: 978-0-9855540-7-1

Dollison Road Books
P.O. Box 1663
Provo, Utah 84603-1663
Published in the United States of America

Contents

To my family
Each one, every one

REGRETS TREE ON FIRE

One
To Disappear

If *I could have chosen* how to have my head sliced into slivers, my psyche stirred into a mash, and my heart splintered into fragments, maybe a year per event would have been reasonable. First big disaster: age 16—fallibility of the parental units. Second big disaster: age 17-caregiver tragedy. Third big disaster: age 18—loved and lost. Fourth big disaster: age 19—best friends . . . how should I put this? . . . best friends spin off . . .? Give me four years to do all that and I'd be twenty years old and ready to hit the adult world, tough and calculated.

I've got five minutes to hit the road, tough and traffic-savvy. I wring the water out of my red bandana and hang it from the back of my hat. Keeps the mosquitoes and deerflies off the back of my neck. I run my hand across my jaw line, feeling my new beard. I stopped shaving during final exams, which annoyed my mother. For a few weeks my beard didn't look too promising because of the sparse patches, but the hair around them has more or less grown over and filled it all in.

My friend Devon peers over top of me into the tiny mirror by the washbasin and I see him rubbing his jaw line, too. "Hey, Walker, I'm giving up the project."

"You'll be deer-fly bait." We're working as flaggers on a road construction crew located near the top of Mudd Mountain this summer. Good and boring. Just what I need.

"But look at this yellow fuzz!" Devon is blonde, so his beard isn't as dramatic as my dark one.

"Give it another week."

"It itches."

"Yeah, but not as bad as deer-fly bites."

"Okay, one more week. Where'd I put my STOP sign?"

I hand it to him. "Which end do you want?"

"Doesn't matter. You took the hike yesterday, so I'll take it today." He whacks me with his sign like it's a tennis racket.

I'm standing in front of a line of cars, a STOP sign in my hand, watching them pile up. Devon signals me on his two-way radio a quarter of a mile up the mountain that he's stopping his traffic flow, so I watch for the last vehicle to come through. Girl in a red sports car slowing down. She rolls down her window and smiles at me. I just stare at her wondering what she wants until she drives off. I signal Devon that I'm sending my line of vehicles through and does he know the girl in the red sports car? He doesn't, but he thinks she's pretty cute. I do, too.

We trade lines of traffic like that for a few hours. It's so perfectly boring that I love it. Devon and I have been friends for so many years that we practically think alike, so I don't ever have to second-guess him. Which means I can stand here and let the mountain sun beat down on me and not feel a thing inside. Exactly what I want.

I see it coming up the mountain from a mile away. It's this massive yellow Hummer. I'm trying to figure out if there's any way to keep some cars in front of him, but there isn't. He's got the road to himself and Devon's line of traffic has already started coming through. I hate this guy in the Hummer. He acts like my steel-toed boots are the stop line. It's not like I can give him a ticket for stopping two inches from my toes. I'm powerless and I know he gloats over it. I try to glare straight into his eyeballs through the front windshield, but he's looking off into the forest with a phone to his ear. I don't exist as far as he's concerned. I send the Hummer on through, glad when he's gone.

Nothing much happening on the mountain. I flex my knees and whip my arms around to ward off boredom. I study the trees and try to count the chipmunks chasing each other, except I'm probably counting them five times over. Then I run in and out of a line of orange barrels like I'm doing a giant slalom. Feels good. I call Devon on our ancient two-way technology. He doesn't have any traffic piled up either. A big forestry truck rumbles onto the road below me, and lumbers on down the mountain.

I try to keep my mind in neutral, but pretty soon I'm wondering if my dad would recognize his working-class son, the clothes, the beard. Haven't seen my parents all summer. They call pretty regularly, though. I'm the same height as my dad, I have the same cheekbones as his (but my mom's eyes), same dark curly hair as him, same shirt size, same . . . well . . . I'm wearing steel-toed boots and he's never owned a pair in his life. And last winter I learned that I don't think like my dad, either.

When he first brought up his vision of the ideal summer job for me, I told him no. That's not how I said it, to begin with, at least. I try to be diplomatic where I can. But I did say no. For two months I said no thanks every time he described his plans. Every time he asked me if I wouldn't rather be working at a job with a future, getting to know how a law office—his—works, I said, "Thanks for the offer, Dad. No." When he put on his scare-ya-ta-hell lawyer voice, I didn't back down. I stayed even and quiet and said *no thanks* for about the hundredth time. When he finally got it, when he finally heard me, it took him a few weeks to re-group and I could see him doing the internal work of it. He came out of it by telling me about a road construction company that was hiring a summer crew. Even gave me some names, which I appreciated.

To be honest, it still surprises me when I disagree with him. I'm not like Howie, my other close friend, who says the opposite of whatever his dad has just said. It grew into a habit with them and they hated each other for it. With my dad and me, it crept up on us kind of slowly. He was my North Star through the murky world of middle school. I used to believe my dad was dead-on when it came to people, moral obligations, right/wrong, seeing things through, getting to the bottom of an issue—all that kind of stuff. But I've learned you can get to the same right places from different directions.

This summer I needed distance. From him. From my friend Howie. After everything that happened last spring, I wanted to take some time off from life. I can't tell you how hard I wished for a way to sort of float for a while and not think or feel. Being a flagger for a road crew on the top of a mountain is pretty close to it. I'd have disappeared if I could, but not the way Howie did. Devon and I promised each other, never that way.

Two
Fire Worship

New Year's Eve at my house involved fire. Lots of fire. The fire celebration at the Walker house! We'd find a little old tree, stick it in a tin bucket full of sand, hang papers on it with our regrets written on them, and then light it on fire in the back yard. A Regrets Tree. For years, that moment of flaming constituted the apex of our pyro-lust.

In order to understand the full wonder of the Regrets Tree tradition on New Year's Eve in my family, you need to understand that Howie and Devon and I worshipped fire. Our interest in all things flaming grew exponentially with our ages, but you could really trace it back to elementary school. Devon's parents, both ER docs and ever sensitive to accidental death and dismemberment, gave the three of us long cautionary tales about boys with matches who caused grief and harm to those around them as well as to themselves.

I'm not sure whether the tales precipitated or exacerbated our pleasure in lighting books of matches, but whole boxes full of matches went up in flame whenever we had enough money accumulated to go to the grocery store and buy them. We had several match-lighting haunts, always on rocks or concrete and away from prying eyes. Somehow we managed to live through grade school without much more damage than a few scorched fingers and some suspicious holes in our clothes that couldn't have resulted from wear by elbows or knees.

We made some of our initial experiments in fire at Devon's house because of his ant problem. Well, it was really his parent's ant problem, but Devon was apparently the only one in the family who saw the ants as a problem.

Devon's house is as much of a scramble as Howie's and mine are images of order. You'd think ER docs would be super clean and tidy, but Devon's parents claim their professional lives require so much organization that they can't stand to keep it up once they hit their own house. They don't have any rules about picking up clothes or eating at the table or what goes where. They can hardly bear any routines at all, so whenever you get hungry you go to the 'fridge and forage, microwave your findings, and take it to your room. My dad says the only reason Devon has turned out to be *an upstanding young fellow* (Dad's very words) is because Devon has spent so much time at our house where the more important rules of appropriate conduct rubbed off on him.

Devon's parents are really worried about safety, though, and have all kinds of warnings for their children about which dangerous activities cause what percentages of the accidents they have to try and repair every day at work. In fact, a favorite good-bye from Devon's dad goes something like this. *Okay, Devon, you can spend the night on Bill's couch if you want, but remember that engaging in target practice by throwing chocolate peanuts at each other's mouths from across the room will result in 65% being dropped on the floor to roll under your feet and create a Slip & Fall hazard, and every one of the 35% remaining chocolate peanuts that happen*

to enter your mouths—*which in all likelihood is not much over 12%—well,
make that 20% because of good eye-hand coordination among teenagers—creates
the possibility and, in fact, the likelihood your chance of choking to death on an
inhaled chocolate covered peanut to be in the probable range of 80%.* That's the
way he talks. None of us has any idea where he gets all the numbers
he throws around. Devon thinks he plucks them out of the air for the
occasion.

So these ants at Devon's house were a constant problem. There
were different kinds of ants coming in from different directions and,
for all we could tell, for different reasons. The first invasion was by a
tiny kind of ant entering the casement of the window into Devon's
basement bedroom. A whole trail of them wound across the floor
and up the wall to his bookshelf. We looked them up on the Internet
and found out they were called 'sugar ants' because—*ta-dum!*—they
like to eat sugar. Devon kept a private stash of candy in his bedroom
in a brown sack in a little cubbyhole of half-shelves behind the
bedroom door where his parents wouldn't see it because the door
covered it up whenever they walked in to say something. The ants
knew exactly how to get into it.

We had a constant war with those ants. We stomped on them,
we sprayed them, and we trapped them. You'd have thought the
obvious solution would be to eat all the candy and—*bingo*—the ants
would give up and leave. We did lots to discourage them, but we
kept refilling the bag with more candy. We needed to fight them at
their own game and win. So Devon took a can of hairspray from his
mother's bathroom (she'd never miss it) and Howie took a cigarette
lighter from his dad's desk (he'd know it was gone immediately).
Howie had chosen minor pilfering that year as one of the grand
challenges of his family life. Our aim was to light the ants on fire as
they marched up the concrete wall into Devon's bedroom window.

It was a great blowtorch. The ants were definitely fried. For some reason the can didn't explode and amputate all of Devon's fingers, so it was a victory all around.

But then we noticed some long black ants—the semaphores of the ant nation—had made a detour of Devon's window and were heading up the side of the house into the window above. So we aimed the can of hair spray cum blowtorch a little higher until we thought we'd gotten them all. But then we realized that actually a big bunch of them disappeared under the siding of the house before they split into the lower and upper bedroom contingents. So, we aimed our hairspray blowtorch at an extreme angle to the house. The can still hadn't exploded and blinded us in both eyes, so we concentrated our firepower under the shingles where the paint was thickest. Perfect. We had a nice little blaze going that discouraged all ants above and below. They were falling by the hundreds. Success. Except that the paint had ignited. We had set the house on fire.

We extinguished our blowtorch and ran inside for pans of water to throw at the side of the house, which hissed and steamed for a good ten minutes. Then we stood back and took a look at what had happened. Not an ant in sight. Definitely success in the ant extermination department. But a rather large blackened area on the side of the house was very much in sight. Even a relatively unobservant adult (which definitely described both of Devon's parents) driving into the family garage would find it unmissable. We needed cover-up. So, we rummaged in the garage for the paint cans left over from the last time the house was painted. But whoever had done the job had been very organized about removing all leftover paint, which clearly meant neither Devon's father nor mother had undertaken the job.

We thought of nailing the blue plastic camping tarp on the side of the house, but it seemed a little conspicuous by dint of color. His parents might notice a brilliant swath of blue hammered into their house. Then we found the quintessential camouflage. A stray board. Devon mused on the existential qualities of the find. Who knows where it had come from or why it had been left in the garage?

Howie said, "Not new. Left behind when the house was built. Oviously."

Howie likes things to be logical. This, therefore That. He hates how life is This but not That, like you'd expect, and instead it's Something Else, which was impossible to see much less imagine. Devon told Howie he should use his imagination more, so life wouldn't be quite as hard on him. Howie punched him in the chest and stomped off.

I grabbed Howie by the arm to keep him with us and said, "In terms of camouflage, the length is exactly right and the width will do." I handed him the board. "Do it." Howie carefully leaned the board at the exactly necessary angle to cover all but the smoky edges of the blackened portion of the house. Success.

The board stood against the side of the house for about eight months. Devon propped it up at least once a week, he claimed, until the winds of winter blew it permanently into the mud. By the next spring his parents said they were thinking of having the house repainted. We thought we'd won the war of the ants.

When spring was over and the painters had left, however, we could see a very large variety of red ant had taken possession of the front steps to Devon's house. We suspected the nest was under the concrete steps because their path wound in two directions from there. One went around the left side of the steps into the base of a small hedge that abutted the house. The foliage was a nice dark green, but it had the wickedest thorns possible. Behind it was the only window of Devon's bedroom large enough to crawl out of in case of a house fire or some other emergency.

The second ant trail went across the right side of the steps into the edge of the front door where they entered and then disappeared. We couldn't find a trace of them inside the house. This did not mean the ants weren't in the house, only that we couldn't see them, which caused us more alarm than you can imagine and resulted in Devon moving into my bedroom. His parents weren't aware of his evacuation because he still spent a relatively large amount of daylight time at home since my house involved a lot of regulations he wasn't used to.

As we surveyed the second column of red ants entering his house and reasoned out the possibilities together, Devon and Howie and I concluded the ants were going straight into either the floor or the walls or both. That possibility sent us into complete frenzies of ant extermination.

The solution had to reside in greater firepower. We found what we needed after more rummaging in Devon's garage. A whole gorgeous box full of fireworks. They didn't look like anything that was legal where we lived. Devon started to speculate on who had purchased them. Which parent was the pyro fiend? When? Why? Did they remember the cache still existed? Did they have plans for it? Howie and I just kind of stood around in awe at the implications of the discovery.

Then we got busy. Devon produced a wad of old cotton socks. We stuffed them with the fireworks and tied it all together with string, soaked it in a little gasoline, and carefully positioned it under the front steps. From there we poured a small gasoline trail to the corner of the garage where we planned to light the match.

We knew we had the ticket to complete ant extermination. Peoples of the planet would thank us. Our names would be held up as examples of ingenuity in the great international battle of man versus ant. We could imagine the nest bursting apart in the air and all the sizzled ants raining down as we three conquerors cheered.

Devon lit the match. It was his house and he claimed the privilege by right. Fortunately, as he threw it, we all had enough sense to run. One second later the front steps no longer existed. At least in a recognizable form. The bang brought out all the neighbors on either side of the street. When we saw this, Howie and I hoofed it in the direction of my house and Devon dove into his open bedroom window through the briar hedge.

Devon's parents came rushing out of the house about then and after surveying the damage for about thirty seconds, wondering how in the world such an attack could have happened in their quiet neighborhood, some sort of parental light bulb went off and they started calling for Devon. They were fairly authoritative yellers when aroused and Howie and I could hear them clear down at my end of the block. Among other things, they promised to come down the stairs and haul Devon out of his basement lair if he didn't show himself immediately.

Howie and I found the goings-on to be completely riveting and sneaked back towards Devon's house, hedge by hedge. We saw Devon emerge with a meekness he's not exhibited again since that day. His parents reacted very dramatically to the sight of their son, dripping blood from streaks of red all over the exposed skin of his body. They immediately went into triage mode and the entire neighborhood got a preview of what might happen to them if they appeared in Devon's parent's Emergency Room dripping blood. Howie and I found the proceedings very interesting.

All the thorn damage pretty much deflected Devon's parents' wrath. They focused all of their energy straight onto flowing blood, not Devon's culpability. Devon looked very pitiful for the next month or so as the scar tracery on his skin from the thorn hedge healed. I looked the other day, and the scars are pretty much gone now.

The explosion backfired in another way, though. We three were not accorded the merit award for being world-class ant-exterminators as we expected. The event brought down such infamy upon our names that for several years we were known widely in the neighborhood as budding arsonists and potential delinquents. On the good side, however, Devon's house got attractive new front steps and the ants left.

About this time Devon and Howie and I also developed a preoccupation with vulgarity. One day after we'd been playing chess way too long, we got the idea to explore our budding notions of unacceptable language by writing down all the really bad words we could think of. We were in Devon's exceptionally trashed bedroom and very bored because we had gotten the idea, somehow, that the chess greats only made excruciatingly deliberate chess moves. Instead of trying to intimidate each other with speed, we'd slowed ourselves down to a trawling tempo, which left us with all kinds of vacant time to add to the list of forbidden words.

Just before it was time for Howie and me to leave, Howie said, "Hey, Devon. Go up to your parent's office. They've got a paper shredder up there."

"So?"

"You've got to feed our bad-words list through the shredder."

"What for?"

"What if somebody finds it?"

"Who?" Devon had been the sole cleaner of his room for several years by then and couldn't imagine a parental toe dipping into the debris on the floor. He liked it that way.

"Our parents, dork!" Howie said.

Devon said he wouldn't do it. There was no need to, and besides, his parents were home. Howie said Devon had to completely destroy the list. Otherwise, the possibility would remain for Howie to get in bad trouble at home for a list that gross. The evidence must not continue to exist in any form.

Devon said he wasn't going to risk wrath needlessly. He scrunched up the list into a ball of paper, threw it on top of an already full wastebasket, and struck a match to the wad of words. Devon thought he'd solved the problem. Except that everything in the basket caught fire. The wastebasket itself was plastic and melted, and the whole fiery mess started leaking all over the carpet. Before his bedroom burst into flames, we grabbed the fire extinguisher his parents (ever prepared for accidents) had hung by the furnace, and doused the fire.

As you've probably deduced, Devon's room was destroyed most of the time. His parents didn't even try to fix it up anymore. The rest of the house was really nice under the clutter, but Devon's room was a total disaster under the clutter. That didn't prevent us from spending a lot of time in it.

This one day we were at his house trying to put together a science project. We had made two different plans already. But each time we were totally organized to go ahead with the project, Howie would say it was stupid, it had already been done, and we'd have to find something totally original. Well, what's original for three kids in middle school to do?

When we harassed my parents for ideas, they had us hunting around on the Internet and doing research in the school library, which got tedious. Howie claimed he could envision a project involving radioactivity that would win first place, so we tried asking Devon's parents where to start on it. They said we had to memorize the Periodic Table of Elements first. We stopped asking Devon's parents for advice. But then we discovered this movie star about our age who could sing the Periodic Table. Yeah, weird but cool . . . so if he could sing it, we could at least memorize it. Still, Howie's project would never fall within the school-imposed budget limitations even if we could figure out what the science was.

Every once in a while we'd have a breakthrough and get going on something sort of original, but this particular year, things weren't going very well. Howie had just said the current project was stupid and wouldn't work. Devon and I were mad at him because we were out of time and couldn't start over. So, we locked Howie in Devon's room while we went to the store to buy the supplies to do the project anyway.

We didn't hate him or anything, we were just sick of him. We figured that if we went to the store without him, he'd have to go along with what we'd planned because all our money would be spent. Each group in the class had a strict budget and had to produce the receipts. If you went even a penny over-budget, the mark for the project was dropped a letter grade, and then one more letter grade for each dollar after that.

We were on our way home carrying two huge bags of materials when, just as we got to the front door, we heard this terrible crash. It practically made the house shudder. Dropping our bags, we raced down the stairs to see what had happened. We found Howie in a heap on the floor, the electric wiring from the light fixture wound around his neck, the fixture broken, and yards of wiring pulled out of the ceiling with chunks of dry wall scattered all over the place.

Devon and I unwound him, thankfully without electrocuting ourselves and before Howie turned blue. Devon's parents were on a twenty-four hour shift at the hospital and Devon figured if he could get a fix-it guy to come to the house soon enough, we could take care of the hole in the ceiling before his parents got involved in the problem. Devon can be persuasively urgent when he needs action. So Bert, the handyman who had painted the house the year before, showed up about a half-hour later.

He stood in the middle of the bedroom looking at the disaster for a while. We were standing around watching him, hoping he'd get out his tools and start fixing things right away. He took off his cap and scratched a bit, and then said, "Hey, you guys think you're monkeys or something?" We didn't think his joke was funny, but he didn't leave it there. He looked around at each of us and said, "Swinging through the tree tops were you?"

Devon figured he'd better go along with the current humor—we needed help bad—so he laughed and said, "Something like that," and looked at Howie. Actually we both did. Why would Howie do a thing like that? We hadn't even been gone to the store that long.

Devon said, "Are you going to start on the ceiling?"

Bert said, "Where else? While I'm at it, how about if I put up some monkey bars for you guys to hang on?"

Devon said, "No way, man."

Bert laughed.

When Devon and I talked about it later, it might have been a lot of fun to have a series of handlebars across his ceiling to swing from. But the thought of Howie hanging with an electric cord around his neck from something as substantial as steel monkey bars was pretty horrifying.

It took Bert a couple of days. He patched and taped and painted and sealed and even re-carpeted. Devon's room looked better than it had in the last five years. Later, I asked Devon if he'd gotten in trouble with his parents for the bedroom ceiling disaster. He smiled and laid his arm across my shoulders and said how glad his parents were he'd had the presence of mind to take care of the problem himself. I couldn't believe it! My parents would have had a fit. "You're joking!"

We were still practicing our early version of bad language, so after Devon finished with a few expletives, he said, "All I got out of it was how glad they were my disaster of a room was cleaned up. Something about a pro-active approach to the basement dungeon."

For a little while Devon and I were careful with ol' Howie. We didn't argue with him as hard as we used to and we never locked him in a room again. But we were pretty self-centered, you know, and after a little while things pretty much got back to normal. That's one of my regrets, but I keep it to myself.

Three
Almost Popular

Last fall when we lined up all our new classes at the start of school, the first thing to smack us in the face was when our AP English teacher said we were going to spend the first month or so on *The Tragedy of Romeo and Juliet* by William Shakespeare. Even if you lived in a non-English speaking part of the world and had never heard of the play before, just the name tells you what's going to happen. Boy, girl, ends badly. There. Said and done. I didn't figure it was information I needed right then. I wanted to know how to have success with a girl.

Devon, across the aisle from me, was looking fairly pleased about things. "A school course on love. Guess that about balances out having to take a school course on sex." He was talking about the new sex ed teacher. *Groan.*

The Shakespeare teacher, Ms. Carmangay, was young and pretty and everybody in the class wanted to please her. She explained that this term we would all learn how to walk and talk at the same time. Everybody kind of laughed because it seemed so obvious. But she went on to explain that walking around while we were speaking the lines, like actors do, was actually quite difficult.

I didn't care if it was. What she had just described meant we weren't going to have to listen to each other drone on in this kind of Bible language followed by horrible work sheets like when we studied *Hamlet* in ninth grade. This year we'd get to stumble around on our feet doing love scenes. Fine with me.

Right off Ms. Carmangay lined the class up in two lines facing each other to shout Shakespearean insults. Things like, "Thou mammering guts-griping malt-worm!" or "Thou pribbling unchin-snouted whey-face!" or "Thou puking milk-livered varlet!" After we got fairly comfortable with that, she changed things up and gave each person a different list with three categories of words that made up the insult. You could read straight across, or you could change them around however you wanted. Since there were four lines on the paper, you had four different opportunities to throw out a line. Once you'd used up all your insults, you had to step back out of the line.

We got to scream, "Thou gleeking crook-pated clotpole!" at the top of our lungs to anybody we wanted to. I thought it was fairly cathartic. Well, actually, I loved it. Everybody loved it. For the rest of the Shakespeare unit we insulted each other before class, during class, and after class. Ms. Carmangay let every insult pass as long as it was inventive and heart-felt.

The insults were fascinating to watch. Devon would insult somebody, exquisitely tailoring the insult to their real-life flaws, then put his arm along the top of their shoulders and smile down at them and suddenly the whole thing transformed into a love scene. When I insulted somebody, I could feel the rhythm of the words in my mouth, like I could almost taste them. For me, it was process rather than result. Howie put his whole bulldog soul into it.

18

After he insulted somebody, they'd have to reach for a bandage to staunch the flow of blood.

So anyway, after we'd been creatively insulting each other for a couple of weeks in AP English, Ms. Carmangay came to class clutching a whole forest of wood sticks. We were to think of them as swords, these three-foot lengths of half-inch wooden doweling, and were to group ourselves into threes: two to duel, one to keep it fair and safe. Howie went after the sword fighting like he could really arm himself against all comers.

Here's the irony of it. I know these guys, and I fully expected Devon to love the love scenes and Howie to love the sword fights. Turns out Devon was awfully good at playing Mercutio who gets killed in the swordfight in the first act, and Howie actually became lyrical over the romantic lines in the balcony scene in the third act. It was like both of them got to address a part of themselves they weren't used to exposing. I'd swear that Devon has never thought about death once in his life, well, except for when Howie brings it up. But usually Howie saves all those kinds of ponderings for me. Yeah, lucky me.

Since words pour effortlessly out of Devon all day long anyway, the clever things Mercutio says when he's dying were totally believable coming from Devon. Then there was Howie, who had never actually spoken to a girl outside of a class assignment or a chess competition since sixth grade. Here he was on his knees declaring undying love to Juliet with more feeling than I knew existed in his gruff old body.

Makes you wonder about casting against type. After all, what teacher (or parent) can accurately guess the internal life of a student when all they have to go on is the exterior? Here's proof. I got cast as the Prince, the peacemaker, because I'm tall and people think of me as being calm, which is absurd. They have no idea what's going on inside of me.

I was half desperate to get to do Romeo's lines, so I memorized them while I was listening to Howie and giving him his cues. Howie learned his lines plenty fast, but he wanted to try them over and over again with all kinds of different actions. Devon, on the other hand, wasn't interested in rehearsing a hundred different ways of blocking a scene. He wanted to do it all on the fly. Mercutio's speeches were long and full of imagery, but after looking at them for about ten minutes Devon could spin them off, laughing and dying at the same time.

Ms. Carmangay said our Shakespeare class was doing so well with the scenes that she had organized a special evening presentation for parents and students from other classes. I figured it was one of those school activities you could conveniently forget to tell your parents about. But Lanny, my little sister, seemed bent on advertising the event to half the city.

Casting was partly by class vote, and Howie got voted to do several of the Romeo scenes. I think that was the first time I can ever remember his parents coming to a school event together. Occasionally his mother would show up, or not, but this time they were both there. The Shakespeare excerpts were on the same night as Howie's birthday and his parents invited Devon, Allen, and me to go to a restaurant with them afterwards, another first. All the time I'd ever known Howie, this was about the first time his parents had acknowledged our existence. It had always been Miss Denise who looked out for us.

As we were waiting to be served, we talked about the scenes and who did what and the close call in the sword fight between Tybalt and Mercutio when Devon slipped. I told Howie I thought his scenes with Juliet were about the best ones of the evening, and Devon said, "Good job tonight, Howie." Allen Mac gave Howie a little jab and said, "Cool, dude. Juliet's hot!" Howie had this big, open grin on his face after that, looking from his mom to his dad and back.

I saw Mrs. Bessamer smile a little at Howie, who immediately became absorbed in staring at the white linen tablecloth. And then Mr. Bessamer cut in with, "Thought it was going to be something worth my time."

I have to say the comment kind of took the wind out of me. I glanced at Howie. He was staring straight at his dad, face set, his voice sarcastic. "No business contacts in a high school auditorium, Dad? Imagine."

"Always thought it was wimps and fags who strutted around on stage like that." Even Devon was speechless after that one, since he and I had both been on stage in the scenes. Mr. Bessamer had complete silence at the table to fill, so he turned to Allen Mac. "Notice you weren't up there fartin' around. So how come you hang with these three?"

Allen Mac was pulling air, opening and closing his mouth, staring from Devon and me back to Howie. Finally he croaked, "We get extra points for attending," and his voice jumped up an octave and cracked.

Mr. Bessamer looked him over and said, "Keep your hormones under control there, kid. I'm just sayin'."

Mrs. Bessamer said, "Howard, remember your early morning conference call? It's a big account. A lot is riding on it."

"So?"

She got a little taller in her chair. "So, I'll drive the boys home."

Mr. Bessamer glared at her and stomped out of the restaurant without another word. He took a lot of the air in the room with him and it took a few minutes for us to recover. Devon and I both tried to make conversation, but Howie sat there like he was made of stone.

Wouldn't touch a bite. Allen Mac offered to eat Howie's order on top of his own, and then did.

I thought maybe a little gift giving might help save the party, so I pulled mine out of my backpack and laid it on the table. It was an old chess book with a scrubby leather binding I'd found on the throwaway table at the front of the school library. The librarian had said it was a real doozer from somebody's estate that the inheritors wanted to get rid of. I had smiled at him and said, "One man's trash is another man's treasure," which is one of those little aphorisms certain adults enjoy. The book was a chess classic in Russian, but you could tell what was going on by the diagrams. I guessed right. Howie studied it for a few minutes, flipping through the pages, and he almost smiled. "Strategy!"

Devon gave him a bottle of decent after-shave. Howie doesn't have very acute nostrils, or something. He'd wear the worst stinky stuff until Devon or I threw it out. Allen Mac said he'd forgotten it was Howie's birthday and would get back to him. Allen spends his money on himself and has never come through with a birthday gift for any of us since his mother stopped buying them in eighth grade. Howie didn't have any expectations to dash.

We all kind of hunkered down, waiting for what his mother would produce. I hoped with every corpuscle in me that it would be a family gift—tickets to a game or a trip somewhere, something a little bit interactive anyway. When she placed the little package on the table, everybody knew what it was just from the shape. Once again, a gift of the newest communication technology under the sun, something Mr. Bessamer got free at work.

His mother had the gall to smile and say, "So we can check up on you 24/7." The smile looked like such a strain on her, it might crack her face. Devon and I knew for a fact that only Miss Denise, their daytime housekeeper, ever checked up on Howie.

The day after the Shakespeare scenes, Howie was almost popular. But he didn't know what to do with it. He didn't relax and glow like Devon did when somebody said he'd been great as Mercutio. When someone complimented Howie on his Romeo performance, he'd look down at the floor and say, "Yeah, well, not bad for somebody with a broken leg." Then the person would look down at Howie's leg and see it wasn't broken, and wouldn't know what to say after that. By noon his celebrity status had worn off.

But when we got to AP English, Ms. Carmangay was rhapsodic, and Howie was popular again for about ten minutes. She said Howie was brilliant. Howie was intuitive. Howie was the perfect Romeo because he epitomized the passionate hope of the naïve. Then none of us were sure it was a compliment, and Howie's popularity waned again.

Ms. Carmangay loved Shakespeare and said so every day. She said the person she most wanted to meet when she died was Shakespeare. She said if she could just attend a season of his plays at the Globe Theatre re-creation on the Southbank of the Thames River in London, she could die a happy woman. Devon whispered under his breath, "Simple woman; simple needs."

Howie said, "Wish I could say the same for me."

I hate listening to all Howie's self-absorbed death wishes, so I said, "Won't work since you're not a woman," which I realized was fairly lame. Howie snorted and glared and I got out of his way.

Everybody in the class wanted to be at the Globe like Ms. Carmangay did. We imagined absorbing Shakespeare with the very pores of our skin like she did. By the end of the term, our entire class came to hold the group ambition of attending the Globe Theatre.

Actually, it lasted long after class ended (well, by at least half an hour). Nobody could have guessed who'd be the first one of us to get there.

So, this one day a substitute teacher walked in and started handing around work sheets. The whole class groaned. Except for Howie who was busy checking text messages. Sometimes teachers get so sick of crabbing about hand-held devices that they pretend they don't see what you're doing, which is what must have been happening in Howie's case. He's never subtle. I could see the blue-metal gleam of the very newest technology. Howie's dad didn't deliver where it counted, but he did deliver every state of the art electronic gadget as it came on the market at his work. Howie turned to look out the window, enough so I could see his face. It was dark, really dark. After class I thumped him on the arm and said, "Hey, you get a message in class, or something?"

"Yeah."

"What about?"

"Somebody wants me to know how stupid I am."

"Battle of the IQs again." All during elementary school kids had wanted to test themselves against Howie's skills. He could remember facts like nobody else. I didn't think he always knew what to do with the facts, but he could quote you information like he was an Internet site himself.

"No. As in stupid stupid."

"Ignore him."

"He wants me dead."

Devon said, "That's serious stuff. Let me see the message."

Howie flipped through to a group of messages he'd isolated. Devon and I put our heads together over this piece of the most gorgeous technology we'd ever seen and read some of the worst hate mail you could ever read. "Who's writing that crap?"

"How would I know?"

Devon asked, "How long has it been going on?"

"A while."

"Be specific," I demanded, channeling my dad.

"Since summer holidays began."

He hadn't even told us. It made me sad and angry at the same time. "How often?"

"Every day."

"Same person all the time?"

"Can't tell."

"Anybody you know? Anyone from school?"

Howie shrugged. "Hope not."

It would be one thing if someone just happened on your number and decided to make your life hell for the sheer meanness of it. But it would be way worse if it was somebody you knew, that you saw every day.

"What a waste of technology," Devon sighed. "What do your parents say about this?"

Howie gave him a glare that said, *you are so completely stupid I can't believe you said that!*

"You're good with electronics, "I said, "There's gotta be some way to block this kind of shit."

"Yeah, I went to the IT guys at my dad's office when he was out of town, and they showed me some tricks. Seems to work for a while, but the network of calls is getting bigger. I have to find new firewall manipulations every couple of weeks."

I looked at Devon in amazement. We were Howie's two best friends, it had been going on four months, and he hadn't told us. I wanted to deck him.

Devon said, "Just turn it off for a couple of months. They'll stop if you don't engage with them." Howie shook his head.

I agreed with Devon. "I don't think there's any other way, Howie. Turn it off. Cancel your Internet connection. Don't give the perverts any satisfaction."

Howie went into his bulldog stance, feet a little too far apart, and his face took on that made-of-stone look he gets. "No Internet access? You'd never do that. Besides, my parents want me available 24/7."

I think Howie wanted his parents to get in touch with him so bad he'd have been willing to walk through fire all day long just in case his parents might have something to say to him. I don't know of a single time they ever did, though. At least not until last spring, which was their last chance.

I'd give almost anything to have known the end from the beginning, what all the cyber-bullying was going to amount to. Maybe I could have done something different, changed something about myself that would have made a difference. But lives don't work that way, no matter how many regrets we might have.

Four
The Code

Sometimes kids at school would make a sarcastic comment about me being friends with a loser like Howie. They didn't understand loyalty or how that shapes your thinking. I had to stifle the urge to punch the kids that ragged on Howie, but at the same time it made me wonder where my loyalty came from. It's not like I gain anything by it. But when I think about walking away from him—like when he's being himself and ignoring other people's opinions and I can't stand him anymore—even then I know I'd lose a lot. My integrity, maybe.

Howie was confrontational with me, unrelenting with Devon, but hardest on himself. He made no excuses, gave himself no credit. If I could have rolled him into Allen Mac so they'd be half of each other, maybe Allen's self-congratulation and Howie's brutal honesty would have made two enjoyable friends.

The thing about Howie is that he resists. Everything. Even when we were little kids, his legs were locked in a braking posture half the time. Suppose the three of us were at my grandparents' lake house and Devon and I decided to catch frogs in the shallows and then organize a frog-leaping race. Howie would say the true test of skill was to race dragonflies. Well, you can't race dragonflies. They have their own set flight pattern and that's it, round and round in great big looping circles. They don't think in straight lines. Neither do frogs, but you can get a forward trajectory out of their hopping by using rearward scare tactics. Still, it would take up half our morning arguing Howie out of the dragonfly racing.

I lived with my grandparents when I was little, but ever since I came back home to live, Howie and Devon have been my two best friends. We were in and out of each other's houses all through elementary and middle school. The housekeeper, Miss Denise, would invite us into her kitchen for after school treats. Afterwards, we'd fool around upstairs in Howie's huge bedroom that contained every toy and electronic gaming device in the known universe.

About five minutes before the first parent was scheduled to come home, Miss Denise would send Devon and I packing. The neighbor's yard had a lot of tall trees in a clump, so Devon and I would stall there for a few minutes, waiting for Miss Denise, until one of the Bessamer cars approached. They always drove separately and walked around to the front door. After the first parent arrived, Miss Denise would leave by the kitchen door and catch the bus two blocks away, and sometimes Devon and I waited with her until the bus came. If we looked back at the house, Howie was usually watching the three of us from his bedroom window.

He's super smart and an ace chess player, but the rest of him is a trial. Sometimes Devon and I would get sick of him and tell him to get lost. Here's a classic Howie argument. *Weekends and holidays are designed to destroy families because they pose unreasonable expectations for family togetherness.* Maybe it was a perverse way to justify his parent's lack of interest in parenting, or maybe he was practicing how to be as cranky as they were, but it sure wasn't how Devon's and my family's worked.

Growing up, I saw my parents as very close. They acted the loving couple with each other and I thought it was completely natural when Devon's parents were the same way. It came as a recurring surprise to me to discover how much Howie's parents actively disliked each other. I didn't know what to do with that information at first. It more or less re-arranged my universe. It was no secret to Howie, that's for sure, and he was openly sarcastic about the stupidity of them staying together to try to be a family for his sake. A few years ago, his father had had an affair with another woman, so then his mother had an affair to keep things even. They tried to patch things over for Howie's sake, but the patchwork had gaping holes in it—holes where the love used to be. Howie said over and over again how he wished they'd get honest, get divorced, move on, make him a statistic.

Devon's parents had hospital shifts that kept them at work on a lot of weekends and holidays, but they had season tickets to the theatre for the whole family and believed taco salad was the basic comfort food. His parents may have had a limited repertoire in the kitchen, but they could discuss just about anything you wanted to talk about. I mean, they're sort of like living with Google Search, live and prowling your house. Most covetable of all, his family went to London every summer to visit grandparents. I told Devon they should adopt me so I could go, too. He asked his mom, and she said she was willing. Sometimes I like to be at his house just to get a fresh breath about how relationships can be. It's fun to watch his mom and dad joking around with each other in ways mine never do.

My parents are way more intense with each other, more deliberate about what they do and say. They generally reserve weekends for family activities, but are pretty good about letting me invite friends. They say it's because my two younger sisters have each other, but I don't have anyone. Actually, I think they still feel guilty for shipping me off to my grandparents for all those years. Maybe that gives them something to write on those little pieces of paper we hang on our New Year Regrets Tree every year.

Howie had developed no optimism about girls, and for me the jury was still out, but Devon had grown up with parents who were best friends. Maybe that was why he took it so hard this year when our high school hired this over-eager teacher for the Human Sexuality unit. She was a substantial woman about six feet tall with coarse black hair to the shoulders, who thought we were all dying to know the details of her sex life. Most of us were grossed out when she announced that no man had ever completely satisfied her. As if anybody could. I mean she wanted to be rich, she wanted to be famous, she wanted to be beautiful. And none of that was ever going to happen to her. Didn't make a whole lot of sense to think a few minutes of sex would make up that kind of deficit.

She had this wooden box with a lock and key on it and we were supposed to write down anonymously all our questions and sexual fantasies. It got worse. She started a First Time segment. The first time you have sex you're supposed to tell this gross, awful woman about it? She had about as much sensitivity as the wooden box.

Some of the boys in my class invented incredible stories to stuff in her box. I think they got them off porn sites, actually. Well, she just about went ballistic with jubilation whenever she'd get one of these gross little nuggets and would bring them to class, her lips practically trembling with anticipation. She'd read them out as being what somebody in the class really experienced or really wanted to know about. It was so awful. We'd just groan and slide down in our seats and try to put our minds somewhere else.

At least that's what Devon and Howie and I did. We made a pact never to take anything Witch Hazel said in class out of the class with us. Yeah, her first name was Hazel. She wanted us to be real comfortable with her and on a first name basis. Invited us to call her Ms. Hazel. We felt pretty familiar with her after we'd called her Witch Hazel Porn for a few weeks. Of course, not to her face.

Devon had taken to wearing this puke-green shirt that was about a hundred sizes too big for him and made his skin look like an extreme case of jaundice. Not just once a week. He wore it every day, so we could follow all its stages from clean down to filthy. We asked him where he'd found this fashion item and he named a big & tall store on the edge of the city biking limit our parents had imposed on us when we were ten. Did we want to come shopping with him some time?

NO.

I was completely into not paying attention in Witch Hazel Porn's class, but I'd more or less wake up from my self-induced stupor for the rest of my classes. Apparently Devon didn't. Ms. Hendrickson, the math teacher, was used to Devon being an A-student and objected to his daydreaming in her class. When she confronted him with it, Devon admitted his body was in class but his mind was definitely elsewhere. She wanted to make her point, so she said, "Daydreaming may be pleasant, but it has very little to do with true accomplishment in life."

Devon told us later, "I didn't want to destroy her narrow world-view, call her into any kind of a crisis over contemplative thought being necessary to creativity. I said I was less caught up in a daydream than a kind of Post Script to life."

"What's that?" Howie wanted to know. "Some kind of new theory about the after-life?"

Howie was fascinated with the possibilities of death and the after-life and wanted to talk about it constantly. We'd already gone the rounds as to what extent the earth was an open or a closed system. This had included frequent trips to the nasa.gov site where it says about 3,000 metric tons of space stuff hits earth daily, which obviously kills the closed-system argument. I said the principle allowed for the same thing to be true as far as God's involvement with the Earth, but Howie claimed there was no evidence that they were parallel phenomenon.

After that science project episode where Devon's parents told us to memorize the Periodic Table of the Elements, I took another aim at destroying the closed-system theory. I said that the principle of half-life in the exponential decay of an element was proof-positive there was an after-life. Nothing, once created, ever ceased to exist. If the elements of our bodies continue to exist on and on, why couldn't our souls? They were made up of matter, too, but matter more refined than current science is able to measure. Maybe spirit matter is too refined to be subject to decay of any sort, at least not in the same way our bodies are.

Howie acted like I was more or less making it all up. Said I didn't have a clue about the science behind it. He was partly right, I guess, because I don't know how to apply physics to the human experience. But he was partly wrong to shoot down an interesting way to think before he knew any more science than I did. Maybe I'll have to major in physics at university, (anything that isn't law, since my dad's a lawyer). I'd really like to explore the idea of spirit matter.

Anyway, Devon snorted at Howie's question about whether a Post Script to life had to do with the after-life. "You dorks. It stands for P.S. As in a Pecker Salute."

"What?" I got the image clear enough, but the idea of straight arrow Devon coming up with something like that caught me by surprise.

"You heard me," he said laughing until he doubled over.

Later, Howie and I got him cornered over poker-chess (I'll tell you about that later) and told him he had to tell us what was going on. Flunking out of school wasn't cool any way you looked at it. This is what he said: "Witch Hazel Porn said something that caught my attention. Yeah, I know, I exhibited total lack of self-discipline to tune-in to her drivel. But she claimed it was considered normal for a boy our age to have an erection that lasted many hours, even all day. That kind of snagged my attention. You can see how."

Devon had kind of snagged my attention with that fact, if it was one. "You've got to be joking," I said.

"So I tried it out."

"How?" Howie asked.

"Easy. You just start thinking of certain things and keep it up all day. (Pun intended.)"

"That's not a pun," Howie said, and Devon flipped him off. "Like what?" Howie pursued.

"Hey, I'm not giving you a list, man," and Devon cracked up. "Witch Hazel Porn has already done that, so don't get all wide-eyed and innocent. But then you guys don't pay attention in class."

I couldn't imagine doing it all day long at school. "You've got to be joking."

Devon looked a little offended. I could see his point. It was like being told your A in Human Sexuality wasn't as important as your A in Chess. Howie and I shut up and stared.

Devon went on, "So then you do it the next day. And the next. The trick is what to think about when all the stuff Witch Hazel Porn talks about starts getting boring."

Howie was disgusted. "You spent three weeks of your life on that!"

Devon shrugged. "Somebody has to do the tough research!"

So. That's how we began using the term P.S. for something quite different from the usual meaning, which is the forgotten information included after the signature on a formal letter. A very useful name, I might add. It didn't matter how openly we used the abbreviation, nobody ever caught on. Howie had a preoccupation with the whole cheerleading squad that fall and would give us a signal if one of the cuter ones walked by. P.S. 3 meant she was a candidate for a three-hour Pecker Salute. Really dumpy girls could be a P.S. point 001 or something like that.

It was all stupid and disgusting and fairly interesting. Like what use was it to invoke all that testosterone when you're a teenager with undeveloped muscle mass and the girls weren't exactly thronging around? To be absolutely honest, we all knew the coding wasn't a real mark. What you think about is what matters, not how sexy the girl is. But the term was exclusive to us, and there's something bonding about exclusivity. You hope you're not going to be a limp mush-head your whole life, but you don't see yourself well enough to see your strong points. Then you run across something that sets you and your friends apart. Well, the P.S. code might not have been fair to the girls or accurate for us, but we thought it was wildly interesting for a little while.

Anyway, apparently all Devon's other teachers had made the same complaint about his inattentiveness. The teachers claimed Devon had stopped answering questions in class, had done no homework since the term began, and had failed every quiz, test, and exam so far that fall. He was flunking out of eleventh grade and he'd only been enrolled a couple of months. I didn't want to even think about how miserable school would be if Devon got himself kicked out.

His parents were called in.

I hovered around the main office until I saw them leave. Everybody looked surprisingly cheerful. "So what happened?" I asked Devon.

"I told them I was involved in a Post-Scripted event that was a fairly private matter, but I'd make sure I paid attention in school and did my home work from now on if they would please allow me to continue to attend."

I didn't have a clue what he meant, so that night over chess I asked him, "How'd you get your parents on your side?"

"They asked me some questions, and I was honest."

"Questions about Witch Hazel Porn?"

"Yeah, whether her ideas were news to me, or if it was stuff I'd heard before. So I told them about what I'd seen on the street in Amsterdam."

"What are you talking about?"

"I was twelve and we were on our way to visit my grandparents in England like we do every summer. My parents found some cheap tickets routing us through Amsterdam, so we took a roundabout route with a layover. It happened right before we got on the canal boat for a tour of the city. A sheet of paper lying on the sidewalk, a porn flyer. I picked it up and studied it for a little while, then hid it in my suitcase the rest of the vacation. I don't know what happened to it after that, but when I was sitting in Witch Hazel's class all those same feelings started again."

I didn't want a conversation with my parents like that. Ever. "So what did they say?"

"My dad said that in regards to pornography our culture is past prevention."

"Meaning?"

"That it's everywhere. Porn is unavoidable because our culture is saturated with it. Even picture books for little kids have images to get them hooked, but disguised, you know."

I hadn't really thought about it before. Pornography was something perverts did in the dark somewhere else, nothing to do with my life. I didn't know what to say.

"Porn is poison, Bill. That's the only way to describe it."

"Why? I mean it's a waste of time and everything, but poison?"

"Poison sickens and kills. Pornography does the same thing to your ability for a beautiful sexual relationship."

I was at a complete loss here. I'd never had a girlfriend and I didn't know all that much about sex, not really. Worse, I felt completely uncomfortable even talking about pornography. Not that I was doing the talking, but I wished my best friend would move on to a subject I liked better.

"My parents said they'd been aware of what was happening in our culture, alert and careful, but still a son of theirs got hooked on it. I told them I was definitely not hooked."

"Aren't you?"

"I refuse to be. Pornography isn't something I ever chose. It just happened to me."

"So can you get cured . . . maybe that's not what you call it . . . like can you stop thinking that way?"

"My parents think the first step is to get me out of Witch Hazel Porn's class. They told the principal she treats the sex ed class like pornography, not health science."

"What!"

"Sorry, Bill, but I'm outta there. My parents told the school that since they are both M.D.s, they'll teach me the Human Sexuality unit at home."

"No way I'm going to that class if you don't. Would your parents take me on, too?"

"Probably."

"I'll take any exam they throw at us, so long as I don't have to sit through Witch Hazel Porn's class ever again."

"Teaching two shouldn't be much different than teaching one. Will your parents agree to it?"

"They'll have to."

Lunch break was over then, and we had to get to our next class. I started to think about how I treated porn. I thought of myself as being above it. I had tried my hardest to think about other stuff in class. But how much had leaked into me? Maybe I was contaminated without knowing it or choosing it.

Five
Hate Mail

Devon asked his parents if they'd teach three boys instead of one. When they finally agreed, we picked up the forms. My parents signed, but Howie didn't even bother asking his. He said he'd signed his own school permissions for a lot of years and his was the only signature the school had on file. No sense confusing things by making it a bonafide legal document.

So we were on our way to the office to turn in his fake permission form along with our legitimate ones, and Howie was browsing his hate mail. Devon and I were speculating about the kind of perverts who would think up such foul things to say. Suddenly Howie stopped. "It's someone I know."

"Know what?"

"Somebody from Shakespeare class."

We looked over his shoulder and read a really lame message using the words, *thou varlet*, at the end. I told him to take it to the school administrators. He had cause right there.

Howie scowled at me and said, "Already have. They say Internet bullying is emotionally painful, but local in nature. They believe I'm being paranoid to imply that it's gone viral or that it's organized in any sophisticated way beyond a local level."

This was major information and he hadn't even told us. Devon and I were dumbfounded. It had never occurred to us that Howie wouldn't tell us exactly what was going on, or how huge the Internet bullying problem had become. We sensed that he was pulling away from us, that our friendship no longer constituted the nexus of his internal life. I interpreted it as disloyalty, and it hurt my feelings. Devon said to let it go. I asked Howie what his parents said about the Internet bullying and he told me to shut up and mind my own business. I shouldn't have followed his advice, so that's one more thing to regret.

I rarely braved visiting Howie when his parents were home, but Devon was busy with a family road-trip the next weekend and I thought maybe Howie could run over some chess strategy with me since I didn't want to lose another match to Allen Mac. Howie's mother came to the door. She didn't exactly invite me in, but then she wasn't hostile either.

Howie's dad, on the other hand, could be a pretty scary hombre. I'd always focus on something in the distance, look any direction but where he was. But Howie would always look straight at his dad. When I asked him why, he said, "You gotta focus on your opponent." At first I thought the topic had slipped and he was talking chess strategy. He wasn't.

I remembered this as a survival technique that night, and looked past Howie's mother to where his father was working at an enormous desk in the high-ceilinged room. He glanced up but made no indication of hello. I'd been trained to greet and shake hands with adults so I marched through with the drill. It was awkward, though. To him I was an interruption.

When I turned to go upstairs, Howie's mother was standing in the hallway watching me. I couldn't tell if she was going in or out, up the stairs or down. It was blank standing, no context. But then she waved her hand at the stairs, so I headed on up to Howie's room, leaping two stairs at a time.

I knocked on Howie's door at the same time as I opened it. He was sitting in a low chair under the corner windows, motionless, staring straight ahead. My entering did not disturb him in the least. He made no indication he knew I was there. I sat on the foot of the bed, straight across from Howie and watched him staring off into space. I waited a few minutes, completely still. "So where are you?"

Howie's body jerked slightly as his mind came back into the present. "Nowhere."

"Right. Like I believe you." A fairly stupid conversation so far. If I sat and watched Howie contemplate the dilemmas of the universe, or maybe only the most recent fight with his dad, it would become a performance. I wasn't going to allow him the luxury, so I decided to do some meditating of my own. I stared off to the side of where Howie sat, both of us immobile. I expected to catch the flick of the eye as Howie checked me out, but it didn't happen. What was happening was this: I was checking out Howie's sincerity of concentration, Howie knew it and didn't care, and I was getting bored. Finally I stood up and left. All of that nothing had taken fifteen minutes.

When I came down the stairs, Howie's mother was still standing at the end of the hall, apparently having made no decision about in or out, up or down. "How is he?" she asked.

"Seems okay." A full-disclosure statement would have been, *your son is sad. Sure, his body is upstairs, but his mind is somewhere far away.*

40

"What's he doing up there?" his dad asked, head down, still working at the giant paper-strewn desk (solid mahogany, I'm sure) in the middle of the great room.

I looked at the ceiling for how to describe it. "He's hearing the silence . . ."

"Sitting there doing nothing," his father supplied.

"Not exactly. He's seeing the unseen, tasting the ineffable . . .." I dislike it when people flap their hands ineffectually in the air, but I caught myself doing just that.

"When'll that punk kid start showing a little gumption!" his father growled.

I made a last effort to make what Howie was doing understandable and acceptable to his parents. "You know, hanging out. Like, everybody does it. "

His father whistled in exasperation, "Where's that kid's motivation!"

In my mind I supplied a conversation Howie would have wanted to hear. From his mother: *Come down and help me mash the potatoes for dinner.* From his father: *We've got tickets to the game, so hurry up!* But, as Howie had often pointed out, the idea of family recreation hadn't really caught on in his household.

I said good-bye to the general space of the room and was about to let myself out the front door when I realized Howie's mother was close behind me. "Did Howie speak to you?"

"No."

"William." She stopped. I was surprised to hear her say my full name. "Would you try again?"

"Sure. When would you like me to come back?"

"Right now. Could you try again right now?"

"He's not exactly in the mood for visitors."

"Please."

She had this pleading look in her eyes, so I said, "All right, I'll try," even though I didn't think it would do any good. When Howie's in a bad mood it's best to clear out and give him space until he comes around.

On the way up the stairs for the second time I decided to get his blood circulating a little. I opened the door without knocking and closed it with a bang. I'll bet his mother jumped. That house was always silent as a tomb. No music. No TV. No talking. I'm sure they could have chosen all those noisy activities, but no one ever did.

The door slam got results. Howie's eyes whipped over to me, and his scowl deepened. Just then his phoned buzzed. He had access to an almost limitless number of ring tones, yet he used the most annoying buzz I'd ever heard. Sort of like an amplified hornet. Question: Why did he have his phone turned on? Answer: He always had it on.

Howie read the message and I watched the color drain from his face. "Give it here," I ordered. He handed it over and I read the coarsest stuff I've ever seen. Witch Hazel Porn's class was training wheels, compared to this. How do you process that kind of filth?

He said, "There's seventeen more on there. Want to see them?"

"Yeah." I crouched down by his chair and he scrolled through the messages, giving me just enough time to get the gist of each message, and I'm a fast reader.

"Now you know what one day is like for me. I get this every hour of every day of every week."

"Why would anybody get a kick out of doing it when they don't get anything back?"

"The IT guys at my dad's work suspect they've created some kind of loop that sends the same messages automatically from multiple sites with ever-changing addresses coming from multiple countries."

"Multiple countries? Amazing! What's the point of it?"

"Money. The cops are working on it."

"The cops know about it? Money?"

"Has to be money. It's always about money. Always."

"So how widespread is the infection?"

"Think they'd tell a grunt like me anything useful?"

"Well, you're the one taking the hits."

"I'm one of many."

I didn't think the fact was comforting. "How do you know that?"

"Logic. What's it to you anyway?"

"You're my friend."

"Yeah, sure."

Howie said it like he was bored. I didn't understand how he could throw out loyalty like that. I thought of punching him. Might knock him out of his blank staring routine. But it seemed a little primitive. "Any idea how your name got picked up?"

Howie looked me over, as though deciding if he was going to tell me. He kind of shrugged and said, "Remember Tanya?"

"With the big laugh?"

"Yeah, that's her. I used to like her when school started. She'd walk by and I'd say, "Hey, you're a P.S. one-point-three.""

"You said that?"

Howie wagged his head at me in that certain way I despise, and said. "Maybe she didn't know it was a compliment."

"Couldn't you tell she was getting mad?"

"Yeah, but I didn't know if that meant she liked me or she didn't like me."

When it came to personal relationships, Howie had to be the most obtuse person on the planet. Maybe it was because he'd never gotten to practice on his family. All the practice he got was with Devon, the housekeeper, and me. School kids don't forgive your mistakes. They're savages.

"Anyway, she moved to a different school," Howie added.

"Good. Well, none of that filth is about you, Howie. It's all about them."

"Doesn't feel that way."

I heard a catch in Howie's voice and looked up quick. I'd never seen Howie with tears in his eyes before. "Hey, let's get out of here," I said. My brain needed some fresh air and my legs felt cramped. Besides, I knew Howie expected a weekend like any other weekend, his parents at their offices or out of town with clients, the time his own, morose and alone.

As we left his house, his mother shot me this grateful look. Howie didn't even bother to say goodbye to them, so I did it for him. I wish he'd try a little bit. I mean, how hard is it to say, *Goodbye, Mother. I'm going to Bill's for the night. See ya tomorrow, Dad?*

I had stuff I needed to do, and Howie grouching around my house all weekend wasn't my idea of fun. However, my sister Lanny irritated him just enough that he occasionally followed her around, which gave me a few breaks. She didn't realize he was being ironic or sarcastic or jocular. She just took him at face value and discounted every grumpy thing he said. For once in my life I was grateful to her.

She told him she needed help with her math and I heard Howie say he'd try. Well, that was a good sign. He's excellent in math, but when kids at school ask him for help he always says he's too busy. When I asked him why, he said it was because thinking that slow turned his brain to sludge. I figured having him help Lanny was a win-win. He was already grumpy, so maybe he'd fall asleep and put us all out of misery.

They stayed at the kitchen table with her math books way longer than I expected Howie could handle. I went by once and he was giving her an algebraic definition for the Rule of Three. "It's a method of finding a fourth number from three given numbers, of which the first is in the same proportion to the second as the third is to the unknown fourth."

Lanny said, "You sound just like the math text book."

I expected him to roll his eyes and say, *Forget it. Math lesson over.* But he actually smiled at her and said, "Thanks. That's where I got it."

"But what does it mean?"

"It means you don't have to know everything to know some things," and he kind of leaned towards her. I was surprised to hear Howie say that. He pressed himself and the rest of mankind to deliver answers. I took it as a sign he'd gradually mellow, grow out of his demands on the universe. "It's also referred to as the rule of proportion or the golden rule," he added.

"The Golden Rule? No, that's what Jesus said. I'm pretty sure Jesus wasn't talking about math," Lanny said with conviction. "You know, *do unto others as you would have others do unto you.*"

"Right. Buddha said it, too. Every culture has a similar truth. And a true thing holds true whether it's about math or about people."

Lanny likes talking about people, but not in the abstract. I heard her tell Howie that she needed to memorize exactly where all the numbers went so she could pass the test. The surprising thing is that Howie agreed to do it. Did he like my little sister or something? I made another pass through the kitchen to get a drink of water just so I could eavesdrop.

I heard Howie begin again. "Okay, listen. If a sailor measures the angle . . ." and he was off on an example about ancient mariners. It had just enough of a story line to propel Lanny along. I looked at her carefully and could see she was enjoying the math lesson. I suddenly felt completely hopeful for them both. Maybe Howie could learn how to talk to a girl by practicing on Lanny. Maybe she could learn how to think with more depth by talking with Howie. It was all going to work out. I was sure of it.

A few days later at Devon's house we were foraging for sandwich-makings in the 'fridge, talking about Howie and other school stuff, and not paying particular attention to who was coming and going through the kitchen. All of a sudden Devon's dad said, "Howie sounds depressed to me. Has all the classic symptoms."

Devon and I sort of stared at each other while his dad took a phone call. For years we had called Howie grouchy and ornery and self-absorbed. We thought of a depressed person as somebody who sat around and sighed a lot—usually middle-aged and female—so we were undergoing something of a paradigm shift.

After the phone call, Devon asked his dad what the classic symptoms were and he said, "Okay, explain what you know about Howie to each other and you've about got it. Sorry, guys, but I've got to head to the ER."

"Cop out, Dad."

"What is?"

I couldn't tell whether Devon's dad was stuffing his pockets with necessaries for the ER, or emptying his pockets of unnecessary junk. Both actions seemed to be going on at the same time.

"Okay, hold it, Dad!" And Devon laid an arm across his dad's shoulders like he always does with me, a big grin on his face. They're about the same height now, so he was definitely in the way.

His dad stopped his pocket rummaging. "Hold what?"

"Take one minute out of your busy life and list the classic symptoms of depression for your son."

"What? Oh, yeah, well . . . that would be . . . uh," and he began a list that got faster as it grew longer. "Moody, irritable, difficulty

46

concentrating, listless, feeling blue, turned inward, trouble sleeping, weight gain or loss, no ability to take pleasure in anything, self-doubt, self-blame, feelings of worthlessness."

When he finished, Devon was still staring at him, arm across his shoulders, smiling. "One minute on the dot. Thanks, Dad. Page reference?"

Devon's Dad shook his head and grinned, then plucked off the long arm lying across his shoulders. "Ever pleased to help!"

"So what's happening in the ER?"

"Some kind of a problem with a pugnacious med student who thinks he knows everything. Talk when I get back," and he dashed out of the house.

Six
Chess, Cars & Dance Class

Besides fire, chess was another total preoccupation that bonded the three of us, Howie, Devon, and me. We all joined the school chess club in kindergarten. No kidding. The club was for all the elementary grades and our parents probably thought it was kind of cute, babies playing chess. But it was definitely our choice to play. Several times a week we'd be paired off to play each other as well as the older kids. We got beaten a lot, won sometimes. Got better with more experience like anything else you continue to do. By the time we hit middle school we weren't interested in the long, solemn games like you see on classic clips. We'd already been there, done that. We had to have something more boisterously competitive. Loud and fast, as though the knights on our board were making a real charge.

So we added a poker component to our chess game. In our eyes, the new version far surpassed the limitations of the two original games. We had created the king of games. We told anyone who would listen that it was a unique hybrid invention that fused the random aspects of poker and the intellectual focus of chess.

"Lifting brilliant competitors to higher levels of sport," Devon would intone.

You had to have two boards of chess going, which meant we always had to include one extra friend, usually Allen Mac. He was pretty smart, but his birthday was a few months later than ours, which put him a grade behind us. These were the rules we invented: At the point where any player lost four or more playing pieces (whether in one turn or in successive turns), both chess games immediately shifted over to poker. Whoever won that hand took back the last playing piece he had lost (pawns included) and the two games continued.

Whenever a king was in check, both games also shifted over to poker, the outcome determining the next move you could make on the chessboard. If you won with a pair, you got to return a pawn to the second row to help out your king (which rarely helped), plus the losers had to phone out for pizza. Devon and I had usually spent all our money, so it was tempting to pretend pairs didn't occur in our hands. Howie, however, was dedicated to Chinese take-away, having experienced the pleasures of very few home-cooked meals in his short life, and saw home delivery as a reward not a penalty no matter who paid.

If you won with three of a kind, you could revive one playing piece (not a pawn) and place it anywhere on the board to save your king (which often helped). If you won with a straight or better, you could resurrect two playing pieces as long as both were placed at least one move away from a queen and didn't put a king in check (which was a lot of help).

Anybody who lost at the poker hand had to remove one article of clothing before they went back to the chess game. We thought it was a wonderfully regressive rule. A completely nude contestant had five minutes, faithfully timed, to win back a piece of clothing or suffer the most ignominious chess defeat known to man: expulsion of the nude body from the house.

The first time we followed through on that rule was also the last time. We were about ten years old and somehow lost sight of the possibility that our parents might disapprove of their sons running nude through the neighborhood.

I was grounded for two weeks because it happened at my house and my dad said I should have known better. Devon had no privileges for about a month, which really cramped our style. Howie's parents weren't home, of course. But Miss Denise, the housekeeper, promised him the next time he streaked home naked, she'd inform both his parents. That was a threat with real bite.

While the rule was technically still on the books, you can see why we didn't follow up in actual play. Besides, we'd gone back to the earlier format of chess as rapid fire moves resembling emotional lightning strikes. The strip poker portion of the game was certain to aid concentration, according to our theory, and would enhance our competitive edge in tournament play. Devon said that with strip poker on the books none of us would have warm enough fingers to type out the online application for a real tournament. Despite his prediction, we all managed to sign up for the school chess competitions each year. It was structured to go from school, to district, to region, to state, to national. From then on we spent every minute we could find battling each other on the board. Howie took to researching the great chess moves of champions past. He taught the plays to the rest of us and we memorized them for future strategy. I think it helped us play smarter.

This year we were facing a regional competition, and needed four long chess-filled days at Thanksgiving, so I put in the request that our family stay home for the holiday this year. Nevertheless, my parents announced that our family would be going to the lake house, same as usual. My grandparents had built the house on the lake when they were first married. My father's family grew up there and the whole family still owns it. It takes about four hours to drive there from the city and it's still my favorite destination. I'd rather spend my time at the lake house than just about any place you could mention. But honing our skills dominated every second of our life not allocated to other areas of survival—such as eating, sleeping, and satisfying the requirements of the various adults in our lives. I began lobbying to have Devon, Howie, and Allen Mac spend Thanksgiving with us at the lake house. My parents' guilt-levels remain fairly constant year after year, so they readily agreed.

I also petitioned my parents to let me drive a second car out to the lake house, since eight people in a five-seat SUV would have been impossible even if five of the eight didn't sport long legs. Dad and Mom own three cars, so I thought it was a simple matter of elimination. The family would take the SUV out to the lake as always, the black Lincoln Town Car doesn't leave the city, so I figured my three friends and I could stuff ourselves into the sports BMW. Simple.

Not. My dad said I was not yet a proven driver. Like I was supposed to have logged a thousand driving hours before I could begin practicing my driving? Did not make sense as a causal event. With the chess tournament coming up, it's not like I could tell any of my friends they couldn't come to the lake house this year.

Devon said his parents laughed when he asked to use the family car. He already had three parking tickets and one moving violation and his license was only five months old. Howie said his parents said nothing, which was a silence they had already maintained for six weeks, and he didn't expect a break in the freeze any time this holiday season.

Devon said, "C'mon, Howie, you're exaggerating. Nobody has spoken in your house for six weeks?"

Howie looked sour and growled, "What would you know about it?"

Devon laid his arm across his shoulders and said, "Come on! Six weeks of nobody saying, *Please pass the butter*, or *Good morning, here's your job list for the week?*"

"My parents eat down town, so there isn't any butter to pass."

Devon grabbed him in a neck lock, but Howie kept going. "The housekeeper writes the job list and does it herself." Devon upped the pressure. Even half-strangled, Howie finished what he intended to say. He could barely gargle out, "Be - sides - si - lence - is - gol - den."

I pointed out it would help things along if Howie actually possessed a driver's license, but of course that meant he'd have to stoop to the mundane, like applying for a learner's permit, taking lessons, and actually passing the driver exam. Howie struggled out of Devon's grip and snarled that he didn't intend to follow high school imbeciles down the beaten path.

Allen Mac wasn't old enough for his license yet, so Devon was our only hope. A week later Devon described the humble servitude he had orchestrated in his effort to move his parents toward favorable thoughts of him. He had positioned himself as a total slave, obsequious to their every want and need. Finally his parents asked him why he was suddenly underfoot all the time. Devon explained how he needed wheels.

His parents talked about it for another week behind closed doors, and then his father came down one afternoon while we were all there and said, "Your mother and I have been thinking, Devon, that it might be a good idea for you to prove your responsibility to the family. We are willing to help you with your wheels problem on certain conditions."

We were about to burst into celebration when his father raised his hand for order. "The conditions are simple. The car will not belong to you." Our enthusiasm subsided.

Devon's father went on. "The car will be a family car—for which you, Devon, are to take responsibility. You have to pay for gas and insurance, which is a lot of money and will be an even greater amount if you rack up any more tickets."

Devon gave a couple of sincere whoops, Howie and I high-fived, and we all trooped off to begin the exhilarating experience of car shopping—in the dumpy end of three used car lots. Five of us left the house together. Four of us drove home in what would probably be the lamest set of wheels in the entire high school parking lot. But that was okay. We were liberated men!

Devon's dad sat all four of us down and said, "Yes, Devon you may take the family's new car to Bill's family's lake house for Thanksgiving. But just barely."

"Oh, the car you drove home in?"

"Newly purchased," his dad clarified, ignoring the sarcasm. "Now listen, you guys, like your life depends on what I'm about to say—because it does. Watch your speed. Speed kills. Speed is the big hazard on today's highways. Speed is the biggest problem with teens behind the wheel. Have you seen what teens look like after they've rolled an auto or smashed into a tree? I'd like to take each one of you with me for one week-end in the ER and then you'd know first-hand what kids look like when two automobiles collide at 75 mph."

Devon's parents met on an ER rotation in medical school. His mother chimed in, "I'd like to show you videos of what comes through the doors of every hospital in this country on a daily basis:

Limbs crushed, lives ruined. Gawkers slow down to look at road kill, boys. Do you want to be road kill?"

So, we drove out to the lake house in Devon's pitiful junker that looked like resurrected road kill, a hulking shape on wheels. However, it had a state safety inspection sticker right there on the front windshield, readily visible to any highway patrolman who might stop us. If I hadn't known his parents personally, I'd have guessed the only way a vehicle in that shape could get a safety inspection sticker would have been through fraud or at least bribery. But that wasn't how his parents did things, so the machine had to be roadworthy.

The insurance papers and the car registration papers were in the front glove compartment, which was permanently locked and could only be jimmied open with a screwdriver. Consequently we were never in danger of losing the documents, but several policemen (sequentially speaking) noticeably flinched when the person in the front passenger position whipped his hand under the front seat and brought out the screwdriver.

The speedometer, while apparently working, was actually all wacked out, giving totally unreliable numbers, so his dad bought a gadget for the car that read out our driving speed along with its primary purpose of radar detection. We were set.

Except for gas. We were short on cash because of saving up for Christmas presents and were feeling pretty low about having to put out our hands for money to our parents instead of being gloriously independent in Devon's old junker car. That's when Howie drug out his wallet containing two different sets of credit cards, one set from each parental unit, who of course couldn't communicate with each other as to what they planned to do for his sixteenth birthday, and had independently conceived of the idea of the coming-of-age credit card gift. Howie said in his deadpan way, "So, who says my parents aren't ever on the same wave length?"

The four credit cards in Howie's wallet were all drawn on different banks. A VISA and a MasterCard from his dad. Another VISA and an American Express from his mother. With the combined credit ceiling his parents had established, we figured we could each purchase a new car off the lot. We spent some time trying to identify which cars most accurately reflected our aspirations in life. Devon said he'd always wanted a sports BMW with a retractable roof and creamy leather seats. Secretly, I wanted something fast and Italian—a Maserati, maybe—but for the current fantasy of what we'd buy with Howie's credit cards, I suggested a communally owned Hummer.

The bubble of speculation burst when Howie told us our imaginations had been corrupted by the ploys of modern advertising and that he, the owner of the credit cards, had no interest in becoming the owner of a car. He swiped a card to buy the first tank of gas.

We jolted along the road in Devon's old junker car—man, that thing had no shocks left—all the way to the little town twenty miles from the lake house, my family's traditional on-the-way junk-food stop. Without that particular fill-up, the family SUV would probably call it quits five miles down the road. Different car, same requirement. Junk food.

It was a great feeling to throw the wrappers on the floor of the car. Think about it. If you've spent all sixteen years of your life trying to figure out what to do with trash in a car and suddenly it doesn't matter what you do with trash in the car, it's a liberating event.

Allen Mac was checking for phone messages, which reminded Devon he hadn't checked his for a few hours, so Allen offered to do it for him since Devon had his hands on the shaking steering wheel. Nobody important, so he dropped it over Devon's shoulder. Howie took out his own state of the art, mega-muscle, lightning fast, most up-to-date-we'd-ever-seen technology. Envy all the way through the car. Turned it on. Groaned. Not the dramatic, for-the-effect-it'll-make-on-your-friends, kind of groan. This was a real gut-busting groan.

Allen Mac was in the back seat with Howie and snatched it. Read the message. "Hey, that's filthy stuff," he said, with his customary stranglehold on the obvious.

Devon said, "You ought to call the police."

"Yeah, my dad would like that!"

"You've got death threats there. You better get a lawyer."

"Oh sure, great idea. Never thought of it myself."

I reached back and grabbed the phone. Read a few messages and wanted to throw up. "They say they're going to re-arrange his face if he doesn't start smiling."

"Along with other parts of my body," Howie whispered, staring out the window.

"Smiling?" Devon was stunned at the stupidity of the demand.

"Going to carve me like a Halloween pumpkin if I don't start smiling."

Allen didn't get it. "So who cares whether a person smiles or not? That's absurd."

"Don't look for logic," Devon said. "This is hate mail. It's worthless, disgusting filth. And that's all it is."

"It's a code word," Howie said grimly. "I know exactly what they want to do to me. And I know exactly how they plan to do it. I just don't know who or when. Most especially, I don't know why. Why me?" Howie concentrated on the passing electric poles with such intensity that I wondered if he thought the vanishing landscape might hold a clue to help him.

The car went silent for a few miles. If something threatened Howie, it threatened us all. We'd get this stopped. I wonder, now, if Howie ever understood that he had solid friends.

When the lake house was in sight I said, "This is abuse, Howie. You can't go on tolerating it."

"Like I have a choice?"

"You've got to get police protection."

"The police say no crime has happened. They can't protect you from a crime about to happen. Laws are supposed to do that. Any more bright ideas?" Howie snarled.

Devon parked his old junker car in front of the lake house then, and I was thinking how a jog around the lake would feel good. But Allen Mac, a total literalist, had gotten bogged down in supplying an answer to Howie's non-question. If Howie says, *Any more bright ideas?* you walk away. But this is what Allen Mac came up with. "Hey, Bessamer, you've got money. Hire a bodyguard."

Howie's mouth dropped open. "I've got civil rights, same as you! Why should I have to buy protection when you've got civil rights to protect you?" And then his fist came up. Fast and hard. Whacked Allen Mac in the head. *Thunk.* Howie literally dove for the door and ran off into the trees past the lake house.

"I'm seein' stars, man," Allen Mac said. "Why'd he do that?"

Devon said, "He's got a point. The Internet bullies are depriving him of his civil rights. There's nothing stopping them from doing the same thing to you or me."

"Should be something his dad would take care of."

"That's a problem, though," I said.

"Why should it be?"

"It's this thing with his dad. Howie loses face if he can't handle his own problems. His dad never gives him an inch and Howie's exactly the same to his dad."

Allen's response was, "That is so stupid. I'm glad my dad isn't a jerk."

Devon shot me a look. There's nothing to say to a comment like that except, "Good for you," which doesn't need to be said. In the friend department Allen didn't have what it takes.

Jogging around the lake felt good in my legs. When I caught up with Howie, I said, "Look, you gotta find some way to shut this stuff off. Like permanently."

"Ya think?"

He said it real snotty like, so I knew he wanted me to shut up and let him get some air in his lungs. We ran side by side in silence. That was the best I could do, but it wasn't enough and I knew it even then. I wish I didn't carry that regret with me, but I do.

Suppertime. My mother is a very good cook, especially when she has all kinds of people to help her in the kitchen and praise her skills. Afterward, we sprawled around the house in a high-calorie euphoria for a few hours. When it wore off a little, I began to tune in a little closer to what was happening around me and realized my mother had been referring to a big teenage party as something she was planning for the New Year.

At first I figured that was her name for the continuing chess wars I had already planned. It wasn't. Mother meant that my little sisters, my friends, and I were all expected to be the teen-age contingent to a New Year's Eve party that would culminate at the Wyndham House. It sounds like a museum or something, but it was really a family home owned by one of my dad's partners in the law firm. Well, fine. We'd show up where we were expected to, and leave before our tolerance levels dipped to dangerously low levels. Independent men with their own car could do such things.

But my sister Lanny's strange mathematics showed me what the real plans were. She came up to me and calculated it was going to be a *bonafide* boy-girl party because if you added all the girl ages together and averaged them, the number would approximate the average age of my three friends and me. "Do the math yourself," Lanny said, flipping her hair.

I wasn't getting her point. "So what?"

"So you're going to dance with us at the Wyndham House."

"What!"

"Like at the New Year's Eve party. Mom said."

I'm very aware of how people can use numbers to manipulate facts, to exaggerate, to lie, but this was the first time I knew numbers could be used to force dancing. Besides, my friends and I don't dance. No way was I going to get dragged into something as lame as that.

I went to my dad and explained the situation. Chess time + party time = okay. But I didn't want anything to do with my little sister's social agenda. He agreed. Motion carried. But Dad hadn't yet heard what Mother and Mrs. Wyndham had agreed on. They both declared how they intended to raise their children to be socially adept in elegant environments. *Ergo*, the New Year's Eve celebration at the Wyndham House would involve dancing of several kinds.

When this was explained to me, I said, "No thanks, Mom," and stomped up the ladder-stairs to the loft above the great room and set up the chessboards for round one. I thought that said it all.

My father launched no counter arguments and my mother was silent as well. I had no idea they planned to trump me the next day after Thanksgiving dinner when the lake house was stuffed with relatives. Another uncle and his big family of little kids were there, running around, making a ton of noise. My friends and I spent our time playing chess in the loft above the great room, though, so they didn't get in our way very much. But, after a huge meal with mountains of all the foods I like best, my mother said sweetly, "Help your father roll up the rugs, Bill. Dance lesson begins in half an hour."

I looked at my dad and he shrugged like it was all out of his hands. He had totally waffled on me. I was furious. My mother pointed out that we four boys would be able to contribute very little to the party atmosphere if we hulked around the edges all night, not being able to participate in the dancing. From then on we had no choice. Social dancing was on the daily agenda.

I thought Howie's eyes were going to pop out of his head the first time he watched my parents dancing together. I don't think it had ever crossed his mind to think of his own parents as a romantic couple—he was the product of immaculate conception, I suppose—but in my family the adults do a lot of public hugging and kissing. If you grow up with it, you assume it's normal. There they were in public, my mom and dad, my aunt and uncle, in a full embrace, gliding around to the music that filled the great room.

Meanwhile, I was counting *one, two, three,* trying not to look at my feet, while clasping my cold, sweating hands onto the backs and hands of various female relatives: aunts, sisters, cousin, mother. And then there was the music to contend with. Miserable as I was while learning how to do all the parts together, I thought I could at least look over at my dad and get a sympathetic signal of some sort. But he was completely involved with my mother. He held her in this wonderful formal embrace and moved across the floor with an aplomb I didn't know the old boy had in him. They glided around the room, heads in opposite directions. He looked where they were going, she looked where they had been. I guess that about covered it, because they never bumped into anybody.

By the end of Thanksgiving Holiday the four of us could two-step, waltz, and do the jive. Dad said we now had something to do with our feet in duple, triple, and quadruple meters, and pronounced our efforts as a fine contribution for the New Year's Eve Party.

Howie didn't think he had graduated from dance lessons to party, however, and the last night at the lake house he went to bed more morose than usual. The next morning he solemnly took my Uncle Brett aside for extra instruction. I thought he was asking too late, though, because Aunt Sandy was already loading the family into their van. Howie suggested that if he could have a little map of where his feet were supposed to be, it would boost his confidence. He was more than unusually intelligent, he told Uncle Brett, but dancing was so out of his competency sphere that he was afraid he might forget the mere details of foot placement.

It took Uncle Brett a long time to make the kind of maps Howie wanted, who hovered and asked questions about everything. Aunt Sandy had to evacuate the van full of restless children, and the little kids scrambling around didn't help Uncle Brett's concentration or Howie's disposition. Finally Uncle Brett handed him a wad of papers, grabbed a kid in each arm, and drove off.

Howie stood there staring at the drawings and trying to move his feet according to the patterns on the paper. He studied them all morning between Allen Mac's chess moves, but as Howie headed downstairs for lunch he shook his head and stuffed the foot maps into his jacket, muttering just audibly that there were too many feet—in the drawings as well as on the ends of his legs.

That Thanksgiving my friends and I spent most of our time up in the loft overlooking the great room playing chess and happened to be privy to a lot of goings-on we'd rather have missed. Grandma Miriam wandered in one afternoon, looked around the room a bit, sighed several times, and then started searching for something around the cushions on all the chairs and couches. After a while she left and I concentrated on the game. Pretty soon, though, she was back again, this time with a table knife. She tried sawing the cushions open with that, but didn't make any headway. So she left. Mother passed through the room and straightened all the cushions and I assumed that was the end of that.

Well, after supper we were back in our spots playing chess and Grandma Miriam came in with a couple of big meat forks, the kind with only two large tines that can really do some damage. She started stabbing the cushions. I thought maybe a couple of my little cousins had been sent to take care of her, but it turns out they were spying on her. I heard one of them say to the other, "See? I told you Grandma thinks there's treasure buried around here." They were close enough to grab the cushions away, but they stayed huddled behind the couch, peeping out and watching. Meanwhile, my grandmother had turned into this wrecking machine, so I stood up and leaned over the railing to call her to stop. Those little cousins went streaking out of there like they'd seen a ghost or something.

But Grandma took no notice of me. I ran down the ladder-steps and grabbed for Grandma Miriam's arms. It was hard to miss getting stabbed with the forks, but I managed it because my arms are so much longer than hers. I started talking to her about how shiny the forks were and how pretty they looked in the sunlight. She let me move her towards the window and we examined the forks as they sparkled in the light. Then she put one over her ear like a pencil and looked up at me, smiling, all gentle and happy like she used to be when I was a little boy and living at her house. I took both the forks and shoved them in my back pocket, put my arms around her, and cried.

Aunt Amy was in the kitchen cooking when I brought Grandma Miriam in to sit at the table. I told her what had happened. She immediately began rearranging the kitchen drawers so that all of the knives and cutlery were above Grandma's sight level. I helped her sort through all the other drawers, taking out every sharp or dangerous object I could find. While we were working, my aunt told me about some of the dangerous things Grandma did. She wasn't asking for praise or sympathy. She was just worried about her mother and knew how much I cared about Grandma Miriam, too.

While we worked and talked, Grandma didn't appear to take notice of anything we said or did. She sat quietly at the kitchen table, hands in her lap, gazing out into the sunshine past where her grandchildren were playing on the soggy, yellow-brown autumn lawn. I don't think she was seeing them. Her body was in the lake house she loved, but her mind was far, far away.

Seven
The Knot

Devon and I were so used to Howie being exclusively our problem that we were kind of annoyed to realize we hadn't seen much of him after the Thanksgiving trip to the lake house. It had taken Devon's parents about three weeks to teach us the entire Human Sexuality class, even with their heavy emphasis on physiology, and after we passed the exams with A grades, Howie stopped coming to Devon's house. Occasionally we'd see him at a distance with one of the school jocks, which was a total surprise. Howie had avoided the group in general, and athletics of any sort in particular.

The next time I saw Howie, he showed up at my house after supper was over, which was unusual, since he knew my mom and dad were cooking and he nearly founders on home-cooked meals. I had been doing research for my dad in his office law library most of the day, so even though it was late I still had schoolwork to do. Howie had a book on Nordic mythology with him and left me alone while he read it. I finished as much of my homework as I could, but my brain was tired and my whole body ached to lie flat on the bed. It had been dark for hours and Howie hadn't made any motions to go home. "You staying the night?"

"Yeah."

"Parents out of town?"

"Yeah."

I threw him a blanket and switched off the light. But then he started mumbling on the subject of my Grandma Miriam dying. What was going to happen to her? Was she frightened? Where did I think she was going? Howie knows she has a special place in my life, and he also knows her growing senility is a very sensitive subject for me. Since I didn't like the immediacy of his target subject, I changed it to a more theoretical discussion. That was okay with Howie, because the topic was still religion and the after-life, Howie's favorite topics.

It sounded to me like he was deeply afraid of death, despite a certain bravado he always took. What if it was just some kind of amorphous abyss afterwards? The fear of death always revolves around endings, and any ending is too soon if you love the person who died. But my family takes the 'happy graduation' approach to funerals, especially for old people. I grew up with the idea that we lived forever with the people we love. Death was going to happen, but no worries. Life had gone on before we got to earth and it would go on after we left the earth.

So here's where I made my big mistake. I assumed Howie would be comforted by my own personal search. When I finished, he let my last words echo a little. Then he said, "You don't have a brain in your head, Walker."

I managed to keep my temper, but I had to concentrate hard on the habit of loyalty and remind myself that Howie was my friend. I just wanted him to shut up and let me sleep, so I ignored him and rolled over. But Howie wasn't about to let it go.

"I'm not afraid of death ending things, idiot," he said. "I want death to end things. I like the idea of everything being over and done with. What scares me is the concept of eternity. Things continuing on and on and on and on . . . indefinitely. Just think of all that eternal busy-ness, all that time to fill up. Time that goes on and on forever. That's what's truly awful."

I tried to explain it wouldn't be more of the same old boring stuff like now, but continual happiness. We'd have important things to do instead of stupid routines like on Earth. Howie didn't get it. He just couldn't get his mind around the idea of being happy, now or ever. If he was depressed, like Devon's dad thought he was, maybe it was self-induced because he was too ornery to try thinking a new way. On the other hand, maybe his imagination was stunted. It was late and I was about desperate for sleep. But Howie wanted to argue. "By the same reasoning, you could say that we are all predestined to eternal misery."

"I don't agree. Good-night."

"Listen. You say that Christ is a god who had to die as expiation for the horrible things people do. You also say that of all the creations, this earth was the only one wicked enough to kill its god. And here we are, stuck in this hellhole of an earth. Living for eternity with the same evil group is not a reward."

"I'd say your life is pretty darn good, Howie. Overall, I mean."

"Off topic, Bill. If I'm on a planet so wicked it would kill a god, then I must be lumped in with a pretty evil group."

"So, be the best of the worst, Howie. Good-night," and I pulled the covers up to my ears.

"What's the point, if we've already been grouped with the depraved and the evil before we got here?"

"Nobody knows that. For all you know, the best and the worst got put on the same planet—balance things out, more or less."

"Your reasoning tells you this?"

I couldn't tell if he was being sarcastic. "Or, maybe just best in certain ways . . . like love, tenacity, endurance . . ." I rolled over and kind of whispered, "Go to sleep, Howie." It had to be my twenty-fifth conversation with him in the last few months on the same topic and I let my mind fade toward sleep. But Howie was in bulldog mode and his next comment jerked me awake.

"I'm so effing sick of everything, you have no idea. You included."

I felt a thump on the mattress by my feet, like he'd pasted it one. I turned on the light, blinking like crazy. No way I wanted a fight. Why didn't he just pack up and go home? He sort of advanced on me like he wanted to take my pajama leg in his teeth and tear it to shreds. I hauled myself out of bed. "Give it up!"

"Try swimming in a little deeper water, Walker," he snarled.

Howie was gunning for a fight and I'd had it with him. "Enough already! You hear?" I whirled on him and started taking little punches against his chest, pushing him back toward the wall.

Howie went silent. Didn't respond. I let up on him and slammed the bathroom door shut between us. Locked it. Took a hot shower to relax. Figured Howie would calm down and fall asleep. When I came out, he wasn't there. Good. Fine with me. I considered a large and profound burp, but decided the orchestration was too much effort, and fell into bed. I was asleep in about thirty seconds.

By morning I was over it. Howie was Howie. Nothing had changed. I told Devon about the episode on the way to school and how I was worried I'd made death out to be too much of a happy ending. "Maybe Howie thinks dying would be a really good solution to his problems."

Devon laid his arm along the top of my shoulders as we walked along, the way he does. "You sure give yourself a lot of credit!"

"What?"

"You think you make the difference in Howie's life?"

"No!"

"Sounds like you do."

I was trying to be totally honest and I could feel a place of recognition opening up in myself. "Well, maybe I do. Maybe I am. Maybe you are, too."

"Take a close look at Howie's situation, Bill. On the down side, his parents don't like each other and they don't like him."

I interrupted him. "I think his mom cares about him, Devon."

"Not the same thing. His mum might care about him, but neither his mum nor his dad like him as a person." That set me thinking. I'd never worried about my parents liking me. Of course they liked me. I'd always thought the point was whether or not I liked them. Devon jerked his arm across my neck to get my attention. "Okay, I'm making a list here. So, Howie is getting harassed on every social media site on the planet and he has exactly two friends: you and me. Everybody else has offered to punch him in the nose daily since first grade."

"Allen Mac counts for at least half a friend, and Merle-the line-backer might count for another half."

"I don't ever hear anything good about ol' Merle. Do you?"

"Not much."

"But going on with my list, Walker, so Howie has assets. Covetable technology, smarts, and the teachers' respect with some really strong grades. Howie's going to pull through. It's just a down phase. Don't make yourself out to be the center of his choices."

Sounded like good advice, so I let my worries go. After last class, Devon and I waited by Howie's locker. I had to make sure things were cool between us. He showed up a little later than usual and pulled out an over-flowing backpack. I tried to smack the contents down inside for him so it would zip shut.

Devon stopped me. "Hey, this sack is getting stuck in the zipper," and he yanked it out.

Howie whirled on him. "Leave that alone."

Devon bit. "What's in the bag?"

"Rope."

"What for?"

"To hang myself."

If that was a joke, it was lame. Devon and I groaned in unison. "Hey, cut the crap, Howie," I said.

"You sound like a text message."

That stung and I shut up. But Devon was pretty irritated. "Don't joke around with stuff like that, Howie."

"Who's joking?"

"If you need attention, this isn't how to do it!"

"Go ahead. Define my reality!"

"Knock it off, Howie," I said.

"My thoughts exactly."

He was talking about death, as usual, and it made me disgusted. "Enough. Stow it."

Devon tried to cajole him out of it. "Come on, Howie! You're not serious!"

"No?" Right there in the school hallway he dumped the contents of the bag on the floor. A length of stout rope. "I couldn't figure out the knot. Crappy Internet diagram. I'll have to borrow a book from the school library, I guess. You guys be sure to return it for me, okay? Don't want to rack up any over-due fines for my parents to pay."

I wanted to throttle him with my bare hands and save him the trouble of learning how to tie the knot. "Stop it. Those kinds of jokes aren't funny."

"Then don't listen." He stuffed the bag of rope into his backpack and stalked out the school door. Devon and I followed, thinking he'd cool off in a minute and we'd still walk him home. But Howie stopped to talk to someone waiting at the school gate, and then Merle-the-linebacker materialized from somewhere, and the three of them headed up the street.

"Who's Howie hanging with these days?"

"Besides the jock? Don't know the other guy."

A few days later, we caught up with him for lunch. When I saw Howie check for messages, I had to fight off an impulse to grab his phone away and chuck it. But Howie got this kind of a half-smile and slid the phone back in his pocket. "So how's the hate mail these days?" I asked him.

"It's over with."

"How'd that happen?" Devon asked.

"Taken care of."

"Who took care of it?"

"This friend of Merle's. I told him what I thought about the situation in a series of four-letter words and he said he'd talk to some people for me."

Something about this made me uneasy. "So, Merle and his friend know the people who were doing it?"

"Is this some kind of inquisition?"

"Not unless you make it one," I said, starting to get mad.

Devon cut me off and said, "I want to understand this, Howie. You were getting a stream of hate mail that even the IT experts couldn't stop. For seven months. Then you meet a guy who knows the right people. He says the word and the hate mail stops."

"That's about it." Howie actually smiled. It had been so long since I'd seen a smile on his face that I had forgotten what it looked like on him. He wasn't half bad looking when he smiled.

"And what do you have to do on your end for this favor?"

Howie glared at Devon.

"Come on, Howie. People who can start and stop cyber-bullying have to want something."

He looked a little confused and disappointed at first. And then he got defensive. "So, I've got friends."

"Friends that want what out of you, Howie?"

"You want a punch in the mouth?"

"You'd have to catch me first." That was Devon's old taunt and Howie fell for it. Devon dropped his book bag and lit out running. Howie dropped his and barreled after him. Devon's legs are longer, but Howie's are more muscled. I wasn't sure of the outcome. I picked up all three of our bags and jogged after them as they headed toward the little park across from the school.

When I found them, they were both covered with dirt and leaves, but nobody's nose was bloody and they were both lying on their backs looking at the trees above them. I don't know what Devon had said to him, lying on the crispy yellow winter grass. But I do know that for the next few weeks, Howie was actually sort of cheerful, almost pleasant to be around when we'd meet up with him for a few rounds of chess.

Eight
The Regrets Tree

When *Christmas vacation began*, enough family stuff was going on that Howie wasn't on my radar for a little while. My parents had announced that for the first time in memory we were going to have Christmas at home. All my life we had piled in the car and driven to the lake house to have Christmas with my grandparents and the rest of the family. Every year it was this big pile of cousins playing in the snow, food served around the clock, and all sorts of games that lasted for a whole week. But this year I had felt different about going. It was because of my Grandma Miriam. To tell the truth, I wasn't sure I ever wanted to see her again. I feel guilty saying that, but it's the truth. I loved her so much the way she used to be, that I couldn't ever get my heart to accept the way she had become. I suppose the psychologists would say I was in denial. Denial of the awful truths about senile dementia.

Whatever it was that had happened in Grandma Miriam's brain seemed to come galloping straight at her with tremendous speed. That was what caught us all off guard, I think. In just a couple of years, the wonderful grandmother of my childhood had become this silly old lady I hardly knew any more. A person who caused havoc wherever she lived, who destroyed everything around her. The Thanksgiving visit had shown me more than I wanted to know about her decline, so I was actually glad when my parents didn't make us spend Christmas at the lake house.

Nevertheless, I still felt the loss of the tradition. We'd spent part of every Christmas there since I could remember, the old house full of cousins and grandparents and assorted aunts and uncles. Presents would be piled up helter-skelter under the tree in the middle of the great room, a blur of color and pattern, all sizes and ages of relatives milling around the edges.

It felt strange to have the gifts stay under our tree at home. But Mother loved having our own private Christmas. "Finally," she said, "I'm having the Christmas of my dreams."

I'll give her this much, it was beautiful. Color-coded. She bought gold and silver wrapping paper and those were the only colors she allowed under the tree. When friends brought over presents, they had to be either opened right then, or re-wrapped in gold or silver to match the décor before they could be placed under the tree. At first I watched for how Dad would respond to this new way of doing things. He took the view that if it mattered to Mom, that was fine, but he didn't want to fuss with it himself.

Through the holidays the ghost memories of past New Year's Eve parties played in my mind. The most important part was our family's First Night ritual of burning the Regrets Tree. The stroke of midnight meant fire! Pyromania at midnight. Regrets Tree on fire. Now that's my kind of celebration.

This is how it worked. We'd all gather for a late night dinner about ten PM. When we were quite little it was hard to stay awake that long, so my parents would wake us up to observe the New Year.

When I became a teenager, my parents agreed to let me invite a friend or two, which meant most New Year Eve events involved Howie for sure and Devon some of the time. Devon's parents were pretty keen on doing family things with him and Howie's were equally keen on not doing family things.

The meal took Mom and Dad a long time to make and it was usually very tasty. After we'd eaten and praised their cooking quite a bit—that was an important part of the ritual—we'd break all normal rules by leaving the food and dishes on the table and move into the living room where we'd contemplate all our regrets accumulated over the past year.

It wasn't really as much of a downer as it sounds. Dad passed around little stacks of white paper strips, a cup full of pencils and some hole-punchers, plus a few million little lengths of white string. The drill was to write down something you regretted, fold it twice, punch it, and tie a string through the hole so it formed a loop that could be hung on the end of a branch.

I used to have a hard time telling a regret from a complaint. I'd write something like, *I regret not getting a puppy for my birthday.* I figured if I wrote it enough times, my parents would spy at least one of my regrets. It never happened. I never got the puppy. Then I realized it wasn't a case of my parents refusing to get the hint. This was one time they didn't cheat. Unfortunately. Those little white double-folded, hole-punched regrets never came off the tree, never got spied into.

If I'd been able to read Jacey's regrets this year (she's eleven) I'll bet you anything she had fifteen complaints painstakingly written out. *I regret not getting a kitten for my birthday. I regret how mean Lanny was about her party. I regret that Bill says I can't go with him when Devon comes over. I regret Mom won't let me play dress-up in her party clothes. I regret Dad doesn't like doing stuff with me very much.* Complaints. All of them.

I've finally got the hang of a real regret. It has to be over something you, yourself, did or did not do. It can't be about what anybody else did or didn't do. *I regret not thanking Miss Denise for every little thing. I regret not spending more time with Grandma Miriam before she became senile. I regret not helping Howie better.* Regrets can hurt. A lot.

I'm not sure why my family does it to themselves every New Year's Eve. Is it a communal expiation-for-sin type of ceremony? I mean, that's really what it is when you think about it. We find a small tree that's been dead for at least one season, or a large piece of some other kind of downed-wood will do in a pinch, and stick it in a pail of sand. Then we hang all the little regret papers on the limbs, and light it all on fire. That's the part I love.

When I was a kid, the other half of the fun was shivering in the cold and shouting at each other not to read private things. Then, we'd go back in the house to check what the TV showed about the celebration on Times Square. For a few minutes we'd flip through the channels to watch the old people dancing with the razzy big bands. Mom and Dad would bring out the ginger ale and turtles chocolates, which we only ever had on New Year's Eve. I don't know why, but it felt as if there must be some kind of rule that you could only have those treats on that one night. And we'd get more and more excited with the build-up.

At ten minutes to midnight we'd go rummaging in the kitchen cupboards, everybody vying for the stoutest wooden spoon and the biggest pan they could carry. On the stroke of midnight we'd check the cheering crowd on the TV set to make sure it really was midnight. Then we'd run out the back door hollering and whooping and beating on our pans, run around the side of the house, and enter by the front door. It symbolized letting out the old year and bringing in the new. We felt kind of profound and silly at the same time.

Then we'd drop the pans and lids and spoons on the floor of the kitchen and continue on out the back door again to the Regrets Tree. Burn it up. Regrets gone.

When I was little, Dad got to be Pyro-Major. As soon as I turned ten, it was my honor to light the Regrets Tree afire. I've been doing it ever since. Every year that Devon has spent New Year's Eve with our family he promises me practically every cent in his bank account if I'll let him do it. He's not much of a saver, so I'm not tempted. Besides, it's my job in the family.

All our regrets going up in smoke. I love to watch the tree flame. We stand there as long as we can bear it, until the cold seeps in around our necks and numbs our toes. Then we dash for the house. My sisters usually get sleepy after the big supper, the cold, and the excitement and wander off to bed. My parents start clearing the dining room table. But I watch from the big window that overlooks the back yard landscaping clear down to the tree line, as the Regrets Tree becomes a torch and then ash in the pail.

We arrived at the lake house for the New Year's Eve party in Devon's junker car, chess moves on our minds. Dancing lessons were a remote memory, sort of like those fifth grade nightmares about whether a girl would embarrass you over Valentine's Day. My Aunt Amy herded us all into the kitchen where we each ate up about fifteen sandwiches without crusts. Whoever in the lake house kitchen thought cutting off the crusts was a good idea needed her head rearranged. Crusts are a growing boy's hedge against four PM starvation.

We hauled our duffels up some ladder-like stairs to the loft above the great room where a series of narrow beds were lined-up end to end with a few card tables and chair groupings between them. The Regrets Tree was calling us, but so was chess. We set up two games according to the rotation we had going, just to get strategy juices flowing.

I could hear voices outside and felt restless. Howie was studying his next move like the fate of the world depended on it, but my body needed some action. I put my claim on my favorite bed, the one closest to the ladder-stairs, by dumping the contents of my duffel bag onto it. I was half-way bent over when I caught movement outside the narrow window that ran above the beds. I glanced up and that's when I saw beauty incarnate.

A girl I'd never seen before ran across the snowy lawn, a pack of my little cousins after her. The snow fell lightly around blonde hair that streamed behind her. Then she stopped and turned. Her face was glistening with a few melted snowflakes and I could almost hear her laughter over the shouts of the little kids through the window glass.

Collette.

She was beautiful in the snow. She was lovely in the sunshine. She was smart in everything she said. She had a French accent that would make you melt in your tracks. She could tell a really good joke in plain English and she could be completely mysterious in French. She was perfect. She smelled like strawberries and vanilla. She laughed over every dumb stunt Devon and Allen Mac and I pulled. She even listened to Howie's long explanations of alleged fact. She was real and perfect and wonderful and I loved her with every ounce of my capacity. I kept trying to think of a really good way to tell her some of that, but mostly I just kind of watched her and smiled.

Finally the call of the Regrets Tree penetrated my consciousness and I invited her to come with us on the hunt for the perfect specimen. She was the new French-Canadian nanny for one family of cousins, so of course the oldest girl in that family, plus both my little sisters wanted to come, too. Altogether, we formed a clumsy caravan tramping through the snowy woods on an expedition to find a superior Regrets Tree. Having Collette beside me was all that mattered.

Devon spent the first part of the trek pushing me out of proximity to her. He's better looking than I am, so he's always in the running with girls. Allen Mac runs at the mouth a lot and says weird things, so I didn't think he had a chance. Howie? He wasn't even on the horizon. At one point in the march through the woods, Collette stopped, the whole column coming to a standstill behind her. In front of everybody she turned and looked up at me. She smiled, took off her mitten, and wiped the melting snow off my cheek with two fingers. That was the signal. She'd chosen me. Devon saw it and backed off. Allen Mac kept on jabbering, oblivious. I don't know quite how to say what I felt except it was light, happy, a feeling as pure as the winter air.

We found all sorts of dead trees my little sisters said would work, but I knew that as soon as we chose a tree we'd have to turn around and go home. I wanted the excursion to last until the exact moment Collette hinted she was ready to turn back. We hiked far enough to find the most perfect tree of our whole New Year Regrets Tree history. It was as tall as me (six feet) and had been dead and drying out for several years in a lightning strike burn area, so it was tinder dry. The little birch—or something like that—had all kinds of brittle limbs that stuck straight out for hanging our white papers, and it didn't have one side all mashed in from lying on the ground for a couple of seasons like others of our past trees. We carried a couple of axes in the group and everybody took a few whacks at the trunk before the tree finally toppled. Then we hoisted it, a long train of people with our right arms around the horizontal trunk, cut-end first. Collette was in front and I was right behind her, let me tell you.

Back at the lake house everyone else went inside to get warm while I hunted around the property for that old tin bucket we saved to hold the Regrets Tree. Because of the New Year's Eve party at the Wyndham House, we had our traditional supper a little earlier than other years and immediately afterward sat down to write out our regrets. We teased Collette about writing all hers in French so we couldn't read them. Not that we ever get to anyway. Then we piled outside with a lot of gleeful pushing and shoving as we hung the little white papers on the tree standing in the pail of sand in the middle of the back yard. Everybody was trying to look at what everyone else had written, or at least pretending to try, but no one really wanted to break the magic of the Regrets Tree.

I yelled, "Stand back, everyone. I proclaim this moment to be the midnight hour at the Walker family lake house!" Based on a technique perfected over six years of prior experience, I lit the Regrets Tree on fire. It was glorious. A roaring blaze of color in the back yard. In a matter of minutes all our regrets became the least puff of smoke. Everything I regretted doing or not doing disappeared. All the old mistakes gone. Or should have been.

Before the advent of Collette at the lake house, I had rehearsed all my objections to attending the Wyndham's party. I envisioned one magnificent blast of logic as a last-ditch stand against the tyranny of the adults in my life. But all of that evaporated when I realized that dancing would give me a bonafide excuse to put my arms around Collette in public. I'd always figured that clothes, a haircut, shaving—all of that was more or less a phase of my mother's social anxieties (or neuroses, depending). But that night it really hit me. Whenever I looked at Collette I knew that being my ordinary Bill self wasn't enough. I had to look better than Devon, I had to speak more intelligently than Howie, and I had to act more self-confident than Allen Mac.

That night, Collette came down the dark wooden staircase of the lake house like a gleaming goddess surrounded by the most glorious dark green color. A vision, skin glistening. Her hair was held in looping curls high on her head that left the whole expanse of her neck for me to adore. I tell you she was breathtaking. Literally.

Then the whole scene began to crash so fast I couldn't keep track of what was happening. I saw a look on Lanny's face that I couldn't figure out except it was all wrong. I quickly checked Mother, and the look on her face stabbed me like an electric charge that started in my hairline and went to my toenails. I remember wanting to make things right, but I didn't know what to grab hold of. I followed my instincts and told Collette she looked beautiful. But those words somehow served to speed up all the wrong that was happening. From then on, all the words in the room sort of evaporated before they could enter my ears and I didn't actually hear what Mother was saying. Her words were swirling around in the ether somewhere, I suppose, but the one thing I did understand were her eyes.

I turned toward Collette to see if she knew what was happening, if she understood what she had done that Mother thought was so wrong. Her face took on this white, shocked expression. Then her eyes grew wider and completely luminescent and I knew that she understood completely what my own body was refusing to know. I saw Collette's self-possession emerge like a shimmer as she steadily met Mother's eyes. Next she looked at my father and read what was in his eyes. Then she turned deliberately, regally, and ascended the stairs.

The next time I saw Collette was at the Wyndham's. She looked beautiful even without the green silk dress, but she had changed inside. The shimmer was gone and her unhappiness was palpable. I saw her as breakable, then, and I wanted to kiss her back to that moment of radiance on the stairs of the lake house when she knew she was beautiful. It was instinctual, the idea that I could create the lightness in her soul again. Completely unpremeditated. I knew I could do it, that it was up to me.

What was it that made me think that way? I tried to place this belief in my own ability within the physicality of the Wyndham house itself. The massive bulk of it, the elegance of a third floor ballroom, the gleaming hardwood of the dance floor, the festive quality of brilliantly lit and decorated Christmas trees scattered throughout. But those weren't the anchors to my self-knowledge.

Then I searched the social structures around me for how I knew I could heal Collette's heart. Perhaps it lay in the invitation to be there itself, which indicated I was part of an exclusive community of guests. The gathering re-created the ambience of another age when there was more time, more graciousness, more largesse. The sumptuous waltzes from the small orchestra positioned in the middle of the dance floor were juxtaposed with the recorded sounds of contemporary dance for a complete aural experience. But that wasn't the source of my confidence, either. I couldn't quite grasp what it was, but it was close. Hovering.

Then I saw my father. Years of observation had unfolded a truth that until now I had refused to acknowledge. Subconsciously I had patterned to do what I'd seen him actually do. But I had no way of evaluating that knowledge then.

I took Collette by the hand and introduced her to the Wyndham family. I've known them from various family events over the years with Dad's law firm, since Mr. Wyndham and dad are partners. Mother and Mrs. Wyndham are great friends, too. They kind of look alike even if Mother is a brunette and Mrs. Wyndham is a blonde. Same height and weight, same kinds of clothes, same style in jewelry, same flair in decorations, same number of children. Mother must have found that fairly reaffirming.

My sister, Lanny, was bobbing up and down. "It's all so Jane Austen, isn't it Mother? The whole ballroom and orchestra thing.

I mean, remember in the movie how they . . . ." I saw Mother give her the arched eyebrow and Lanny shut up like a clam. Howie was standing by her when the music started, so they moved onto the dance floor together. Two of my biggest problems had found each other. Good!

Then I found Collette and took her in my arms for a waltz. At first just the touch of her gave me brain freeze. I was a blob of protoplasm oozing around the room. But gradually I relaxed into the process and discovered there are many levels to the social institution of dancing. There's dancing with your female relatives. It's sort of like working out in a gym. You feel a lot awkward, you get a little sweaty, you think about where your feet are, and mostly how mad you are at your mother for making you do it.

Then there's dancing with the girl of your dreams. Until I loved Collette, I didn't appreciate how valuable it is to have a socially approved way of holding the girl you love in your arms, pressed tightly against your body, while swaying to the rhythm of the music. Since the low degree of separation between you and your dance partner can continue after the music stops playing, the embrace becomes a public demonstration of adoration that cannot be mistaken for mere friendship.

My dad thought he could be the dance-distance police at the Wyndham house party, but it's a tough job and I'm pleased to say right here that he failed. One of his maneuvers was to make the rounds of Howie, Devon, Allen, and me to remind us of our Duty Dances with all the females who had suffered with us through the Thanksgiving vacation lessons. Right off I looked around for Aunt Amy, but couldn't find her. The idea she wasn't invited niggled at me until finally I cornered dad over the chilled sushi platter at one of the little tables by a Christmas tree. "Are you planning to ask Aunt Amy to dance, Dad?"

He looked at me, genuinely surprised. "She's not here, Bill."

"So we see." I wanted answers. Why had Mother made Collette so unhappy? Even better if it cost my dad a lot to keep the topic off the table in this company. "Select exactly who fits and reject anyone with a slight bit of variance."

Dad was angry enough to have to stifle his scare-ya-ta-hell lawyer voice and the effort was causing the color to creep up his neck. The darker red his neck got, the more pleased I felt. "I didn't make up the guest list, Bill," he growled.

"Oh?" I didn't even try to act naïve. I let the sarcasm hang in the air. "So you and Mother didn't tell the Wyndhams who would be coming from the lake house? They seemed to expect my friends and me."

I could tell Dad was a little unnerved that I would defy him like this—I don't believe I ever had before—and I wondered for just a moment if he would back down and say, *Sorry*. He didn't.

"You know what I mean, Bill." He said it low and with a certain level of menace so I'd let up on him.

"Yes, I believe I do," I said and walked off. Straight toward Collette. Took her in my arms for a dance. I hoped he was watching. I didn't look his way the rest of the night. The sheer number of people in the room insulated me from his displeasure and I relaxed into the safety it offered. I began to enjoy what seemed like a kind of immunity. Fragile and time-limited, but still a distance had been established. I wanted a chasm.

Collette was a great dancer, and I didn't wonder about who had taught her. It didn't cross my mind. Quite obviously she had been born that way. All the guys in the room wanted to be her partner. A lot of them didn't know how to dance and had to stare from the sidelines. Seeing them slouched by the wall lent me a new perspective on the misery my mother had put us through during the Thanksgiving dance lessons. I was almost grateful.

If anybody wanted Collette for more than one song, I'd cut in, which seemed to keep the single males stirred up. I could tell by their eyes that they approved of what they saw, even if my parents didn't. When I'd wrap my arms around her for another slow dance I loved to feel her body all limber and heated up from the fast dances. I wished I could have remained with her, swaying to the music, for all time and forever. I had no inkling of fatigue, of the finality of the midnight hour approaching. If it's possible for time to cease, it did that night.

It wasn't like I spent the night getting up the nerve to kiss her in public or anything like that. It happened completely naturally that on the stroke of midnight our lips met. It happened so wonderfully that there was no need to break away from our kiss when all the cheering began. The actual stroke of midnight became abstract in nature. A few seconds of time before or after the midnight hour separating the years was not an event worthy of celebration compared to the corporeal fact of Collette's body pressed against mine, our arms entwined, our lips touching. The kiss was the first in my life. I'll remember it forever.

The moment of my kiss with Collette had been so intensely private that I had completely lost track of the fact we were in a room with sixty other people. It had been a personal event of deepest significance. That it was innocently committed in a public setting would have completely escaped me for all time and memory of the event, if it hadn't been for what happened next.

I remember clearly this freight train, my father, roaring toward me from the far end of the dance floor. Before I was armed to prevent it, I found myself in the junker car with Devon behind the wheel. Collette was in the family van with my father at the wheel, and we were all headed back to the lake house.

I wanted to take Collette aside and find out if she felt all the things I did, but Mother kept her busy helping with the early-morning New Year snack in the kitchen. After we'd eaten, my mother sent all of the girls off to bed for their beauty sleep, as she calls it, and Collette trouped after them. My parents were making a show of having the boys help them with dishes, but there were too many arms and legs in the kitchen to be efficient, so I left to find out if Collette had really gone to bed.

She was standing on the edge of the living room in a spot you couldn't see from the kitchen. I didn't say a word, I just began kissing her again. We didn't dare risk letting the others hear us, so we tip-toed up to the loft above the great room and fell on my narrow bed up there. She began to return my kisses like there was no tomorrow.

I knew what she'd say if she had spoken. She'd have said, "I love you Bill. I love your kisses. I love your body. I love your mind."

That's what I would have said if I'd vocalized what I felt. "I love you, Collette. I love your kisses. I love your body. I love your mind."

Collette kissed me back like we were approaching the end of the world, like our survival depended on it. I can't tell you more because I don't have words for a lot of it. I was overwhelmed with how my body and mind could encompass such enormous feelings at the same time without ripping me apart. I thought I was going to explode with the joy of it all.

The next thing I heard was the freight train again. But this time it had to go uphill—the ladder stairs, to be specific—and I was able to prepare myself for a few moments, stand up, and tuck in my shirt. Collette had darted over to a chair by the chess table and picked up a magazine. She was quietly sitting there reading it by the time my

Dad finally climbed the almost vertical stairs to the loft. It's amazing how you can spend years of your life admiring your father, thinking he's the wisest, smartest person in the universe, and then all of a sudden he's this stupid, bellowing object.

My mother came up the stairs after Dad shooed Collette off to her room and had a few things to say to me. I had a few things to say to her. "What was the green dress episode all about mother?"

She drew back from me with a white face and I knew I'd hit something. I just didn't know what. So I pursued it. "Tell me, Mother. What was that whole green dress thing about?"

It's hard to describe how I figured out what it was about. My mother disclosed nothing, but suddenly I knew. The knowledge nearly flattened me. I had to face the truth of who my mother was in about two seconds flat. I remembered Lanny's face, her plain, little sister face. I remember mother looking from Lanny to Collette. I saw the recognition of reality on her face. A kind of horror, or desperation—maybe that was it, or a combination of them both. And then Mother told Collette the dress wasn't suitable.

What I had seen in her eyes was a kind of maternal hope that had morphed into jealousy, narrow and ugly. Mother had created a beauty in Collette she would never be able to extract from her daughters. I tried to put my mind into neutral, but I couldn't dodge the parallels to some of the stepmother stories that are part of our culture.

I thought my knowledge of my mother's real heart would destroy me. But it didn't, and I fell asleep. The sleep of a heart wrung to its limits.

Nine
Several Mothers

I awoke to one more insupportable fact. My parents had sent Collette and my cousin home, back to the cousin's house where Collette worked as an au pair. Sent them both off in the van with my dad, who would put them on the bus for town. I had slept through the exit.

I had also slept through another event, one that had awakened my friends. The sounds of my parents fighting. "They were loud, man!" Devon was saying.

"I didn't know your mother had it in her," Allen Mac was saying. "She's really got a mouth on her."

Howie had his back to us, looking out the window, and didn't say anything.

I didn't know what they were talking about. I was just barely awake and my best friends were telling me Collette was gone, my parents had a fight, and my mom uses bad language. This was a nightmare.

Devon said, "Hey, we're outta here, right?"

I panicked. They couldn't leave me there alone. If my friends were leaving, I wasn't staying either. Just because my house had suddenly turned inside out and upside down, didn't mean I had to stick around and sort out the pieces.

I told my mom we were taking off for town. She offered us breakfast. Devon declined with thanks and we threw our bulging duffels into his junker car about two minutes later. I hoped we wouldn't pass my dad on the little country road and have to slow down, roll down the window, talk to him. We didn't even stop at our junk food mecca. Devon said we had enough gas to get to the next little town.

Nobody was saying anything in the car. But I had to know what had gone on, so I started asking questions. Apparently my parents' fight had something to do with Collette, although I didn't see why. Mother had already made her point to me in private.

Devon said, "I always thought your dad was pretty level."

Allen said, "Yeah. We always thought we could talk to him about anything."

"Was it over Collette?" I mumbled.

Howie said, "You deaf or something?"

When we pulled into Howie's street I offered to help him carry his gear. Usually he says no, but this time he handed me his duffel. When we got to the door he said, "Sorry about your parents, Bill. All these years I thought they were so different from mine. Looks like we're stuck with the same kind of stupidity after all."

I knew he was trying to extend consolation, but knowing what his parents were like and how he felt about them, his evaluation of mine nearly broke my heart. All these years of being his friend, of trying to help him through his life with dysfunctional parents, and it had all dissolved into nothing. To my friends it wasn't my loss of Collette that was the tragedy, it was my parents. And they didn't even know what they'd ruined.

I began to put together what I knew about my mother. Things I had discounted or pushed to the back of my mind, things I had seen years ago but pretended I hadn't. The further back I went and the more I tried to remember, the more things started to form patterns. That's when you know that what you're learning isn't going to destroy you. You make a pattern, and after a while the new truth can be grasped.

I'd always known my mother was not a stable, reliable person in my life. My father treated her like spun gold, almost with a reverence. But I had to look with my own eyes. It had begun when I was very little, about three years old. If I wanted to I could probably work out on the calendar the day I left home because it would have been within a few weeks of the day my mother gave birth to Lanny. I don't remember the sound of my Mother's crying exactly, but I remember my father's answer when I asked him about it. He said Mommy was crying, *because she has to. She can't help it.*

I remember tugging on his hand and saying, "Make her stop."

He said, "I'm trying, Son." The way he accomplished this was to take me to my grandparents at the lake house. I missed my mother, the mother who was happy and took me on walks in the morning, not the crying mother who held a tiny baby on her lap and couldn't stop weeping.

I lived with my grandparents for the next couple of years, until finally, one day, all my clothes were packed into the suitcase, all my toys into boxes. I knew I was going home for good, and I thought I'd cry my eyes out to leave my grandmother.

Then the next calamity struck our family. I remember the day I was led into Mother's room to see the newest baby. Mother was crying again. She cried even more. She cried and cried and cried. This baby copied her and cried and cried and cried, too. That was Jacey.

The older baby was a little girl now, walking around and trying to talk. And she never cried. Never. Little Lanny would stumble on a rock and skin her knee. Tears would be rolling down her cheeks, but she wouldn't make a sound, never cry out in pain. She'd just go find a grown-up to take care of her knee. I thought she was very brave and very cute and I liked to entertain her with toys while all the crying was going on.

Soon I went to live with Grandma Miriam at the lake house where everybody was happy. It was the place I was used to, a safe place, one that held everything fun in the world. I spent my mornings at the kindergarten in the town twenty miles away from the lake house. It was a long drive on the bus, but I got to sit in the front seat behind the driver and watch the road and everything on it.

My Aunt Coco came to the lake house to live and soon there was another baby there with us. This baby didn't cry and neither did Aunt Coco, and I was as happy as I could imagine being, living with my grandparents.

My dad seemed to think I was sad about not getting to live at home and kept promising me I would be able to come home soon. It seemed more of a threat than a promise. He said I needed to understand that Mummy loved me very much, but wasn't ready to take on the raising of a boisterous, running, jumping, first-grader. I didn't see the problem. I loved things how they were. My parents came to see me at the lake house most weekends, and about the time all the crying began, Dad would take the ones doing the crying, plus little Lanny, back home to the city. And all would be peaceful again.

I loved my grandparents. They were the center of my life. I didn't know it was happening, of course, but Grandma Miriam was the de facto mother of my childhood. I didn't come home to live permanently until the new baby, Jacey, was nearly three and

I was eight years old. Nobody asked my preference, which would have been to stay with my grandparents at the lake house. When my parents insisted I live with them for the school year as well as vacations, I felt like a short grown-up in a house with two baby girls. I took care of them and helped them and tended them, but I didn't ever play with them in a parallel way as a sibling does. And my father took care of my mother.

As soon as Jacey could spend mornings in nursery school, mother went back to her old job working part-time in a medical lab. She was very good at it. Everything was clean and precise and absolutely responsive to her touch. She knew what was going to happen every second she was there and loved it. Home-life, on the other hand, was chaotic for her. But I have to give her this, she tried. I could feel her trying.

I felt a little formal around her. If she came into my room, I immediately stood up. My father insisted on polite behaviors around girls and women, so I always showed her that kind of formal respect. She came from a family that didn't show physical affection in public—no kissing and hugging at all—and my father's family did. So, Mother made the effort to learn how to do it. I would watch my mother think through how to pat Lanny on the shoulder to acknowledge what she'd said. It was deliberate. I could see her thinking through how to respond to Jacey with a hug because the psychologist had told her Jacey craved physical affection. But Mother could never manage a spontaneous response that began in her heart and showed itself as a hug. I wonder if it would have made a difference to her if my sisters had been beautiful.

With me, Mother simply tried to get it right. A few weeks before I turned ten Mother asked me if I wanted to have a birthday party. I said, "No, thank you." I thought that was plain enough. End of topic.

Not so. The next day at supper she said, "William, I've thought of a fun idea for your birthday party this year." I looked up, very surprised. "I've found a farm outside of town that has these darling little ponies that are perfect for children to ride."

I was just staring at her with my mouth open because I'd already said, "No, thank you," and I couldn't figure out how this was a logical extension of the conversation.

Marc," she said, turning to my father, "these little ponies are so cute and clean. Not at all huge and dangerous like a full-sized riding horse would be. Doesn't that sound like a lot of fun?"

He said, "Great idea, Lana. You're a lucky boy, there, Bill."

Mother drew up the guest list, mailed the invitations, double-checked with the mothers, rented taxis, and arranged for everyone to bring little bags with clean clothes. That way, after the horse riding had ended, there would be a clean group of children to open presents and eat cake and ice cream in her home.

It's not like I hated the day. It was very interesting and the children she had invited were good kids. It's just that I didn't really care whether it happened or not. That's the way it tends to be with us. We are very careful with each other, and yet—I know she loves me because she says so all the time and she does kind things for me. What she doesn't realize is that they are loving actions on her terms, not mine. Sometimes I wonder if she knows me well enough to even know what my terms might be.

Mother did her very best to love her children, but she loved my dad easily. Loved him with every part of her soul. I was in awe of this kind of love. Wondered about it. Hoped to have it for myself one day. Then adolescence hit. I began to focus on how to win a girl's love and memorized all Romeo's lines.

So, I grew up with two mothers. One was fragile and one was

sturdy. The duality took me through junior high school. Grandma Miriam gave me a base, a touchstone. Then, a couple of years ago when I was visiting at the lake house I realized she had changed. Somewhere in my brain I had already collected a certain amount of data about this change, but on this particular day I was forced to address the entire catalogue of how she was different now from when I had lived with her as a little boy.

I watched her conduct music in the air, waving a wooden spoon around as though a melody only she could hear was wafting through the air. Then she turned to the side and said, "Of course, I don't think your father meant you. He was talking about that other boy." I tried to see who she was talking to, but there was only the tree fern anywhere near her. Then she straightened her bent little back up to full height and said very sternly, "Stop it right now, Marc. I won't have that kind of nonsense in this house."

I touched her gently on the shoulder and said, "Grandma Miriam, it's me." She turned around and smiled, reached up and smoothed the hair away from my eyes. "Of course, it's you, William darling. I'm sorry you missed Marc and Douglas. You could have told them what's what."

"What do you mean?" I asked her.

She smiled at me with her twinkling eyes and said, "William, don't tease me like that. Of course he's your son."

I was named after Grandpa, and apparently she was reliving a scene that had happened years ago when Grandpa was still alive and before Uncle Douglas took off. When I told Mom and Dad about it, they thought she might be suffering from loneliness after Grandpa died. So my parents took her back with them to live in the guest room at our house. All day long while my parents were at work and the rest of us were at school, Grandma Miriam would wander through my mother's hyper-organized house messing up drawers, pulling things out of closets, dropping food on the kitchen floor.

Then she started trying to get out of the house when nobody was watching. When we'd try to stop her she would accuse us of threatening to strike her. She'd raise her arm over her head as if shielding herself and would start to whimper. She would whine about all kinds of absurd indignities against her person. When the girls took a shower with her to help support her, she would cry out that they had used scalding water. When my mother would tie her shoes, she would sob that Lana had pinched her toes until they were black and blue. It was awful to watch all the chaos.

My mother began to have her crying spells. Then Jacey joined in. Good grief.

Naming a thing makes it easier to grasp, somehow, but none of her doctors could reliably decide on a name. Dad called Grandma's problem senile dementia, which is not a kind name. After a few months of the chaos, my mom couldn't handle it anymore and my parents began to investigate assisted living centers for the elderly. Each weekend we'd go as a family with Grandma Miriam to take a look at one of them. We'd meet the staff, have lunch in the communal dining room, and view an empty bedroom. Some of the residents were so obviously batty that my sisters were all about refusing to leave Grandma Miriam in that kind of company. But then, some of the residents were very nice, just slowed way down to trawling speed. To my mind, Grandma Miriam would fit in nicely with both groups. But she showed no interest in the excursions. They meant nothing to her.

Then one weekend my parents got a call from Aunt Amy who said she wanted to take care of Grandma at the lake house in exchange for free room and board for her and my Aunt Coco's children that she was raising. I believe my dad did the math pretty darn fast and realized it was a far cheaper alternative to any of the expensive care centers near their home in the city. So it was all arranged. Our house went back to normal, basically. But I was still anxious about whether the unseen around the corner would hold a bridge or a chasm.

Ten
Way Too Much

O *ne night last winter* in the middle of a snowstorm, my family sprawled out in the chairs in the great room, relaxing after supper, which doesn't happen all that often. The falling snow padded the sounds of the city and we were encircled in this huge quiet. I looked around at each person in my family and I felt good. I can't say I'll ever feel really close to my mother after what she did to Collette at the New Year's Eve party, and I keep a respectful distance with my dad. But still, I don't harbor a bunch of hostility that would make me feel terrible all the time. I've watched Howie's anger at his parents and it's kind of like he's drinking the poison so they'll feel the pain. Doesn't make sense. Besides, I was deep into fantasies about how to see Collette again, and was nearing the desperation point over a couple of scenarios I thought might work.

Mother had served little white cups of thick, smooth, dark cocoa. I concentrated on thinking about how she tries to make an ugly world beautiful and that was a good thing. I was just about getting there. I have to force myself not to see Collette's face when I do it, so it takes a lot of self-discipline.

The house phone rang and not one of us moved to answer it. Finally my dad couldn't stand the ringing—maybe he's got a more highly developed civic conscience than the rest of us, or something—and walked into the adjacent study to pick it up.

He said, "Hello, Aunt Thelma. How are you this evening?" He's always kind of formal like that, even though he's known Grandma Miriam's sister practically his whole life. She never has earth-shaking news. It's usually just to thank us for whatever gift Mother has chosen for the family to give her. Sometimes to say a relative is sick, or getting married, or there's a new baby. But never that a relative has gone missing.

I couldn't understand the words at first and asked Dad to repeat himself, even though I know he hates doing that. The second time through, I more or less started to understand what he was saying. Grandma Miriam had disappeared. Vanished.

She had been happily ensconced at her sister's home, remembering old times together and enjoying life. Aunt Thelma said she had phoned in the week's grocery order the same as always, and had walked down to the corner store to pay for it. The delivery boy always helps her back to her condo with the groceries. But when they returned to the condo Grandma Miriam was gone. She'd taken her very best woolen dress coat with the sheered lamb collar, her fur-lined leather gloves, and her black dress purse. Aunt Thelma knew for a fact that she had only $62.43 in her purse, because that's how much had been in the dish on the pantry shelf where Aunt Thelma keeps a little cash for incidental expenses. The dish was empty.

"She couldn't get very far on that amount of money," Dad said. He grabbed his coat and boots, and I followed behind him. For hours we walked the streets and alleys in the blocks around Great Aunt Thelma's condo. The snow was fresh and falling, filling up our footprints as we trudged along. There was no sign of Grandma Miriam's little feet.

We were cold and tired and it was getting late, so we went home where he sent me off to bed. No way could I sleep knowing my daffy grandma was probably wandering around in the cold somewhere and didn't have the wits to save herself. I could hear Dad upstairs phoning everybody he knew in the city. He knows a lot of people. He called every neighbor, every one of Grandma's acquaintances, every person at church, everyone from his university days, all my school friends' parents (although I thought that was stretching things). Nobody had seen her.

About midnight I could tell Mom and the girls were finally in bed, so I went upstairs to help him out. His face was grey and lined and dark circles were forming under his eyes. I said, "Dad, it's time we go to the police."

He put his head in his hands and said, "I know."

We met the officers at Great Aunt Thelma's condo and gave them all the information we could. It never occurred to me to go to school the next day, but Mom made my sisters go to school to get them out of the way. Both she and Dad called their work to say there was a family emergency and they wouldn't be coming in. Actually, we couldn't think of anything to do with ourselves once the police began to work on finding Grandma Miriam. In the waiting, the heaviest thing to bear was the knowledge that the longer she was lost, the less likely it was she'd be found alive. The weather was cold January. Bitterly cold.

About noon I realized that Dad hadn't yet called Uncle Brett. I'm not sure why he was so slow about it. Maybe something to do with that darn New Year's Eve party. I don't know, really. But it seemed to me like he'd waited way past when a brother should inform another brother. I also told Dad he should call Aunt Amy, too. Maybe she knew something. He snorted at that—a lawyer type of snort that I really hate, so I won't give a translation of it. Just let me say, he didn't want to make that phone call, either. Strange, isn't it? He'd called every person he'd known in his whole life, and the last two people he calls are his brother and sister. Maybe it's his way of taking responsibility in his family. He's such a take-charge kind of person that if something is out of his control he can hardly bear to admit it. Seems to be a fairly dysfunctional approach to me.

During a crisis like this I soon realized it didn't help when somebody brought up the same information or line of reasoning you've already thought through. It's better to be silent and hope that fresh thinking will bring new ideas, new hope. But Mother didn't get the hang of that. She kept saying the same regret/complaints over and over. *If only Aunt Thelma hadn't gone to the store and left Grandma Miriam alone. If only we'd kept her in the care facility for the elderly. If only it weren't the dead of winter and snowing so hard. If only the girls would go to their rooms and do their homework without having to be told. If only Aunt Amy had helped Grandma more. If only Dad would open up and tell her what he was thinking. If only I would go to the store and get some balsamic vinegar, so she could make a refreshing spring salad to lift our spirits. If only Grandma Miriam hadn't gotten senile.* If only . . . if only . . . if only . . .

The if-onlys in life are crazy making. There are plenty of places it's not smart to take your mind. Listening to my mother took my brain to every one of those non-productive places. Then I picked up on how Dad was watching her. It was almost clinical, like he was measuring her. Then I heard what he heard. Mother's nerves were unraveling rapidly. To him it was the well-known pattern starting again. In her controlled world, she was a gracious mother and hostess with her little white china cups of cocoa. Add a big dose of uncertainty, and twenty-four hours later she was near wailing-pitch asking unanswerable questions.

I heard the hysterical edge to her voice and wondered how much longer Mother could hold herself together. I didn't want the crying to start. What if Jacey picked up on it? It would be a nightmare. We were already in a nightmare, for all that, and I didn't know how long my dad could hold up under the strain of his mother's disappearance along with my mother's distraction. If he started yelling, what would I do?

I went upstairs to my parent's bathroom and opened the medicine cabinet behind the sliding mirrors above the sink where they keep prescription drugs. I started reading labels. It took me longer than I expected because there were so many bottles, but at last I found what I was looking for and pocketed the vial.

As I came down stairs, Mother came out of the kitchen, arms cradling a large empty soup tureen. She said, a sob in her voice, "What kind of a family is it that can't keep track of its own members, Marc? Are you listening to me, Marc? First there was Richard. Richard and Charlotte, popping in and out. Never knew where in the world they were. Literally. Douglas disappears for seven years, reappears for your father's funeral. Not a word from him since. He could be in jail or dead for all he tells the family what he's doing. Then Amy goes off and comes back, goes off and comes back, over and over. Five addresses in five years. Then your little sister Coco goes missing. Gone nearly a year now and never lets us know. Never tells us a thing. Who knows where she might be? Now, Mother Walker . . . just walks away from everything . . . leaves. Disappearing isn't appropriate behavior in a family, Marc. Everyone knows that! Why don't the Walkers know that?"

Dad said, "Now, now, now, Lana. Just calm yourself."

As if she could. I'd give almost anything if Mother could calm herself.

"People aren't supposed to lose their relatives like that, Marc. Really! After all! It's up to you, Marc. You're the last sensible one left. You really must take care of this problematic behavior in your relations!" She ended on a little hiccup of a sob and returned to the kitchen where I heard her turn the water on full blast.

I cornered Dad in his study and told him he'd better sedate Mother before things progressed any further with her. He took the pill bottle I handed him and went into the kitchen where Mother was hand-washing a set of dishware we haven't used in five years. The water was so hot that steam was rising and her hands were bright red. How could she stand it? And then I realized she was too distracted in her mind to feel what her body was telling her.

Dad put his arms around her and drew her away from the sink of hot water, ran some cold water in the shallow sink next to it and gently placed both her hands in the cold water to take down the burning, all the while talking to her gently, telling her how lovely their vacation in Jamaica had been last year, how he loved to watch her salsa dance in her red silk dress, how her eyes flashed like a Spanish beauty, and on, and on, and on.

I watched Mother, half-hypnotized by the sound of his voice and the images he was creating. Her mind was far away in a happy place and she was being held close where it was safe. He drew a glass of cool water and placed the pills on her tongue. She swallowed each one carefully and deliberately. He led her upstairs and I knew he would have to undress her and pull up the covers over her limp body as it fell numbly into a place of gentle certitude.

Two days later, I knew. I was sitting in my room and the house was quiet. I wasn't reading, wasn't listening to music, wasn't thinking through chess strategy. I wasn't doing anything. My mind was blank. And then there appeared this knowledge. I simply knew. *Grandma Miriam is dead.*

Later I learned that my grandmother had taken a taxi to the lake house she loved and had died of a stroke in the cold great room, alone. It had been very sudden, probably a very short passage. But the awful thing was that for several days no one found her. Apparently Aunt Amy, who was supposed to be taking care of the empty lake house, had gotten the 'flu and was sick in bed with a high fever. Consequently, she didn't do her chores for a few days.

Dad's response to his mother's death was to get angry with every single person who was even remotely associated with her death or disappearance. He shouted around the house for a few days in his blustering lawyer-voice until he got over it. He started to ease up on Mother's sedation then, and I thought they were both going to be okay.

Once Dad stopped yelling, a strange thing came over me. I started crying and couldn't stop. I was down in my dark bedroom when the sensation started. I felt like I was sinking down and down and down, and then the racking contractions in my chest began. The tears flowed and my nose was snotty and I felt half-suffocated. I wondered if what was in my mind was making my body drown itself. Maybe that's what Jacey and Mother feel like. The difference is Jacey stands on the stairs and cries so it vibrates the whole house up and down. The voice as weapon.

For me, though, I intend to hide it. What if I have the same problem as my mother? The world doesn't need another crier. I'll never let on. That's one chasm I know I can create.

As the day of the funeral approached, I knew I had to be clinical about my crying, had to know what thoughts started me off, what kinds of thoughts helped me quit. I discovered that images or sounds from the past set me off crying and specific activities in the present stopped me. I'd think about Grandma Miriam catching one of the outside cats at the lake house for me so that I could hold it and feel its warm fur on my face and my tears would roll. Then, I'd think about each action for lunch. Walk to the 'fridge, lift out the mayonnaise jar, open the can of tuna fish, slice the pickle, slice the tomato, lay out the slices of bread, build the sandwich, hand the plate to somebody hungry standing beside me in the kitchen. Do that over and over again and I would start to feel fine.

I think I've pretty well got it down. At the lake house before the funeral I lost it a few times and then had to pull myself up really sharp, so I know I can do it. Nearly chokes the wind out of me when I shove the tears down deep inside, but I know I can stop.

The day of the funeral the whole family assembled at the lake house. Dad had partially lifted Mother's sedation and she was busy controlling us all. That helped her a great deal, I suppose. She had all sorts of rules about what we could do and could not do, and who we could talk to and who we could not talk to. She didn't exactly spell out that I wasn't allowed to talk to Collette, but I knew that was part of the agenda. Everybody was so sad about Grandma Miriam being gone that nobody argued with Mother. We all just did what she said. Or, in my case, didn't do what she said. But I didn't argue with her, either.

When I saw Collette for the first time since the New Year's Eve party I had the impulse to burst into tears and to laugh hysterically. Both. I wasn't sure which my body would do. She had just arrived with my uncle's family and was carrying suitcases in from the van. I started toward her, not knowing if it was laughter or tears that would come out.

Collette turned to me with these cool eyes and after a moment, slowly turned her head away. She had just told me we were nothing to each other. That made me angry and I stalked after her. She kept various cousins between us as she emptied the van, but on her last load of suitcases, I held the door closed so she had to stop. She looked straight into my eyes with this kind of pleading expression on her face that said, *Let it be. Just for now.* I whispered, "Later?" and she nodded. A little hope was enough. For the first twenty-four hours until the funeral was over, we conspicuously ignored each other and that helped put all the adults at ease.

Funerals are more than the ceremony itself. They're a performance, in a way, and certain public kinds of things are expected of you. I was fine at the funeral. It was when I got back to the lake house that I was worried about coming unraveled. A fast walk in the cold air down to the lake and back helped.

Towards evening on the day of the funeral I was down at the boathouse taking my mind off things. I was looking at Grandpa's old wooden boat that he used to row out on our little lake. I was thinking about being little again and how enormous the boat and the lake had seemed. I sat down on a concrete bench out of sight of the house and let my mind drift. I was imagining what it would be like to be out on some really big water, one of the Great Lakes maybe, or a sea, when I heard a rustle. I thought it was one of the outdoor cats that ran around under our feet all summer long. I turned to look.

Collette.

She didn't say anything, just moved close, slid her arms around my neck, and kissed me. That was the best medicine a person who's in danger of crying could possibly get. Complete distraction. I kissed her back, let me tell you. I didn't feel the cold or anything. I kissed her until I thought I'd fall into her soul and we'd meld into this kind of floating being.

From then on, I'd catch Collette's eye somewhere on the other side of the room and she'd know what I meant. I'd slip out one direction and a few minutes later she'd follow from a different doorway. We made out like mad all over that lake house property, snatches at a time. Since we couldn't risk being heard, what little we said was in a whisper. Collette had this way of whispering in a French accent that was so funny, I'd nearly choke trying not to laugh. We'd chase each other around a little bit, but then we'd have to crouch down behind whatever was shielding us from view of the house.

Sometimes, as we began a whisper, our lips would brush together so that we'd kiss instead, the half-formed words evaporating off our tongues, wafting away from our minds. I loved her. I can't tell you how I loved her. It was so sweet and painful and forbidden, and so present.

I have to admit that between kissing Collette and trying not to cry about Grandma Miriam, it really took it out of me. I was exhausted. The day after the funeral Collette and I had found a new spot and were kissing behind the stack of wood on the north side of the garage when a voice called her name from the back door. My aunt wanted help with something or other. After a few minutes I circled around to the front door and went up to the long loft above the great room where a row of single beds had been set up as a kind of boys' dormitory. In about two seconds I was sound asleep.

I woke up groggily to the sound of voices below. I recognized all of them and it seemed like a family meeting of some sort. At first I only half-listened, but when I realized what my dad was saying, my heart started pounding so loud my ears were full of the roar of my own body's response.

This was basically it. He was blaming Aunt Amy for not taking care of the lake house well enough. If she had been doing her job properly, he said, she would have discovered Grandma Miriam before the tragedy of her death occurred. His inference was that since Aunt Amy's store had gone bankrupt the summer before, this was another proof that she was not a capable person. With no formal training beyond a high school education, he believed that Aunt Amy was not a stable person to be guardian of Aunt Coco's children. I didn't get a clear picture of who Dad expected to step up and take in two more little boys in the family, but I could make a pretty safe guess it was not going to be my mother.

I could see how my dad was reasoning things, but the weights and values of his thinking were all messed up. I couldn't believe it was him talking. Aunt Amy yelled at him, which he completely deserved. Uncle Brett and Aunt Sandy tried to do some of their peace-making stuff, but Dad just kept barreling on. I wondered how long he'd taken to think these things through. They seemed like raw rubbish to me.

He said we didn't have enough money in the family accounts to pay for Grandma Miriam's last expenses, much less the hospital bills Aunt Amy was claiming for Aunt Coco (that nobody had heard from for a year). He said he had figured out a way to juggle the trust fund for Coco's boys in order to help out a little, but the up-shot of it all was that we needed to sell the lake house property. When I heard that, it felt like all the water in the whole lake had come smashing down on me and I was sinking to the bottom, drowning.

Aunt Amy was sobbing, Uncle Brett was arguing with my dad, and Aunt Sandy and my mother were talking loudly at the same time to whoever was closest. Everybody was angry with everybody and it was my dad who had caused it all. The meeting was over. I wanted to tell Dad what I thought of his treatment of the family, but I didn't have any words that would stand up to his. As I slowly came down the ladder stairs, I caught his eyes and stared him down hard. I could see the realization flood over him as to where I had been during the meeting. He knew that I had heard everything, and he looked away.

I walked out of the room without saying a word, eyes straight ahead. I couldn't bear to look any of my aunts or uncles or cousins in the face. I went straight for my coat and told the girls to hit the car. They took one look at me and scrambled. Jacey dumped the cat in her lap and Lanny grabbed for her schoolbooks. We were all out in the car with our seat belts fastened by the time my parents appeared. I thought the biggest shame that could fall on a family had just come to us. The new truth I had to face was that my father was no longer bedrock.

When I got home I didn't know what to do with my parents. I didn't want to be near them. I didn't want to smell their skin. I didn't want to hear their voices. I didn't want to have any kind of scene with them. I didn't want them to justify themselves to me and talk soulfully about the ways of the world. There was no way they could justify what either of them had done—Mother to Collette or Father to Aunt Amy.

I wanted to be left alone. I wanted a chasm.

Eleven
Cave Life

*I*retreated to my basement bedroom and rarely left it. Maybe my parents thought a few days of solitude would heal me, so they didn't try to force school on me. They more or less staged the information they wanted me to pick up on. Like, I would hear my dad calling to Jacey asking her if she wanted to go on errands with him because Mother and Lanny were having a mother-daughter shopping trip. Normally, all he'd say is, "Hey, Jacey, let's go," so the rest of the speech was for my benefit.

A few days later my dad insisted I come up for supper and staged another news item for my benefit. While we were serving ourselves at the table, family style, he asked Lanny if she had heard from her cousin, Adele, recently. That was the oldest cousin in the family that had hired the French-Canadian nanny. Collette!

She said "No. Mom, make Jacey pass the potatoes."

Dad said, "Well, you might want to call her."

Lanny was completely focused on the remaining creamed potatoes, so it was up to Jacey to ask why.

Dad said, "Because their French tutor left in the middle of the night of the big ice-storm last week."

If I could have played it cool I would have. But I choked on my potatoes.

Lanny rose to the occasion. "Oh, that's just awful. Where did she go?"

"Nobody knew for a few days. But finally she phoned her parents to tell them she had eloped with her boyfriend."

I was way past choking by this point. I was frozen in mid-motion. What could he possibly be talking about? I was Collette's boyfriend. And I was sitting at the table with my family.

Lanny squealed with delight. "Eloped? David and Collette? They were so in love. I knew it! I just knew it!"

Knew nothing! Lanny knew nothing about love. She wouldn't have recognized love if it had been sitting under her nose. Which it was. My love. For Collette. Exposed on my face for everyone at the table to see.

Mother said in her most controlled voice, "Is there something you know that you would like to tell us, Lanny?"

Lanny's mouth began to work, but I didn't hear any of it. It didn't matter. Collette. Oh, Collette! How could you do a thing like that?

In the back of my consciousness lurked another thought. Maybe Collette hadn't eloped. Maybe somebody got a scrambled message somewhere. It couldn't be true. If it couldn't be true, then it wasn't true. Was it?

I went down to my room to figure out how to think, but I wasn't getting myself sorted out. I didn't have the impulse to cry or break up furniture like you might expect. It was like I was going deeper into myself, trying to find a bottomless place of nothing.

That's when Devon walked in. He didn't even phone first, just showed up at the door. "Hey," he said, as he walked into my room.

I looked at him real hard. "Did my dad call you to come over here?"

Devon looked genuinely surprised. "No, why would he? Does he even know my number?"

"Your parents."

"Well, that. No, he didn't."

I trust Devon. He tells tall tales, but he doesn't lie. There's a difference. I'd planned on keeping what I'd heard about Collette at suppertime a dark and hidden secret from all mankind for the rest of my life. Devon comes over, and in two minutes I'd blabbed the whole thing to him. It all spilled out of me. Maybe I don't have as much self-discipline as I like to think.

"She was gorgeous, Bill. I'd trade places with how bad you feel now, just to have kissed her, you lucky dog."

I could feel the crying coming up from my belly. It was inching its way up and I was pushing and squirming against it.

"It's okay, Walker."

"What is?" I knew if Devon named it (the crying), I'd burst like a busted dam.

"Hey, I've got the talking-points worked out for you. True friend— that's me." He started clowning a little to get me to lighten up.

"About what?" I was gulping for air like a goldfish.

"About this thing you're trying not to do."

"Go home, bird brain." Crying was one thing I had no intention of discussing with Devon.

"So, you know it doesn't really matter if you do it in public."

"Like you'd know."

"Yeah, well . . . so everybody's doing it," and he looked at me hard.

Devon and Howie and I use that line for all the lame choices we come across. We hear about some kid we used to respect who's started tweaking and we look at each other dead pan and say, *well, everybody's doing it*, meaning *that is so entirely stupid.*

I was trying to anticipate how this conversation was turning around when Devon said, "Repeat after me. The curriculum of self-esteem says . . . Come on, Walker, you know it. Give me Witch Hazel's line."

I'd stopped gasping by then and mumbled her stupid mantra along with Devon, "You are wonderful just the way you are." He went on, "By the way, Walker, whether or not you cry in public has no bearing on your personal worth because no one's watching you anyway! What did you think? That you make any impact whatsoever on your community? You are so entirely full of yourself."

"I could give you a good counter-argument." I knew that's what Devon was after. If I channeled my dad, maybe I could get past this.

"So?" And Devon sat back with his arms folded.

"Never cry in public because it's so, like, over-done. You know, weddings and funerals, christenings and baptisms, all the various award ceremonies."

"Yeah, and it makes people around you uncomfortable because they don't know what comes next. And you end up going a lot of places alone, unless you like that."

"Right, and your tissue usage increases so that you end up supporting the paper product companies more than a really green person wants to."

"Plus, your sympathy cohort is age five and under, and they tend to stare."

"You might not know this, being fairly inexperienced as you are, but it makes you feel kind of sick for a while afterwards, with the attendant dehydration and all."

"Didn't know that." Devon pulled the remnants of a package of caramel corn out of his backpack and leaned back to see how high he could toss a kernel and still catch it in his mouth, one at a time.

He stopped for a moment, considering. "Besides, loud crying has a distinct pitch and very few people are able to match it to common household motorized machines. Think of the dissonance going on in any given kitchen."

I was grinning at this point, kind of getting into the whole ridiculous conversation. "Did you know that if you cry at unpredictable moments, you could find yourself incapable of crying when it really counts? Your body doesn't have enough water on hand to make the requisite tears. Known hazard of crying in public."

"I'll keep that in mind," he said, ignoring the growing litter of caramel popcorn around his chair. "Besides it's a-cultural. Our culture prefers fists, knives, and guns."

I snatched the caramel popcorn bag from him and tried catching a few. "Yeah, and criers don't get no respect."

"I hear it's hard to multi-task while crying."

Which meant he didn't think I had a very good catch ratio with the caramel corn. There was a lot of it lying on the floor around me. "It can be done, but your boss probably won't give you a raise for achieving it."

"Let's try it out the next time we go down to your dad's law office."

"Go home, Devon."

He said, "Okay," and got up good-naturedly. "See you in school tomorrow."

I didn't promise him I'd be there, but I kind of planned on it. That is, until I woke up the next morning. I got as far as getting dressed. And then I felt like I'd been loading bricks into a truck all day. Exhausted. I fell into my chair and was asleep in a couple of minutes.

When I didn't show up for breakfast my dad came down to my

room. I told him I needed a few more days off. He didn't get on my case about it, which I have to say I appreciated. I guess there are a few perks for being an A student.

For the first time in my life I did nothing day after day. I didn't leave my room except for the occasional meal. I never answered a phone call. I didn't read. I didn't play music. I didn't even think. It was like I had entered a dormant phase. A nothing state. A satori.

After a few days of this, somebody sent Lanny to get me, but I growled at her and she left. Then somebody sent Jacey down to tell me something. I pretended I was too heavily asleep to wake up. You can't growl at her or she'll start crying. Good grief.

I wasn't hungry and I didn't do anything. The boredom was oppressive, and yet I couldn't think of anything to do that would be any better. I have no idea what time it was when Devon showed up. He just walked in unannounced. We sat there in the semi-darkness of my room for a few minutes, but I could tell Devon was getting twitchy. Watching him fidget was the most interesting thing that had happened in my world all day. Finally the words broke out of him. "Hey, Walker, either you meet me on the corner in the morning for school or I'm coming down here and I'll drag you out."

"Try it!"

"To quote the ER docs who rule my house, *you've got two depressed friends, Devon. Do something about it!*"

"I'm not depressed; I'm just taking a break. Work on Howie."

"I will. Now, listen up Walker, the world's been turning while you've been hibernating."

"No duh."

"We both saw Howie change when the hate mail ended, right? He was actually happy during Christmas. Cool with your sister at that dance. We thought he had come out of his depression, right?"

"Yeah, you should have heard my sister."

"Hey! She likes him?"

"I guess."

"Well, we thought things were going good for ol' Howie. But yesterday in class I saw him take out his phone and glance through messages. It was like a dark curtain went down over his face."

"So the hate mail has started up again."

"Must have. He lit out after class so I couldn't ask him about it."

"Wonder what's up. Ever ask Howie who Merle-the-line-backer's non-student friend is?"

"Yeah, the first day back at school I saw Merle waiting for him and made some kind of comment to Howie about Merle's shadowy friend in the park across from the school. Howie flipped me off. Then said he was the guy that keeps the Internet safe."

"Do you believe it?"

"Well, if he can, that's a lot of power. The whole thing gives me the creeps." Devon stood up to leave, "You're on the corner at 7:15 AM, Bill! Unless you want my fist against your head."

I was there. I didn't want to be, but I was there. The reason? After ten days alone in my room I didn't feel one bit better. Solitude had given me no solutions to my problems. Maybe Devon's dad was right about the depression diagnosis. Anyway, my body was in school, but my mind wasn't functioning. As I scrunched into my desk for math class, I hoped I could rest on my former laurels as an A math student for one more day. I couldn't think about quadratics. My mind just stuttered when I tried to force it, so I let it take me anywhere it wanted to go. Images of Howie flickered in and out. When my mind hovered over Collette, it felt happier there.

I let my memory flee to a time years ago when my mother had taken me with her to visit a friend whose baby had died. The grieving mother had wanted to preserve absolutely every memory and every thing her little boy had ever touched. I remembered seeing some little bronzed baby shoes sitting on the bookshelf in the living room and I knew what they were without having to ask. That's what I did with every memory I had of Collette that morning during math class. I protected it, bronzed it, so my memory would never slip and slide over her, what she looked like, what she said, how I loved her, loved her, loved her.

Howie didn't meet us at the lockers. We waited for him a good fifteen minutes on the school steps, watching as most of the students cleared out of the school. Finally, Devon and I shouldered our backpacks and headed toward the parking lot. Opposite the school gates there's a mini-park, mostly used by the smokers of the school-world, where cigarette butts collect in leftover tide-pools of refuse. We saw a body curled up under a bush and walked over to see what was up.

Howie.

We rolled him over. He was conscious, but so shaken up that at first he couldn't speak. His face was starting to color into deep purple blotches and both of his lips were bleeding. No teeth missing, as far as I could tell. Devon and I concentrated on getting him into the back seat of Devon's junker car. We were on our way to Emergency when Howie peered through his swelling eyes and mumbled, "This isn't my street!"

"Hey, man, you need stitches, "Devon said.

"And from there we're taking you to the police station," I added.

"Stop!" he shouted, grabbing for the door handle. "Stop! Stop!"

I thought he had to throw up or something. Devon pulled over to the side of the road as fast as he could. I was half way out of the car when Howie shoved past me yelling, "Let me out of here!" He didn't double up, retching, like I expected, and staggered down the street a few steps.

I took his shoulders to turn him around, get him back into the car and to the hospital, but it was like he went hysterical. He started to fight me, screaming, "My dad can't know. He can't see me like this. Don't let my dad see me!"

All the action started the blood flowing. He needed some stitches pretty quick. I got my arms around him and pushed him back into the car, holding my fist over the manual door lock so he couldn't get out. "Your dad's not the problem, Howie."

"You don't know. You've never heard him," Howie kept yelling.

I tried to reason with him, but he wasn't listening. "No way!" he shouted again and again, lunging for the door handle, trying to peel off my fingers. I yelled for Devon to step on it. He had an irrational friend pummeling me and bleeding all over the back seat of his car.

As luck would have it, the ER physician who pulled back the curtain to the cubicle where we had been ushered, was Devon's mother. I loved what her eyes did when she saw Devon standing there. Then she saw Howie and turned into a professional. First, she addressed his anxiety with a fast-acting medication, then cleaned up his wounds taking a few stitches here and there. When she was through, she said, "Howie, this is not your fault. There is no shame involved in getting beaten up. You go down to that police station, and you tell them everything you know."

Howie seemed to gather his resolve as we drove along, because he got out of the car on his own, walked into the police station ahead of us, and asked for a particular officer by the name of Patron. Devon and I eye-checked each other, because this meant he had to have been there before. Sure enough, the officer walked in and said, "Howie, introduce your friends and then tell me exactly what happened."

Devon and I introduced ourselves, and Howie mumbled, "Got beat up."

Officer Patron said, "Who?"

"Don't know his real name."

I asked, "Was it Merle-the-line-backer's friend?"

Howie looked at the floor way too long, then nodded his head. "They call him B-Twelve."

The cop was studying Howie like he had a plan in mind, so I backed off. He said, "Tell me about it, Howie. I can't help you if you don't."

Gradually Howie admitted that when Merle-the-line-backer had offered him friendship he'd been a little surprised that a jock would notice a chess nerd. But it felt pretty cool to be a little more popular than usual and he decided it was something he could get used to easy enough.

"What did you have in common to talk about?" Devon asked.

Howie didn't say anything for a few minutes. Officer Patron bent forward in his chair, concentrating on Howie. Finally he answered. "Mostly the shit coming in on my cell phone. He didn't even seem surprised, kind of acted like it was normal. I started to feel like I wasn't such a stupid schmuck to be a target. So then he introduced me to B-Twelve."

"Another football player?" Officer Patron prompted when Howie stopped.

"No, non-student. B-Twelve said the hate mail would stop for any friend of Merle's."

I was starting to get the picture. Howie had glimpsed himself as popular, accepted by the jocks and their powerful friends, and had basked in their attention week after blissful week. And that was the Howie my sister had a crush on.

Howie said, "The week after school started up in January, the hate mail started up again. I saw Merle after school and asked him,

Hey, what's up? I'm getting hammered again. Merle said, *I'll set up a meeting with B-Twelve. See what we can work out."*

"Where did the meeting occur?" the officer asked.

"In the little park across the street from the school, same place we always met up with him. So B-Twelve tells me I need protection. At first I didn't get it. And then I realize he's saying I have to pay him to be my bodyguard." Howie looked down at his hands for a few moments.

"What did you say?" Officer Patron prompted.

Howie looked up at him. "I told him, *No way! I've got civil rights just like everybody else in this country.* B-Twelve just grinned at me a little, like I was a kindergartener, or something, and said to Merle, *Let's give him a few days to think it over.* So, I thought it over for a few days. And the more I thought about it the madder it made me.

"I was dreading the sight of Merle, but yesterday he told me B-Twelve had a solution to my problem, and I needed to hear him out. I had a few pithy comments I wanted him to hear as well. Like how people were born free and equal. That kind of stuff. So, today after school I went with Merle over to the park.

"B-Twelve was waiting for us and said, real cocky like, *I've run your situation past the Druj and they've jumped up your price. Sorry, kid, yesterday's rates ain't possible.* I said, *Price? What price?* He said to Merle, *Hey, I thought you told us he was a smart rich kid. Seems he's a pretty stupid rich kid.*

"I wanted to know exactly what the price was, and B-Twelve said, *Usual entry-level figure is $100 a week, but you've already had four weeks of protection. You can keep the discount price if you pay $500 up front. Now.* I was starting to boil over and yelled at him."

The police officer interrupted. "Tell me exactly what you said."

"I said, *Who's getting this money?* B-Twelve stood up and said, *Your bodyguard needs a fair shake!* and he pasted me on the mouth. Knocked me to my knees. So he grabs me by the shirt and pulls me up real close. *I'm your bodyguard, kid, and I'm the best in the business. You don't wanna mess with me. I don't go easy on the no-pays.* Then he hit me half a dozen times on the face and dropped me in a heap on the ground. Merle walked off with him and I could hear them laughing. I couldn't get up, and things went pretty dark.

"That's when Bill and I showed up?" Devon asked.

"Yeah, I guess. So I'm already stuck in the middle, even though I haven't agreed to anything. I haven't handed them a red cent. And I'm not going to. They can do what they want to me, but I'm not giving them protection money." Howie looked up at the officer, his whole bulldog soul engaged in defiance.

I had this sinking feeling. It was all bigger and uglier than anything I had ever imagined. Howie might not value his life, but I did. Howie's life was part of mine. Maybe a bodyguard was the logical answer. But I wouldn't make a very good one. I don't have the skills. I looked over at Devon and knew he wouldn't be any match for B-Twelve either.

Howie wasn't finished. "Officer Patron, I've been here a couple of times already. You've heard me out and sent me on my way. Every time I come I get the idea you know more than you're telling me. Tell me what you know. What's going on? I want it straight."

Officer Patron's body position seemed frozen in place. My guess was he had no intention of making any significant disclosure to three high school boys. I said, "Howie's life is on the line here, Officer Patron. That's no exaggeration. You're not protecting him by not telling him. You're exposing him to even more danger."

Devon said, "These guys thrive on fear and silence, officer."

I was trying to think like a lawyer, trying to channel my dad. "There are a number of civil liberties being violated in this case."

The officer looked us over a minute and made his decision. His body softened a little and he said, "The whole thing has blown up real fast. Up until now schools were correct in believing that bullying is a local matter, more or less done for the perverse fun of meanness. But last fall things changed when we could see it was all connected with a viral Internet thing. Some IT detectives started working on it because so many of these cases were popping up all over the country."

He stopped. I felt like there was more to come and waited, but when I could see that was all we were going to get out of him, I asked the inevitable question. "What do we do? Back at school, how do we handle ourselves?"

Officer Patron said, "Be each other's protection. Stay together."

Devon's eyes met his. "High school students don't do that. But then you know that, right?" and I saw a flush creeping up his neck. "Is this condescension?"

Howie growled, "Thought I could count on you for something a little more pro-active than that."

"Boys, I'm telling you what I can. You guys have to figure out how to be your own safety in your school. You can't count on anyone else. Ever. I know that's harsh. But I'm giving you the realities of this world we live in."

I understood that Officer Patron was talking about loyalty. "So you're telling us that a sort of protracted huddle will keep us safe?"

"The main thing is to keep up your awareness. Keep track of the kids who seem vulnerable. Offer them friendship. That's the biggest protection students could give each other." He looked at our faces and sighed. "If they'd just do it. Get over themselves and just be nice." When none of us had an answer, he looked over at me and with half a smile asked, "Any chance high school students could ever start being kind to each other?"

I didn't think his question was cynical, like he was aiming a put-down at teenagers, although maybe Devon and Howie thought so. Officer Patron held me with eyes that were almost hopeful, so I considered the question. Thought about what kind of changes would have to take place in my school to create real friendships. Could it co-exist with competition? I glanced at Devon and Howie. Were we friends despite competition for grades, girls, chess?

Officer Patron waited, still hoping. When he saw I couldn't come up with an answer for him, he sighed again and looked at Devon hopefully. Devon tried to lighten the mood, ease us all through it by clowning a little. "A serving of niceness, coming right up! Over-easy or sunny-side up?"

Officer Patron looked us over sadly and muttered, "Three men versus human nature . . . I'm sorry . . . Really, I am so sorry."

Something deep inside me opened up and I said, "No, we all start out knowing what good is and wanting truth and justice. That's human nature. Kindness is what makes the unknown bearable."

Back in the car I asked Howie if he wanted to stay at my house for a few days.

"No. Miss Denise will be there for me. My parents are away on client trips—Grand Cayman for Mom and Mazatlan for Dad—yeah that kind of business trip. Anyway, I should be pretty normal looking when they get back next week. Not that they would notice."

I looked at Howie's bruised and battered face and felt an impulse in my fists to do the same thing to B-Twelve, to Howie's dad, to anybody else I thought might be culpable. It was an awful feeling, made me sick inside, but the impulse was stuck there in my mind.

I thought I'd be able to go to school the next day, but the truth is I got as far as the front door and couldn't open it.

Twelve
Tournament

When Devon came over after school he was full of energy, which I found excessively annoying. He said we needed to warm up our chess skills since the big regional tournament was this coming weekend. I'd more or less forgotten about it. I got out the chessboard and as we set up I unthinkingly reversed positions of the kingside knight and bishop. Devon silently corrected my setup. He drew his eyebrows together like I was deliberately being a problematic opponent, but didn't say anything. On the second move he had me in a fork, by the third my bishop was pinned, and in two more moves my king was in check and all I could do was scurry around delaying the inevitable. Devon let me do it for a couple of moves and finally took my king with his queen's pawn. Yes, it was pitiful chess. I'd played better in kindergarten.

"So, tell me about Howie," I said.

"He's been at school every day."

I was genuinely surprised. "Bruises and all?"

"Bruises, stitches in his fat lip, and wearing a sign."

"What?"

"Yeah, he wrote a big sign and hung it on his back between classes. He'd take it off to sit in his desk. The sign said, *THIS IS WHAT HAPPENS TO FRIENDS OF B-TWELVE AND MERLE-THE-LINE-BACKER.*"

"That would get a bunch of attention." Howie had guts. That was the way to stand up to them. I had to admire him.

"It did. The whole school was buzzing with what had happened and who B-Twelve was. I didn't see Merle anywhere. But during afternoon classes Howie got called down to the principal's office. I guess the coach thought that kind of public accusation violated Merle's human rights. Howie had to stop wearing the sign."

"Did Howie comply?"

"He took the sign off, but by then the word was out. He carried the sign in his hand everywhere he went, but he didn't wear it. So I heard them call him down to the office again. This time they told him he had to get rid of the sign. I guess he told them where to go."

"So, is he kicked out of school?"

"No, apparently they couldn't come up with enough grounds. Howie carried a new sign the next day that said, THIS SIGN DOES NOT TELL YOU THAT MERLE-THE-LINE-BACKER IS PART OF AN EXTORTIONIST RING. So this morning I carried a sign that said, GET IN THE PROTECTION GAME. YOUR CIVIL RIGHTS DO NOT EXIST. By noon, a lot of students had sprouted signs."

I felt deeply ashamed that I'd hidden in my room when Howie and Devon had had enough courage to go to school and make a statement. I was kicking myself up one side of my head and down the other for not rising to the occasion. "That does it. I'm coming to school tomorrow with a sign of my own."

"What will it say?"

I thought about what my own fight had been. "How about, YOUR DEPRESSION MEANS THEY ARE WINNING."

"That's a little personal for you, Walker. Sure you can handle it?"

Could I? "If you think about things very long, some of us can't leave the house. I'm not going to be part of that group." Decision time.

Devon set up the chessboard again and after opening up his back row in a couple of moves, he made one of the lightning strike attacks with his queen that he'd learned from Howie's Russian chess masters book. Beat me in a total of five moves. Normally that would get me going. I'd feel a surge of adrenalin and all my competitive nerve ends would start to whang. But try as I would, I couldn't seem to focus. Finally, I said, "Listen. This is rotten chess and I don't want to make it habit forming. I'll be there in the morning, okay?"

And I was. But it didn't mean I could hear a single word that was said. It was all sort of weird, like an under-water experience. I was there in body, but I couldn't count on my body to make appropriate responses.

I went to school Friday, as well. My sign for that day read, DEPRESSION SAYS THEY HAVE ALL THE POWER. TAKE BACK YOUR POWER. People would stop and talk to me, but Devon had to answer for us both. I tried, but I couldn't seem to get the words to come out. Devon's sign read, YOU'LL KNOW A REAL FRIEND BY WHAT S/HE WON'T MAKE YOU DO.

Half the school was wearing signs. Some of them were pointed and political. Some were clueless. But one thing for sure, no way would a proclamation from the principal's office stop that surge of solidarity. It was scary, but the loyalty felt good. Administration was silent. I looked for plain-clothes officers in the halls, but couldn't identify any. Maybe they hired really young-looking officers to blend in. Or maybe they weren't there.

Friday evening Devon came over and announced, "Time to concentrate, Walker."

He set up the chessboard, but all I could do was stare at it. At that point in my grieving I couldn't see how it mattered whether I could play a game of chess or not. We went through a few games, one after the other, fast as can be. I was going through the motions of thinking, but I couldn't make my mind do it, which felt completely strange. Like I was watching myself not play. If Devon could play expertly, then that was enough for both of us.

I sat back and looked at him. "Play for me, Devon. Please. Take all my games at the tournament."

"I'd do it if I could, Bill, but it's against tournament rules."

"Oh, I forgot." I really had. I'd also forgotten how to play.

Finally, Devon swept the board clean with his arm, pushed away from the table a little, and studied me for a few moments. "Okay, I get it."

I looked at him with more concentration than I'd had all night, and I could see he really did get it. He knew I couldn't do any better than that. I was performing at my personal best from a place I'd never been before. "Maybe Howie or Allen could gear up for a win with you," I suggested as I put the board away.

"Yeah, maybe."

I knew Devon was pretty disappointed after all the thousands of chess hours we'd spent together, but I was relieved to know he understood. He proved it by not pushing me to do what I couldn't do.

When I told my dad I wasn't going to compete in the chess tournament Saturday, he said he needed some help at his law office. Sometimes he sends me on errands to get to know all the other firms in town. I detest that courier job. I have to do it on bicycle because traffic is so dense downtown. Every day that I face traffic in the city core while perched on top of a bicycle, I think I should get hazard pay and be awarded accolades for merely surviving.

But on a Saturday morning I knew the other firms were closed, so at least I wouldn't be pedaling around town. I hauled myself down to the little law library he and his partners keep, found the memo he'd left for me, and pulled out the volumes on case law. I couldn't make my brain track the meaning and felt pretty rotten about it. Nothing like a sudden drop to an IQ of 50 to finish destroying my sense of place in the world. The outdoor cats at the lake house were smarter than me.

I hauled myself back home and mother had a list a mile long of things for me to do. I guess they'd decided *Keep Bill Working* was a viable road to mental health. I swept the garage, cleaned an oil spill off the concréte, organized tools on the bench, vacuumed the SUV, put together a shelving unit to hold sports equipment, and when I was finished I still felt rotten and went to my room.

I had sat there in semi-darkness for a while—no idea whether it was twenty minutes or two hours—time was all the same, when Devon showed up. Eventually I roused myself enough to say, "So what's up?" Devon didn't say anything, which was uncharacteristic, so I said, "Are you here to report your brilliant performance at the chess tournament?"

Devon wasn't his usual exuberant self when he said, "I did fine. Won all my matches."

I congratulated him and asked what level the next round would be. He didn't answer, didn't seem excited at all. "Wish I could have been there," I added.

"Me, too."

Devon was usually so effusive about everything I was surprised at having to dig for information. "So how did Allen Mac do?"

"Good," he said, nodding his head abstractedly.

"How good?"

"He won the first three and lost the fourth."

"Bet he lost to Howie, right?"

"That's the thing, Bill. Howie didn't show."

"What?" Howie not showing? Howie was a bulldog of a chess player, even if he was covered in bruises and stitches. The only way a match with Howie would ever end was because it was timed. Howie would never admit defeat unless the clock did it to him. Not to show up wasn't an option for Howie. "Is he sick or something?"

"I asked the school to call his house when he was late for the tournament start." Devon paused.

"And?"

"And they acted kind of slow and dense, same as usual. I asked them again when the first matches were over. This time they were slow and dense in a different way. I suspected they knew something they weren't telling me, so I kept pestering them until they finally told me Howie had withdrawn from the tournament. Then the Principal put on his way creepy 'kind' smile, and in this super distinct official voice he said, *Do your part for both of your absent friends, Devon.*"

"Meaning me. So where is Howie?"

"In the hospital."

"You're joking!"

"I wish. After lunch the gossip started to trickle in that Howie had gotten jumped in the boys' washroom, taken to Emergency in an ambulance."

I was completely focused for the first time all week. "Have you gone to see him?"

"Not yet. I came to get you."

I grabbed for my coat and ran up the stairs. Dad was sitting in his favorite chair. I told him Howie was in the hospital. I saw his eyebrows hit his hairline, but that was all the information I had time for. Devon and I headed out the door, grateful that his lame old junker car still had inflated tires and a motor that turned over.

When we got to the hospital, Howie's parents were just leaving his room with a doctor. His father looked both of us square in the eye, from Devon to me, and then back again. I expected he'd be glad we came, but he wasn't. He seemed angry, and Howie's mother pretended we weren't there.

His parents had hired a couple of private security guards, so Devon and I had to show ID outside his hospital room. One of them took our Driver Licenses and said he'd ask Howie if he wanted to see us. In a few minutes the guard returned with our licenses and we opened the door. A young nurse was standing at a small monitor, apparently entering some data. Howie was hooked up to an IV and a couple of other lines, his skin pale, a little grey.

"What happened?"

"Three guys jumped me in the restroom . . . before the tournament started."

"Fists?"

"Knives. Said they'd carve me like a Halloween pumpkin."

"Why?"

"Said I didn't know how to smile."

Devon and I eye-checked each other. Smile? "What's the smiling bit about?"

"Code for protection money."

"How'd you get away?"

"Couple kids and their dads came in for a pee. Broke it up."

The nurse stared at Howie and then looked so shaken that I felt sorry for her as she scuttled out of the room. She was young, maybe not much older than Collette. She probably hadn't had enough experiences with the bad awful stuff people can do to one another to get toughened up. I hadn't either, actually.

Devon whistled a little and went to the window. I sat in the chair, immobilized by the image of an army of high school kids walking down the hall with smiles plastered on their faces to tell the world, *I paid my money. I'm safe today.* Devon pulled a chair to the side of the bed and took Howie's closest hand in both of his own. "We're with you. None of us is going to pay either."

Suddenly furious, Howie yanked his hand away. Pulled the sheets off, tore open his blue cotton hospital gown. Bandages up and down his arms and legs. "This'll make you change your mind," he yelled. He peeled off a large patch of gauze and tape on his chest. "Take a look. Take a close look. Get it in your brain." He kept on yelling, "Oh, yeah, we're all brave until the knives come out!" And he started tugging off the bandages wherever he could reach. Howie's body was a patchwork of stitches.

Devon grabbed for his hands and I ran for help. The security guards burst into the room and helped Devon wrestle Howie's hands away from the bandages. A male nurse at the central station came running with arm restraints and an injection, then stayed on, quietly talking Howie through his terrors. Told him he was safe, that the situation was under control, that everyone would help him, that his life would be better. All the soothing words Howie had wanted to hear from his mother and father for the past sixteen years.

The nurse adjusted the IV lines and waited silently with us until the hospital drugs took Howie into quiet. The grey left his skin as he settled into pale sleep.

Sunday afternoon Devon and I returned to the hospital and the same security guards were there. They recognized us, but had to do their job in asking for ID and getting Howie's okay for us to visit. Howie was sitting up in bed and his color was better.

"So how's it going?" I started. "Good food?" and I grinned, expecting Howie to complain about the hospital food like everybody else.

"Yeah, real good. Five star, I swear." I thought he was being ironic at first, but he was so earnest, maybe not.

"So when are you getting out?" Devon asked.

"Tomorrow. If I leave my bandages alone from now on."

"Going to?"

Howie scowled at him, which was fairly normal behavior.

"You okay with going back to school?" I asked.

"My dad says he's hired those security guards for at least a month."

"They're coming to school with you?" I was trying to imagine how something like that would work.

Howie glowered, "People who pay money get a bodyguard."

"But . . ." I started.

"Yeah, I know," Howie interrupted. "I refused to pay, but my dad insists on paying. Who's the smart one here?"

I was trying to think through the logistics of eleventh grade with a bodyguard walking you from one class to the next. "Wonder what the school will do. Did your dad check about the rules?"

"My dad says the school's rules aren't good enough. He's got his own."

"What does that mean?" I asked. "Sounds like he thinks he's above the law."

Howie looked tired. He whispered, a deep husk in his voice. "Listen, you two. I will never pay money to be free. I am already free. That is my right."

Devon took Howie's hand again and said, "Remember we're with you on this."

Howie jerked his hand away and said. "Go home. I'm tired." As we were walking toward the door he added, "But thanks."

Thirteen
Rearrangements

woke up Monday morning knowing I had to face school from now on. Every day. Sometimes it takes a shock to get the system going again. I'd gotten some big ones. The funeral for my grandmother had lent me a corona of grief that had widened and darkened with the news about Collette's elopement. But the attack on Howie picked me up and shook me upside down. Woke up every nerve in my body.

I actually began to look forward to the routine of school as a salve to all the raw places in my soul. Funny how boredom can be such an irritant that you're desperate to get rid of the same ol', same ol' that school often amounts to. And then you look at it from a place of chaos and school is the routine that induces pattern and calm. Weird how the truth can be two opposite things.

First thing when Devon and I walked into the school, the guidance counselor nabbed us. Asked us to come to the office for a few minutes before class—she'd make sure we were counted as present and on time. We were ushered straight into the principal's office where he and the vice-principal and Officer Patron were sitting around the desk. They introduced him as the officer investigating the incident at the chess tournament and requested we co-operate in answering the questions he'd ask. I half expected the school people would pick up and leave, but they didn't. Officer Patron didn't make any indication he'd met us before, which saved him unnecessary explanations to the administrators, I suppose, and began by asking us what we knew about the attack at the school over the weekend.

I hadn't been in the school, so Devon told him what he knew. It was all hearsay, because he hadn't been present when the attack happened, either. When it looked like Officer Patron wasn't going to tell us anything he knew, Devon politely began to interview him. At first the officer took a noncommittal stance, but finally Devon said, "Howie Bessamer has been sliced up and down his body because he won't pay protection money and you're not going to help his two best friends stay out of harm's way? How many more kids are going to get carved because they refuse to pay for protection? Or maybe they can't pay for protection? Not everybody in this school is rich. But I guess you know that."

Officer Patron paused in his brusque routine for a few moments as he looked hard from the Principal to the V.P. and back again. "We've got a situation here. If we say too much it could start a panic in the community. If we say too little, more people could get hurt. I'm on your turf. What's it going to be?"

While the principal and V.P. agonized over the decision, I asked, "Could you please tell us more about the size of the Internet ring your detectives have discovered?"

It was like a screen came down over Officer Patron's face and I knew he was more than a little irritated I'd opened up the dimensions of the problem for scrutiny. The school administrators stopped talking and stared at me.

"Oh, sorry," I said. "I assumed Officer Patron had told you the extortion ring had gone viral. If it's Internet, then it's got to be international in scope. Right, Officer Patron? Heavily funded start-up costs somewhere along the line, right?" Officer Patron looked startled at first, then a little angry.

Before he could answer Devon cut in. "Keeping it a local matter for now, we'd like some straight up information, Officer Patron. Who is working the terror at the local level?"

Officer Patron was on the spot, now. I wondered if there was any chance he'd tell us something we didn't already know, but school administrators are good at getting the information they need to run a school. It was sort of like watching an adult staring contest.

Finally Officer Patron began his chilling narrative. He described how a social persona who called him/herself Supreme Maelstrom would surf the web chatting with schoolgirls who wanted to seem cute and sexy to their friends, or boys who wanted to be somebody but who would never play football or be a rocket scientist.

"Well, that's about everybody in the school," Devon said.

I added, "Basically, everybody in a high school is a wannabe for some reason or another."

The officer explained how Supreme Maelstrom looked for personal web sites that were lame or calling out for attention. "He coaches them Online, helps set them up to be the foxes of their school. All they have to do is become a Nix. When the girl asks what a Nix is, Supreme Maelstrom tells her to point out somebody in the school who needs a makeover. Who are the geeks, the total losers? SM supplies an email address with the Subject line 'Nix.'

"The student then posts as much information as she can get, with phone numbers, email and home addresses, personal habits. For each bit of information, SM enhances the girl's personal page with stylish chitchat, imaginary friends, airbrushed photos, smooth profiles, and if she's a really top notch Nix, he sends her allowance money. With the Supreme Maelstrom at her side, a Nix is promised she can achieve any social goal she wants. She can be the most popular girl in the school with all the guys standing around drooling.

"Supreme Maelstrom approaches boys a little differently, searching for those whose personal pages hold some alienation, dissatisfaction with their place in society, who want more action, more power. He recruits his Druj with offers of making them into fighting units who could take on the geeks and losers of the world, all the stupid people who merely take up space on the planet. For every successful "ambush" he sends them money, with promises of bigger things to come."

When Officer Patron paused to take a long drink of water, I saw the look of horror or fear, maybe disgust, on the faces of the Principal and VP. They questioned each other as to protocols that would cover this kind of an emergency, finally agreeing to have a whole-school presentation the last hour of the day. In the meantime they would alert the people on up the command chain in the school bureaucracy.

Devon and I left the office with a sick feeling in our stomachs. I really thought I was going to throw up and went to the restroom, but I was too spooked by it all to go alone and made Devon go with me. We made it to our first class without getting jumped. Then the next. And that's how it was for us, the whole day. We didn't stay for the all-school presentation. Instead, we left school early to visit Howie on his first day back at home.

Two security guards were working the front of the Bessamer house and we didn't even get to knock on the door. They asked for our ID, spoke into a small device, and then told us, "Sorry, boys. The Bessamer family doesn't want any visitors for a while."

The next day at school, conversations were buzzing all over the place about Howie and school security. Devon and I didn't join in. What was there to say? But that didn't stop the rest of the kids from saying plenty of nothing all day long.

For all that I was sitting in my assigned seat in Room 402, I still wasn't really present in class. During AP English I couldn't think of anything except Howie, and Ms. Carmangay left me alone to do it. We had started a new Shakespeare play that I couldn't get into, *The Tragedy of Julius Caesar*. A whole lot of people were arguing and I knew enough Roman history at the time of Julius Caesar to know it was going to end badly. I hate tragedies. If an author hasn't got life figured out enough to get his characters out of the messes they get into, then he shouldn't be writing. No more tragedies! Hear that, Bill Shakespeare?

All class I felt Howie's absence, the empty place where he should have been. But as much as I tried, I couldn't bring up a polish-perfect version of him. The only Howie that came to mind was the person who'd been my friend, both loyal and annoying. Howie had been so earnest in defense of Devon and me when we were both twigs in fifth grade, that even though Howie didn't have a clue how to throw a punch, his bluster actually made him an effective bodyguard. Kids like to take on the twigs of the world, punch them in the nose, throw their book bags around. But with Howie walking between us it was like Devon and I were taking our own personal bulldog to school for the day. After Devon and I had finally developed a little muscle mass to balance our growth spurts so that we finally looked a little less like a couple of cranes, we in turn had felt fairly protective of gruff old Howie. That was part of the balance of our friendship, a part that underlay all the heat of fire, chess, and hormones.

I felt somebody shaking my elbow. Devon. That meant English class was over. Devon knew that only my body was in school and steered me into the lunch line. We talked about going to see Howie after school and what we'd say to encourage him. On the way to math class after lunch, I asked Devon, "Why did they target Howie? Why not you or me?"

"It could be either of us tomorrow. Or in half an hour." He pulled out his phone and checked for messages. "Not yet, anyway."

I checked my messages, too. For all I knew, some stupid Nix had labeled me a loser who needed a makeover. I wondered if all the kids in the school were scared of the same thing, popular kids or not. A grudge here, a whisper there. What would happen if they started forming their own protection groups like Officer Patron had thought was such a good idea the first day we met him? School would turn into dozens of armed camps, all wary of each other. All out to be the most powerful. Did that mean the flip side of loyalty was an anarchy of interest groups?

A few days later, after the last bell had sounded, Devon and I joined the stream of humanity headed outside and went to visit Howie again. There were a couple of new security men again, but this time we were allowed inside. Howie was sitting in a big chair in his bedroom not doing much of anything when we came in. He nodded hello, so Devon and I rattled on about the dailies—school, home, all the stuff you assume makes up an ordinary, normal life. I had to wonder what Howie would look like without his bandages. He had a slice down one cheek, but all the rest would probably be covered up with clothes.

Finally Howie said, "Tell me about the chess championship." So Devon told about the next level of the school chess competition and who had won. Him! Howie's eyes smiled and he said, "Brilliant." That was pretty big praise from gruff old Howie, so Devon described some of the more distinctive plays. Seems as though somebody from Tanya's school—the girl that was Howie's first crush—had read the Russian chess masters, too. Devon still beat her and we high-fived one another. Devon described how the school had electronically connected all the chessboards to large TV monitors around the school gym so the audience could watch all the matches at the same time (and nobody could cheat). The technology was awesome. *And nobody else got knifed in the boy's washroom*—but we only thought the last part.

On Friday after school when we went to visit, Howie's eyes were kind of dull. At first I wondered if he'd been drugged for some reason. Devon tried to pep him up a little by describing the goings-on in Shakespeare class. How *Julius Caesar* was full of sword fights in the last act, but not one single love scene to make it all worthwhile.

Howie seemed to respond, so I started telling him how to think through the new material we were learning about in math (I hoped I still knew what was going on). Howie cares about grades a lot and we knew he'd be feeling the pressure about being behind in class. He must not have been listening to either of us very much because he suddenly demanded, "Tell me where my parents went."

I looked at Devon. He looked at me, equally stumped.

"Did you text them and they didn't answer back?"

Howie nodded.

"When?"

"Sunday."

"So they haven't been around since then?"

139

"Came to see me the day I was admitted to the hospital. Period."

I couldn't get my head around any excuses for them. This was neglect. Always had been. I was trying to think of some way to help him and blurted out the first thing that came into my head. "Dad needs me to do some law research this Saturday. Interested?"

Howie shifted a little in his chair. "Can't. Still hurts to move. About all I can do that's pain-free is blink my eyes and swallow."

"Maybe next week, then," I said.

Devon, on the other hand, was completely enthusiastic. He can hardly wait to talk the particulars of a case with my father. It works out that Dad gets two-for-one when he sets up tasks for me at his office. Beginning last fall, the two of us ended up giving Dad almost every Saturday morning, plus a lot of the school holidays. I'm not sure why Howie wasn't interested, but he never came with us, not even once.

On our way home we stopped at the police station for an appointment with Officer Patron. Would the security officers be allowed to guard Howie at school? What role would the police be playing? His response was ready-made. "Our first step is to interview students at the school."

Really? What kid whose gotten mixed up in social media bullying is going to come forward? It would be like volunteering for a stint in juvie. "Any takers?" I asked.

"We have a few leads." His face was fairly closed off, which gave me the impression he was going to give us as little time and information as possible.

Devon asked, "How has the wider Internet search been going?"

"We can see outlines of the network, but attaching a specific real name to a code name is very difficult. We can't afford to make mistakes, blame a kid for something he or she didn't do."

Devon and I felt frustrated. We wanted to see people in handcuffs. We wanted to see perpetrators sitting in jail. We wanted to expose everyone involved for the dirt-bags they were. If any progress was being made, neither of us could detect it.

The next day, Devon texted me, *Think Howie's ready for school tomorrow?*

I wrote back, *Let's go find out.*

Any visit to Howie's house when his parents were home made us essentially intruders, but in all the years I'd known Howie, his parents had only answered the door a few times. When we were little, Miss Denise let us in through the kitchen door. Later on, Howie opened the door himself. But this day, we couldn't see any guards as we approached the house. As we stood there in intruder mode, hoping that Howie was watching for us, I half expected a guard to pop around the corner.

I rang the bell. We waited. Rang the bell again. Waited. Rang. Waited. Just as we started to leave, Miss Denise came to the door. When we asked how he was doing, she shook her head, which wasn't promising. We ran past her up the stairs.

Howie's room was a complete mess with clothes and books strewn everywhere. Howie was standing in the middle of it all, completely distracted by the chaos. Two suitcases were open on the floor, and they were the only surfaces in the room not covered by clutter.

"Hey, what's going on here?"

"I'm moving out."

"What?"

Howie looked vacantly toward the suitcases, but didn't explain.

Devon said, "We saw the guards were gone. Kind of thought things had gone back to normal."

"No, it means my dad had a fight with the high school principal. For all I know the commissioner of schools weighed in. Maybe the whole school board, the mayor of the city, and the governor of the state all had their say. Who knows, maybe Dad took my fate to the Supreme Court and the President of the United States."

I stared. I'd never heard Howie do hyperbole before.

"Meaning?" Devon asked.

"He lost."

"Which means?"

"My dad can't lose. He has to win even when he loses."

"So why the suitcases?"

"He's sending me to a private school. Soldier Ridge Academy."

I'd heard of it. A kind of military academy that had somehow escaped change during the touchy-feely movement in the seventies. Still a boys-only school. "He can't do that!" I said, realizing it was a stupid comment even as it was coming out of my mouth.

But Howie didn't snort and tell me I was stupid like usual. He looked kind of soft around the eyes and said, "Yeah, but nobody tells my dad that."

"I'm having trouble with this, Howie," Devon said. "When did he decide that?"

"Can't tell, really. He might have been planning it for months, or even years. But the timing worked out for him. He got the acceptance letter a few days ago."

"Do you want to go?"

Howie shot me a look that was so full of pain that I flinched and looked down.

"How soon?" Devon asked.

"In the morning."

Howie needed help. More help than Devon and I knew how to give. But there was one superficial service we could do. "Where's the packing list Soldier Ridge Academy sent?" Howie dug around in a motley pile on the bed and pulled out a rumpled paper. Devon took it from him and we began to fill the two suitcases with the items the letter listed. When it was full and latched, I started picking up books from the floor and lining them up in the case. "Want to take any books?"

"No books on the list. Guess they have their own. Or maybe this is a school where reading is frowned upon." It sort of sounded like he meant it to be funny, but it came out so mournful that I was more inclined to cry than laugh.

Devon and I hugged him goodbye, the first time we'd ever done that. I didn't want to let go. It was like somebody was going to walk off with my arm or my leg and hadn't promised to bring it back.

The next morning Devon and I got a text from Howie at the airport, *Okay, I'm outta here.*

We texted back, *Invite us for spring break or whatever, okay?*

I guess he boarded about then, because he didn't text us back.

Fourteen
Vision in Black Spandex

A battery of exams took over our lives for a while. And after the exams were over, our parents started imposing their own agendas. Devon's parents were planning a massive garage sale and needed his help, they said. My dad started giving me more and more errand-type stuff to do at his law office. I have known my whole life I was expected to be a lawyer. My grandfather William had been in family law, and since my father is a trial lawyer, everyone thinks I'll be a lawyer too. My dad won't force me. I won't let him. But still he expects it of me. That's pretty strong stuff—expectations.

My dad invites me to do enticing (at least to him) legal-type jobs. One I hate is being office courier. The regular courier was on an extended sick leave or something, so I was really glad to hear it when Dad's firm hired a temporary courier. One legal-type activity I actually like is watching court proceedings where Dad's got a jury and has to interrogate witnesses. He wants me to know clearly the differences between TV and reality.

Devon and I were on our way to court to see how Dad was going to prove that a particular Slip & Fall was a load of crock. He claimed it was a totally bogus racket against insurance companies since the woman had six different Slip & Fall claims going at the same time. Not that he thinks insurance companies personify altruism, but he hates when the rest of us have to pay for somebody pulling in money on a fake injury. Devon and I were both pretty eager to see him go to work on the poor jerk trying to pull it off. We were not at all prepared for the vision in black spandex waiting for us in the office. The new courier/file clerk.

Brooke was one of these aloof girls who is gorgeous but doesn't know it. Most of the pretty girls at school are so completely informed of the fact that it's a total turn-off. But somehow Brooke had missed out on getting the information. Devon was smitten. Written all over his face. We hung around until Ms. Martin, the office manager, practically stumbled over us and then remembered to introduce us to the new employee.

The next day, even though my dad hadn't said he needed any help, we beat it to the law offices after school. Ms. Martin's door was ajar and we could see into her little office where Brooke was standing. We heard her say, "I called you in, Brenna, because I have your pay forms ready to sign."

Devon and I looked at each other, *Who?*

And then Brooke said, "Thank you, Ms. Martin, but please call me Brooke."

The office manager said, "It seems a bit unusual to me . . ."

"My birth certificate name isn't the name I go by. Just a family quirk. If it's not too awkward for you?"

"No, no, it's just fine. I've just got to remember the name is Brenna on the pay stub and Brooke in the office," and she laughed.

We heard Brooke's voice take on this cheery tone as she thanked the office manager and said she'd go start on the filing. Devon and I just had time to duck into my dad's little law library so Brooke wouldn't know we'd been eavesdropping.

From that moment on, Devon's mission was to charm information about Brooke out of the office manager. Little by little, it dribbled out, despite Ms. Martin's best intentions. Brooke was a high school senior who had finished all her courses a semester early, so that's why she could take the job. She was a year older than us. I told Devon an older girl was off-limits. Only one of us needed to suffer the Collette factor. He didn't buy it and begged Ms. Martin to tell him when Brooke's birthday was. She clammed up and claimed adherence to privacy laws. There was no way she could divulge private information to satisfy his curiosity. But Devon knew she loved French pastry. For three days running he turned up with *milles feuilles* in a box wrapped with glossy white paper and tied with red satin ribbon.

Finally Ms. Martin caved. "Oh all right. But don't you dare get me fired for this!"

It turns out Brooke was only seven months older than Devon even though she was a grade ahead, which meant they were the same age five months out of the year. That was a green light for Devon. Maybe I'd have given him a run for her, if it hadn't been for Collette, that is. But every time Devon looked at Brooke I could see he'd have wagged his tail if he'd had one. It would have been pretty heartless of me to go after her and try to beat out my best friend. Besides, my dad was always lurking around—it was his law office, after all. So, I decided to hold off on Brooke for several good reasons.

Devon asked her if she liked playing video games. She grinned and said, "Yeah," kind of slow, like there was a lot more to say on the topic.

"What's your game?"

"Mud-Raiders."

Devon had to whistle under his breath at that one. There isn't a faster, harder game on the market. No blood, no gore, just wild speed. "Tonight?"

"Sure. Where?"

"Do you know the Gaming Center a block from the high school?"

"I'll find it."

"Let me pick you up."

"No need. I'll meet you there! Eight?"

Devon has top-notch hand-eye coordination and expected to beat her flat out. That's not what happened. She was a shark, totally aggressive in this completely unselfconscious way. We both loved it. Some girls put on this butch thing and swagger around to show how equal they are, but Brooke simply was equal. She knew how to play and she went for it full out.

She won the first game against Devon with some strategies we'd never seen before. I think he was too stunned to play his best. When she tried them on me, I worked harder than I ever had at a game. Who knows if I could have won against her, because the laser shorted out and we had to stop in the middle. The management was good about refunding the match and gave us a do-over card.

We stopped for pizza and while we were waiting in the booth, Devon laid his arm across Brooke's shoulders like he does, and peered down into her face. "So, Miss Walton. How did you learn to play like that?"

"My uncle. He raised me ever since I was a little girl."

"Raised you to be a shark?"

"Among other things," she grinned.

"I've got to meet this uncle who's a wizard at Mud-Raiders," Devon said.

"He's on an extended business trip right now, but I think I've figured out how to beat him when he gets back."

"Way to give the guy a welcome home," I said, teasing her.

We managed to do something with her every weekend after that, mostly getting-to-know-the-city kinds of things. Devon armed himself with Chamber of Commerce commentary until I wanted to tape his mouth shut, but Brooke was big on facts, I guess. She'd listen to him and her eyes would glisten.

I felt a little awkward, like an add-on, and asked Devon if he wanted to take her on dates alone, you know, get to know her a little better. I said it in a way that he knew I was talking about him making out with her. He let his eyes get kind of cold and stared at me a minute. Didn't say anything. I was kind of surprised, I have to admit, since making out with Collette had been such a compelling experience for me last winter. Didn't Devon think of Brooke that way?

They'd talk and talk and talk and talk. Well, Devon's always been good with words and I was interested in the way Brooke responded to all that talk. But what I particularly noticed was that Devon never kissed her. Not once. He never put his arms around her like she was his. But when he looked into her face, it lit him up like a marquee. I asked him about that and here's about how the conversation went.

"Hey, Devon, if Brooke's so hot, why don't you act like it?"

"Well, how would that be?" he said slowly.

"You know, kiss her, put your arms around her, pull her close."

"Hey, I'd love it."

"So what's holding you back? I've been watching her, and the girl thinks you're way better than just an okay buddy."

"Yeah, I think she does."

I was having to pry the goods out of Devon and was starting to feel annoyed. "So aren't you physically attracted to her?"

"Sometimes I can hardly concentrate on what she's saying because the attraction gets in the way so bad."

I was getting this. "Hey, I don't have to come along with you."

"I want you to come."

"Why?"

Devon looked like he was trying to sort himself. "It goes back to the load of crap Old Witch Hazel Porn dumped on us"

"She was a pile of crock, ol' Witch Hazel Porn."

"I wish I could burn up all the rubbish she taught us."

"Cauterized brain cells might be a handicap. Remind me not to partner with you in chess."

He couldn't treat it like a joke. I guess he still felt acutely the damage from Witch Hazel Porn. "Everything that came out of her mouth was putrid. I want to look at sex differently from anything she ever imagined. Witch Hazel Porn taught us the physical act of sex was ordinary and predictable, commonplace. She trained us to think of it as being all about what our own bodies wanted and needed. I want to burn it out of my mind."

"Yeah, burn up the trash."

"The course in Human Sexuality didn't end when I took the exam, you know. My parents still talk to me about it a lot."

No, I didn't know that. Glad it wasn't happening at my house. Think I'd rather be dead, actually, than discuss pornography with my parents. Still, it was kind of weird to know Devon was having a problem with something I didn't really understand. "So, what do you do when the words and images start coming into your mind?"

"I substitute them with ideas I want to have.

"Like what?"

"Okay, like if I'm reading and thoughts start, then I deliberately take my mind to another place, maybe some new chess strategy. Happy song lyrics are pretty powerful for me, too."

"And that works?"

"Mostly. Sometimes it helps to change what I'm doing, too. Like if I'm by myself, then I go see who else is home and start visiting with them."

"Can you ever get away from the thoughts?"

"It's hard, I'll admit that. I've learned that pornography becomes addicting when a person uses those images and thoughts to help them feel better."

I didn't understand. "How?"

"Like if they feel lonely, or insecure, or unloved. It's self-medicating. Makes you feel better short term, like tobacco or drugs or alcohol."

I hadn't ever thought through the why of pornography. Devon was pretty calm talking about it. Not at all embarrassed like I was, I hate to admit.

"So Mum and Dad made a guess that I hadn't gotten that far, that I wasn't addicted yet. For me, it was like a bad habit I had to break. I still felt respect for girls and they wanted to make sure that didn't get destroyed." Devon's face took on that marquee look he gets. "I want Brooke to know I love her without me ever putting my hands on her. I want to know for myself that I can make that kind of love happen."

I thought of all the kissing and making out Collette and I had done at the lake house and here was Devon, taking his love in a different direction. Had to wonder how it would turn out for him. Well, I had something of a ringside seat.

You'd think a chess game would be about as neutral as it gets where sex is concerned, but I guess your attitudes go with you. In high school, most of the boys do the *har, har, har,* stuff about girls and sex if that's what their dads do. So this is what happened at chess club. Devon and I had only attended sporadically after Howie moved to Soldier Ridge Academy. Our heart wasn't in it any more. But Allen Mac was still pretty dedicated. This one day, he'd hounded Devon and me until we finally agreed to go.

Allen and Devon were matched up, but nothing interesting was going on. Devon knew all of Allen's moves because Allen didn't know how to change up his strategy to make the tactics in Howie's Russian chess master's book original to the situation. I'd beaten my partner and she'd gone home, as had the rest of the club. But Allen Mac had subscribed to the slow and excruciating defeat mode. I wanted them to get it over with, and was more or less standing around staring out the window when it happened.

Allen said, "Hey, saw you in the Game Center a few weeks ago with a real hottie."

Devon's face jerked up from the chessboard, startled. "What?"

Allen started to smirk, and repeated himself. "Yeah, a few weeks ago at the Game Center. That Brooke's a real hottie."

Devon rose straight up out of his chair and pasted Allen one. Right in the mouth. Punched him so hard that Allen Mac fell out of his chair. Allen stared up at Devon in disbelief. I had no idea Devon would do something like that, either. The look on Devon's face told me he was struggling with a rage that wanted to pound Allen to bits. Devon started to go for Allen, but I got to him first. I pulled him away from the object he wanted to pulverize and yelled at Allen Mac that if he had any sense he'd get out. Now!

He grabbed his book bag and sauntered out extra slow to show Devon he didn't care. At the door, Allen Mac turned, his lip puffed out and bleeding, his voice full of injury. "All I said was, *That Brooke's a real hottie*, and he tries to deck me." He said it like Devon had been totally unreasonable to slug him.

Devon's legs began pumping again, like he was trying to run after Allen and pound his face in. Good thing I still had his arms in a lock. I started talking to Devon, trying to work him through it.

Finally he said, "Let go of me. I'm okay."

I put away the chessboard and handed him his book bag. We took the stairs down two at a time and when we hit the sidewalk, the air had never smelled so sweet to me. I stopped Devon and said, "Okay, take some deep breaths." Devon did it. I think he was trying to sort himself and if breathing the spring air would help, he was willing. "So what was that all about?"

"Sorry I lost my cool back there."

"Tell Allen Mac."

"Yeah, I will."

"So what's going on?"

"He took everything ugly from Witch Hazel Porn's mind and smeared it on beautiful Brooke. I'm not going to let that happen."

"Why are you so sensitive about it? I didn't hear him say anything stupider than usual. Everybody talks like that."

"I flipped out because he doesn't get what real love is about."

We talked some more about it as we drove home. The part he kept coming back to, the part he couldn't endure, was to have what he felt for Brooke be compared to the concepts of sex we'd learned in Witch Hazel Porn's class.

Fifteen
Changes

*D*evon knew Brooke's birthday was coming up and began to dream up a birthday extravaganza. He likes drama, so I knew it would be fun. But all of a sudden while he was making plans, reality smacked him in the face. The temporary job at my dad's office ended and Brooke was gone.

Devon was astounded. No goodbyes, nothing. Why would she jilt him like that? I pointed out that we'd been preoccupied with term papers and hadn't exactly communicated our own schedules. Why would she think she needed to hunt us down to say good-bye when we'd only seen her once in the last two weeks?

Devon's eyes were huge with alarm. "She knew how I felt about her!"

"Did you tell her?"

I wished I hadn't said that when I saw how it deflated him. But then he went to work on Ms. Martin to give him Brooke's address. This time it took five boxes of *milles feuilles* delivered one a day, but finally she caved. Two minutes later we were on the road in Devon's car, expecting, I suppose, to find Brooke in the middle of a Mud-Raiders battle with an expansive uncle who would generously offer to help hone our skills to peak performance.

Instead, we found a frowsy motel with worn carpet, stale air, and a world-worn ambience that could never have housed a classy lady like Brooke Walton. Devon refused to believe it, so he hounded the front desk clerk until the man looked up the records just to get rid of him. After a few minutes, the clerk shook his head. "No one by the name of Brooke Walton has registered at this motel in the last two months."

"That's impossible!" Devon exploded.

I was worried for the front desk clerk, who was looking fairly uncertain. Then he recovered himself and snarled, "I've gone out on a limb to help you guys, now get out of my lobby. Come on. I've got better things to do than help out a couple of punks harassing me about finding their girlfriend."

All of a sudden Devon remembered. "Please, sir. Is there a Brenna Walton?"

The front desk clerk glared, but he scanned the records for a few minutes, then looked up and said, "No one by the last name of Walton has stayed here. No Bobs, no Bessies, no Brennas and no Brookes. Now get out of here. At least figure out what your girlfriend's name is next time!"

Devon apologized profusely and we left. He kept muttering over and over, "It doesn't make sense. She was not a fake kind of person. It's not something she'd do. This doesn't make sense, Bill."

What did I know? Maybe I could have helped him a little before Collette came along. But every time he said, "It just doesn't make sense," all I could say was, "Yeah, I know."

Devon moped for days.

And then I began moping because Devon's parents announced the reason for their up-coming massive garage sale. They were picking up the family and moving to England. Devon's mother has a British accent, so I knew she had grown up there. But I thought all the doctors in England wanted to leave their rotten socialized health care system and come to the U.S. and get rich on American hypochondria. Devon's parents said that was how it used to be, but nowadays the U.S. health care system was so broken that they were going back to where people's needs drove the system, not the greed of management companies.

Apparently his parents had made an agreement with each other back when they were doing their ER residency that they would spend half their professional lives in each of their home countries. It was his mother's turn to live at home and his father's turn to have the engaging accent. For a couple of years they'd been investigating possibilities as they turned up, because repositioning dual careers would take time.

Devon hadn't been remotely worried about it happening before he left home for university. All of a sudden an opportunity had developed that seemed custom-made for his parents and they announced the move—the summer before his senior year. Cruel and unusual punishment, in my opinion.

Devon was caught off-guard. He was indignant. "You don't spend all your life in a town, make friends with everybody you can, fall in love one fine spring day, only to have your parents announce you're moving to a different continent. Am I supposed to say, *Sure, I'd love to change countries and leave everything I care about?* Bill, I'll never be able to find Brooke again from half-way around the world."

I hadn't seen Devon this close to tears in many years. It may sound a little heartless of me, but I told him he'd be crazy to miss out on a chance like this. He could take his International Baccalaureate while he was in England, same as here, and the next year we'd enroll in the best undergraduate program that would take the two of us. Between school years I'd help him hunt the planet for Brooke. I hate to admit I actually said there were other Brookes in the world.

Devon got steamed about it and I knew he was going to retaliate with *other Collettes in the world.* He might have even activated his right fist. I valued my face, so I began embroidering it all with every tourist destination in England that I'd ever read about, from Stonehenge to Hadrian's Wall, until his impulse to slug me passed. The more I talked about all the places he'd see, all the great things he could do over there, the more mollified he seemed. Gradually I began saying how much I wanted to move when he did, live with his family, spend my senior year with him in London.

And that became my truth.

When Devon told Ms. Carmangay, our English teacher, that he was moving to London, she nearly swooned. He was going to be the first person in our Shakespeare class to realize the class dream, she said. I told her I planned to move with him, and she congratulated the two of us, shook our hands, and beamed with delighted envy.

Talking about the move to London in such concrete terms made it an imminent reality. The more I talked about living with Devon and his parents, the less I could see myself living at home for another year. From then on, I spent a lot of time figuring out how to position London as an academic necessity when I announced my decision to my parents.

We had to tell Howie, so we texted him to set up a Skype connection for that night at 8 PM. He had said it was only allowed under the direst of circumstances. We promised him this qualified, and he said he'd get the necessary permissions.

When I first saw him on the monitor, it was so good to see his familiar old face that it was almost like getting my missing leg or arm back for a little while. "Hey, good to see your stupid face," I said, grinning ear to ear, which was a fairly standard opening for us.

Howie responded quite formally, and tipped his shoulder so we could see that another person was standing behind him near the door. He'd just said, *Keep it on topic. We've got company.* Right away I was a little disappointed. I wanted the old Howie back, with no one listening over his shoulder.

Devon understood the signal and went straight to the point. "Hey, Howie, the reason we're calling is, well, first of all, we miss having you around."

I said, "I hate to admit it, but A's are harder to come by without you as a study partner."

We waited a moment for him to say something, but he was looking down and we couldn't see whether his eyes were smiling or not. Finally he looked up at us in the monitor and his eyes were as close to expressionless as it's possible to get. He didn't say anything at all.

"So how are things at Soldier Ridge Academy?" I asked.

"Good. Goin' good," he said, his head nodding up and down mechanically.

"Well, Devon's got some news. Kind of good, kind of not, depending on . . ."

Devon shoved me over and said, "What Bill's trying to say is that my parents are moving the family to London. The move is set for the first of August. So I wanted to invite you to come to England and visit. Maybe before school starts in the fall? Bill says he's . . ."

Devon's voice kind of trailed off because we could hardly believe what Howie was doing. He took it like he'd been shot. Staggered backward like a bullet had slammed into his body. Then he dropped onto the bed and slumped forward with his head in his arms. He didn't look up at the monitor or say another word.

Finally Devon said, "Hey, guess we'd better go, Howie. We'll talk later, okay?"

The guy by the door was walking forward, hand in front of his face until it filled the camera, so I didn't see his features. The connection cut.

Devon said, "That was weird. I had no idea Howie would take it that hard."

I thought it was more than weird. "It was wrong, Devon. Something about it was wrong."

"Yeah, I know."

We sat there for half an hour tossing around ideas, but nothing we dreamt up was going to be of any practical help to a friend in a school three states away, a friend who obviously hated being where he was.

The next day after school Devon said, "We've got a re-do waiting for us at the Gaming Center. I think we owe the memory of Brooke a re-match."

I'll play a game of Mud-Raiders any day of the week, whether it's dedicated to true love or not, so we threw our book bags in Devon's old junker car and headed over. You can practically smell the testosterone as you walk in the door. At least that's what I said. Devon said it smelled like sweat and stinky socks to him. Which describes his bedroom perfectly, so I guess he should know. Oh, well. We dropped on our headgear, took our stances, but before he flipped the switch, Devon solemnly intoned, "In honor of Brooke Walton the Magnificent, wherever she may be."

I repeated the salute. "In honor of Brooke," and we went at it.

In the game of Mud-Raiders it's possible to come to a draw, with no winner. This frustrates some people, but I kind of like the idea that there doesn't always have to be a clear winner and loser. It suits my idea of justice, a reality ruled by something other than rivalry and competition. Some people truly can be equally matched. That's what happened to our scores that day, and it helped me feel connected to the universe in a general sort of way.

"Think Brooke's been improving her game, same as us?" Devon asked.

I smiled at him. "Sure she has!" He really had it bad, and I felt genuinely sorry for how much he hurt. I was about to challenge Devon to another round when this guy came up to me.

"Hey! Where's yer friend?"

What's that supposed to mean? So I just looked him over. Couldn't place him from anywhere. Just then I heard a big laugh behind him, and this girl stepped around him to the side. Tanya. Had to be her. Nobody else laughed like that. "Hey, Tanya," I said. "How's it going? Playing any chess these days?"

The big guy beside her reared back a little to look her over. "Chess?"

She shook her head so all the curls bounced around and said, "So how else do you think I know a nerd when I smell one? 'Course I played chess—in fifth grade!" and she laughed that big sound that made me want to stuff something in her mouth.

Devon said, "You look familiar. Friend of Merle's? Football?"

"What's it to ya?" and he swaggered his head. "I'm askin' about the kid that don't smile. You a friend of his?"

Devon looked at me to see if I knew where this was going. I thought I did, and didn't like it. But I didn't know how to take it a different direction.

Tanya did her big laugh again and said, "Give him a name, Manny. Their friend's name is Howie. Isn't that right, Bill?" And she laughed again.

This time I realized what was wrong with that laugh. It was as violent as if she had smacked my cheek with her fist. I didn't want to reward her with even a second's worth of attention. I wanted to burn the sound of her laugh out of my consciousness. But that was a dangerous laugh and I had to watch carefully to see what she'd do next.

"Yeah, Howie. So where's Howie these days?" Manny smirked.

Something told me this guy already knew where Howie was. I turned to leave, Devon ahead of me, and Manny yelled after us, "Give Howie my best the next time you Skype."

I kept walking, but my heart was racing. How did he know about our Skype call? I wanted to go back and pound the guy's face in. Our two doors slammed shut on Devon's old junker car and we peeled out of there. I pulled out my cell phone to check for hate mail. I couldn't help it. I just knew I was on somebody's list. When we pulled up in front of my house, Devon did the same thing.

"Not yet," he said.

"Same," I said, staring at a few safe messages from people I knew. We could feel it coming.

Sixteen
Fugitive

My dad was the North Star of middle school, but my grandfather, William Walker, Senior, had been the North Star of my childhood. He was a huge presence in my life, all six-feet 4-inches of him, and when he died a steady light in the universe inexplicably went out. I was nine years old and believed in heroes. Whenever I'd complain about something, he'd say, "You have to grow up some time, Bill." He'd say the same thing whether it was my toy that had broken, or a kid who'd been mean, or a teacher who'd been unfair. Always, "You have to grow up some time, Bill." Eventually I figured out that he meant something like *I can't make life fair, Bill, so suck it up.*

That's true, of course, as far as it goes. But I think it was pretty harsh to learn what I needed to know about being an adult in a single year of one disaster after the next. I couldn't do anything about some of the disasters, like Grandma Miriam or Collette, but I was convinced Devon and I could help Howie, even with him away at a military academy. A road construction crew with his two best friends for the summer was the answer. We were sure of it.

We texted Howie that another momentous thing was in the offing, and to please set up permission for another Skype visit. When his face appeared on the monitor, I almost didn't recognize him. He'd lost so much weight that he was as skinny as Devon and I had been in elementary school when Howie was our bodyguard.

"Hey, Howie! You're vanishing, man," I said. I almost barreled on with, *Hey, aren't they feeding you these days?* But Howie gave me a face signal that said, *Don't go there!* So I choked off the comment.

"Signal's good on this end. You guys having trouble?"

For Howie to deliberately misunderstand startled me. Once again, he tipped a shoulder to let us see the person standing in the background, apparently monitoring the conversation.

Devon said, "No, everything's good. Hey, we've got some good news."

"What?"

I said, "You know how I don't want to work in my dad's law office this summer? Well, he finally gave it up. But he told us about a road construction crew that's hiring. Devon and I are getting our applications ready and want to hand in one for you."

We watched Howie's face go remote and still. Then he said in a controlled voice, "I've been advised that the best recruits at Soldier Ridge Academy attend the summer session. I need to improve my rankings."

Devon had heard the tone, too, but he still whispered, "Say, yes. Please, Howie."

Howie kind of smiled, then shut it down. "Super to talk to both of you. But I gotta go now. Some heavy-duty studies coming up tonight. My grades aren't what they should be."

That was the one thing Howie could say to us that we'd never believe. There wasn't a stronger way he could tell us that his life was upside down and totally messed up. When the connection ended, Devon and I looked at each other. "What's happening at Soldier Ridge?"

"Nothing good."

"What should we do?"

Neither of us could answer that question, even though we went over and over it. Should we tell our parents? Should we go straight to Officer Patron? Should we pay Howie a visit to see first-hand what was going on? What were the chances they'd let us see him? We phoned Soldier Ridge Academy and didn't get further than the secretary. The answer: Not a chance.

We decided the next step was to go see his parents. Maybe they'd talk to us about what was going on. Friday after school, we headed over to Howie's place and Miss Denise came to the door, invited us in. We got right to the point with her. What had she heard from Howie?

"Nothing."

"He's been gone two months and you've heard nothing?"

"Sorry, boys, nothing to report. Interested in something to drink?"

We brightened at that, so she got out the juicer and a bowl of fresh oranges. When we'd finished the best 8-oz. treat in the world, Devon said, "If his parents are home, we'd like to give them a try. We did face-time with Howie yesterday, and things seem a little weird at that school."

"Why? What's the matter?"

"Whenever we've talked to him, things don't feel right. He's never alone, and he says stuff that isn't him."

"Like what?" Miss Denise asked.

"Like his grades aren't good so he has to take summer school."

Miss Denise shook her head. "No, that's not Howie." We heard the sound of the garage door raising. "Time for me to go home, boys. I'll ask Mrs. Bessamer if she'll visit with you. Come wait in the foyer while I ask."

We followed her and stood on the same spot where we'd waited for the past eight years. Finally, Miss Denise came out and nodded to us as she left. Mrs. Bessamer followed her and said, "Hello, Bill, Devon. How can I help you?"

"We wanted to ask for news about Howie," Devon began.

"He's doing fine. Just fine, boys. Soldier Ridge Academy appears to be exactly what he needs."

I said, "In terms of structure, discipline, that sort of thing . . . but we . . . "

"Yes, all the things Howie needs to learn. Well, thanks for your visit. Come back any time," and Mrs. Bessamer opened the door for us to leave.

Translation: *Go away and don't ever come back, because I won't tell you anything, even if I knew something to tell.* I wanted to paste my fist into the door as she closed it behind us.

We stood around outside Howie's house for a while and tried to think of the next logical step, but nothing was coming to us. Finally, I got nervous about how late it was and checked the time. Mother is big on family dinners, so we headed home.

My little sister Lanny heard me come in and said, "Hey, Bill, you've got a visitor." Usually she'd be all bouncy and energetic about that sort of an event, but she was watching me like she had a secret pasted all over her body. I don't like that.

"Yeah, who?"

"Howie."

I couldn't have been more surprised. "What! Where is he?"

"In your room."

I ran down the steps and found Howie in a lump of sound sleep on my sofa. I watched him for a few moments, saw how his cheekbones were severely defined above gaunt hollows, how his nose protruded large and hard, and the sunken darkness around his eyes. It was like seeing a stranger who was completely familiar. A thoroughly dislocating experience. I draped a blanket over him and went upstairs.

Mother had just come back from the lab and was still wearing her white uniform. She reminded me that she and my dad had plans for the evening and to order in pizza or barbecue or Chinese— whatever my sisters and I wanted. I thought she'd worry if she knew that Howie was asleep in my bedroom, so I didn't mention it. And I hoped my sisters wouldn't, either.

Lanny and Jacey wanted pizza, but Howie is always half desperate for Chinese, so that's what I ordered. When the doorbell rang, Lanny brought the food down to the bedroom, but I blocked her from entering. I shook my head at her and she turned away, disappointed. But she would have been even more disappointed if she'd come in to visit. The Howie in my bedroom was not the person she had a crush on from the Wyndham house party last New Year.

Howie ate at a frantic pace, the little white paper cartons held close to his mouth. I was hungry, too, so I phoned for a couple more items, fried rice with snow peas and some shrimp in a sweet sauce. Then, just as suddenly, Howie stopped. "Lots of food . . . kind of makes my gut ache . . . sorry . . . been empty lately."

"They put you on some kind of diet?"

"Yeah, mine was called subsistence."

"You've lost a lot of weight."

"I know. They control us with food. If you're labeled non-compliant, you get just enough food to keep you alive."

"That's gotta be illegal!"

"That's just the start of it, Bill . . ."

"Are you on some kind of school break?"

"Yeah. Permanent one. I'm never going back."

"How are you going to pull that off?"

"I'm working on it."

"You staying the night?"

"Yeah, if your parents don't mind."

"Why would they?" Howie had never considered whether he was invited to sleep over in all the years I'd known him.

"I'm a fugitive, Bill. I ran away. They'll probably come after me."

"Naw, you're paid up for the year. Private schools care mostly about tuition fees."

"Not this one. Tuition is petty cash compared to the money changing hands at Soldier Ridge Academy!"

"What's going on, Howie?"

"Each student is assigned to a senior student who is a Guide and Protector." When I looked up too quickly, Howie went on, "You're right, we had to pay for protection there. They knew all about my refusal. Stripped me naked to taunt me about all the scars. Promised me some more scars on parts of my body I'd never miss—yeah, you can guess what that meant—and told me the price would double afterwards—that is, if I still thought it was worth staying alive. I paid them, Bill. I swore I wouldn't, but I did. I feel like a whore now, but I wanted all my body parts. I wanted to get out of there and live my life. I didn't know life would feel so precious."

And then Howie told me what life had been like for him at the school. Told me things I had no way of imagining.

I'll bet my mouth was hanging open for a few minutes there, it was so hard to take in. I pulled myself together and said, "I'd have done the same thing, Howie. You had no other choice."

There was a knock on my bedroom door, and when I opened it, Lanny was standing there holding a white sack with our second order of Chinese food. I reached to take it from her, but she shoved past me and set the bag on the table in front of the sofa where Howie was sitting. "It's really good to see you, Howie," she said, sitting down beside him.

"Thanks," he mumbled.

"Bill missed not having you around. So did all the rest of the family."

Howie looked at her and his face sort of crumpled. "Thanks."

Lanny leaned forward and kissed him on the cheek, light and quick, and dashed out of the room, a little shy, I guess. I'd never seen Lanny do shy. Bossy, yes. Complaining, yes. Tattling, yes. Shy was a very nice change on her. Howie sat back with his arm over his eyes for a few minutes while I opened the little paper containers.

We ate in silence for a while, Howie more or less pecking around at the food. What I had just heard from him was a mélange of extortion and coercion, and I wanted to figure out a plan for tackling all the injustices Howie had suffered. After I had taken all the empty containers to the kitchen, I told him, "Let's get some police protection for you."

"Problematic."

"Why?"

"I've got a plan, Bill. If they don't find me at your place during the night, my plan will work."

"What is it?"

"You're better off not knowing."

And that's all he'd say. I quizzed him some more about the school, but he just waved off the questions. What he did want to talk about, though, seemed like a strange topic to me—the various religions of the world. I hadn't been doing the same reading, so I couldn't really get into most of the ideas he wanted to debate. I just told him the way I believed as simply as I could.

"In case you don't remember," Howie said, "I don't think too much of a god that knows what everybody is going to do before they do it. Predestination is about as grim as it gets."

"The theory of relativity gives another option," I pointed out. "If the closest distance between two points is a curved line, and if time travel is possible because of the folds in time that contract distance, then from the vantage point of another position in the space-time continuum, say Kolob—the home of the gods—then God could know the end of everything from the beginning. Which means Earth-life is nothing but freedom of choice."

"I wonder," was all Howie said.

We didn't say anything for a while, but I was feeling really nervous about whether or not something violent was going to happen if his Guide and Protector from Soldier Ridge found my house. Howie, on the other hand, seemed a little more relaxed. From the looks of him it would have been about the first time in months that he'd been able to kick back with a full stomach.

His eyes were closed when he said, "What if it's all mythology? That's what my dad calls religion."

"What?" I was deep into a possible armed encounter with extortionists and trying to figure out what in the house we could use for self-defense. My only hope was a good kitchen knife or two. And here was Howie talking religion.

He said, "Mythology. Religion. Two sides of the same coin."

"Mythology seems to start with truth," I said, "and then it gets distorted over time."

"Religion is a word that means you happen to believe a particular story is true. Everybody who doesn't believe the religion calls it mythology. Poor ancient Greeks. They got outvoted. Nobody believes their stuff is true anymore. Well, except Percy Jackson."

The doorbell rang and we both jumped. We could hear rapid footsteps heading for my room. Howie stood up and faced the door, despair on his face. Half a minute later the door flew open. Devon. He stopped dead still when he saw Howie, then burst into a smile, and grabbed Howie's skinny body into a tight, back-thumping hug. We brought Devon up to speed as fast as we could. His first impulse was the same as mine—take Howie to the police station and request protection.

Howie said, "No, my plan is better." But he didn't argue with us, he just stopped talking.

Devon stayed the night, of course. Every once in a while it felt like old times when we were three boys who believed in heroes and who knew our personal freedom was an inalienable right that could not be compromised by greed and the lust for power.

When morning came, Howie was gone.

Devon and I bolted down some breakfast in the kitchen where Lanny was making pancakes. I thought she was going to cry when I told her Howie had already gone, and she's not a crier. She stood there holding the pancake flipper. "So where did he go so early? I thought he'd love some hot pancakes."

I'd never done this before, but I put my arm around her shoulders and said, "He didn't tell us his plans, but we picked up on some hints."

"Like what?"

"We're going to the police station first, and from there I don't know. Cover for me with Mom and Dad, okay?"

We went straight down to the police station and asked to speak to Officer Patron. They said he was out. We said we'd wait. They said it could take a while. We said we'd wait.

We sat there watching people come and go. We were off to the side in a little indented corner space between the window and the water cooler. Nobody paid much attention to that space unless they were walking over for a free drink of water. That's how we happened to hear Mr. Bessamer when he came in, steaming mad.

It took us a while to piece together what had happened. Apparently, when Howie left my house in the early morning, he took a taxi to the police station and asked for protection. The police said no crime had been committed. It didn't matter that Howie was terrified that one would be committed—on his very person. So Howie decided to commit a crime, if that's what the police needed. He walked directly over to the convenience store closest to the police station. In full view of the security camera, he pinched the key hanging beside the cash register, opened the glass sliding doors to the cigarette cabinet, stuffed as many cigarette cartons into his backpack as he could, and walked out. That's when the store manager spotted Howie, came barreling after him, and knocked him to the ground. Howie let it all happen. The police came—Officer Patron, actually. Howie returned all the cigarettes to a very annoyed store manager and walked down to the police station in the company of Officer Patron, who put him in a cell and called his father.

Why hadn't Howie factored in his status as a minor? Or had he? Devon and I still puzzle over that one. Was he documenting his whereabouts for whoever might be watching? Was he demonstrating that the police and his father were on his side? That he had strong male authority figures in his court?

Anyway, while sitting in the nook between the water-cooler and the window, Devon and I witnessed the picking-up-of-Howie-by-parent. Mr. Bessamer's hands trembled with pent-up fury. He paid the fines, and literally collared Howie for the walk out to the car. I hoped Howie wouldn't get beaten up at home. Paid thugs were one thing; his dad was quite another.

End of the year school projects pretty much got in the way for a few days, but we called and texted him. His answers were monosyllabic. When we went to see him, his room was even a bigger mess than when he was packing for the move to Soldier Ridge Academy. Howie didn't even say *hi*, just stared at us a few moments and then started rummaging in his closet, pulling everything out on the floor. We'd had a fair chance to look his face over, though, and it didn't look like he'd gotten beat up—at least not in the last couple of days. There were greenish-yellow patches on his arms, though, that looked like old bruises. I wanted to ask him about them, but he didn't give me much of a chance.

From inside the closet, Howie began pulling all his clothes off the hangars and throwing them over his shoulder into the middle of the room. Then he started throwing his shoes really hard one at a time at the walls. I thought this was bizarre and said so. He ignored me and handed me a box. Then he handed one just like it to Devon.

When I lifted the lid, the first thing I saw was the Russian chess masters book I'd given him a few years ago. Underneath were all kinds of papers, bits and pieces of things I kind of recognized but hadn't seen for years, including pictures of Howie and me. It was like my whole friendship with Howie was in this little box. Every note I'd ever written the gruff old guy in grade school, movie stubs, every tiny little bit of trivia from all those years was in the box.

I guess Devon's box was about the same because when I glanced his direction, he was staring at Howie with his mouth open, holding the latest birthday gift from Howie's parents—a hand-held device of colossal computing power (so the advertising goes.) Devon's mouth is not open and silent very often, so this was an historic moment.

I was trying to get a clue from Howie's face about what all of this meant. If it were a gift he was happy about giving, maybe he'd have a kind of smile of satisfaction lurking around his eyes. But Howie's eyes were vacant. Nothing was there. Suddenly a little light flicked on in his face and he began abruptly, "Hey, you guys know what a Nix is?"

Apparently he wasn't going to tell us what the boxes of stuff meant, so I said, "Well, if you nix something, it means you veto it, forbid it, that sort of thing."

Devon said, "Yeah, I nix—I prohibit—the formation of Internet gangs."

Howie's eyes actually smiled a little and then he said, "Actually, a Nix is a female creature from Germanic folklore. Unfriendly to man."

I was nudging a few of the trinkets in his box around and said, "Never heard of it before."

"Yeah," Howie went on, "it can take many forms, but usually it's a woman or else half human and half fish. Lives in a beautiful fresh-water palace."

Devon said, "So Supreme Maelstrom knows his/her Germanic mythology."

Howie nodded.

Devon was standing at the window. "Makes you wonder about the kind of girl that would get sucked in. She gets promised everything she thinks she wants. Popularity, power, material stuff, and all she has to do is point out somebody to be a target."

"Sick," I said. "What's in it for the boys, do you think?"

"Power. The chance to use some gross muscle mass."

"Does Druj have a meaning?" Devon asked.

Howie answered, "Yeah. Zoroastrian word for *lie*. As in falsehood." He glared at each of us, a little of the old bulldog stance emerging. "Don't you tell me he's a misunderstood genius. He's got an Internet dictionary and way too much time on his hands. That's all!"

From then on, Howie more or less faded. He said nothing, moved little. I wondered if our visit had exhausted him, so we picked up the boxes of stuff he'd given us and went home.

Devon and I had to work in my dad's law office that Saturday. We called Howie to come with us, even though he never does. He didn't answer. Sunday afternoon no one opened the door at his house when we knocked. We walked around to the side of the house to throw a few pebbles at his window, but if he was there, he didn't respond. Howie's house was still closed up on Monday after school. But on Tuesday and Wednesday there were panel trucks parked out front and workmen flowing in and out. By Thursday we were burning with curiosity when Miss Denise finally met us at the door.

Devon smiled at her and said, "Sure busy around here! What's up?"

She stared at us soberly for a few moments. "Howie tried to burn down the house."

"What!"

"The fire trucks got here in time to put out the blaze before the rest of the house caught fire, but it destroyed his room."

"Where is Howie?"

"In a hotel."

Howie chose an empty hotel room instead of my place? Why? I couldn't make sense of it. I thought he needed to be in a psych ward, but I knew his dad would block that option. Devon asked Miss Denise where his parents were.

"They're on *his and hers* client business trips, if you know what I mean."

What kind of a crazy family lived this way! "So when is Howie coming home?"

"I'm picking him up in a few minutes. I'd invite you to come along, but I don't think he could handle it. I don't want him to bolt. Maybe you could wait here until I get him home?" Miss Denise's face was lined with cares and her eyes had dark circles under them. I hadn't realized how hard this was on her.

Devon and I went up to Howie's room to wait. It was completely changed. Gone was the carpeting and all the furniture, including the big bed with the carved wooden headboard. Instead, the bare plywood flooring was painted black and the walls a howling lime green. His new bed consisted of a single mattress on a piece of plywood anchored by steel industrial chains to the beams in his ceiling. A thin black cotton drape hung from the ceiling on all sides of his bed platform. There were no chairs to sit on while we waited, so we sat on the plywood bed.

After half an hour we were ready for some kind of diversion. We hunted around in Howie's garage until we found his hammock, tied one end of its rope to the fence post at the back of the yard and the other end around a tree in the lawn. Our plan was that when he came home we would entice him outside into the fresh air, out of the house, out of his own tragedy.

When Howie came home he was not glad to see us. Both of his hands were wrapped in bandages. Burns I guess, but I didn't ask. He was completely silent. It was like he could hardly endure the idea that friendship still existed in the world. Devon and I tried to think of some way to prove our loyalty to him, but part of us felt repelled by the awful colors all around us, the silence in the room, the emptiness that was Howie.

Seventeen
Hearts on Fire

Devon and I had excused absences from the first two classes of
the day to meet Officer Patron down at the station. Finally,
he had something concrete to tell us. He said extensive media
coverage had slowed expansion into new U.S. schools, so recruitment
operations seemed to have transferred to Asia, at least temporarily.
Apparently SM didn't realize that the police in other countries aren't
as hampered by laws protecting criminals as they are in the U.S.

As Devon and I walked along in the sunshine we tried not to
think about Howie. Other than him, things looked pretty good.
Officer Patron's report had been upbeat. Our summer job on the
road construction crew was going to be out-in-the-open-air kind
of work with good pay. Devon's parents had said I was more than
welcome to live with them in the fall, so our plans to get together in
London for school were doable. I was still figuring out how to tell my
parents I was moving out, but I was really excited about a change of
scene. Things were looking good, we told each other.

That is . . . until we walked into the school.

As soon as we opened the doors we could feel the jittery energy. Allen Mac was waiting for us around the corner. "Have you seen it?" he yelled.

"Seen what?"

"Howie. It's practically gone viral." Allen had the video running in an instant and held it up for us to watch. We could see Howie lying asleep in the back yard hammock. Someone wearing a black facemask lowered himself over the high back fence. The next bit showed it all in slow motion, the tiptoe to the hammock, a hand reaching out, tipping Howie out of the hammock, and voices shouting, "Booo!"

Howie hit the ground with an audible crack of the head. He scrambled with his bandaged hands and pulled himself up to face the Druj. They were laughing and shouting "Kill him! Get him! Waste him!" They didn't advance on Howie and they showed no weapons, but their screams of laughter might as well have been knives glinting in the sunshine. Howie began screaming. He screamed and screamed and screamed into the camera. The video ended on a still, with a long shot of Howie's open silenced mouth.

Devon and I couldn't even look at Allen Mac. This was something ugly that his sense of humanity should try to cover up. Why was he excited to have us see it? Like a gawker over road kill. What was the fascination with misery?

Obviously, the whole thing had been completely staged. The person filming it had scoped out the situation for angles and shots, which made it all the more cynical. Howie was the victim, but he wasn't the audience. Not really. The high schoolers feeding off the vicious scene were the piranhas it had been filmed for. The video was bait for bigger feeding frenzies via the Internet.

Devon and I turned on our heel and left that school. Headed straight to Howie's house. We pounded on the door, but no one came. We kept it up, pounding and pounding and calling Howie's name and shouting our own names. Finally Miss Denise opened the door a crack, keeping the safety chain in place.

"Miss Denise! Where is he?" I gasped, trying to control my breath.

"Hello, boys." Her voice was absolutely cold.

"Please, Miss Denise. We've got to see Howie," Devon said. "We just saw what happened. Please let us in!"

"I'm sorry, Howie is unavailable." Her face was frozen, like she didn't even know us. That didn't make sense. We'd been visiting there all our lives and it never occurred to us to think of Miss Denise as an obstacle.

Devon said, "Please tell us where Howie is, Miss Denise!"

She got this closed-door look on her face, like she'd never seen us in her life and repeated the same thing. "He is unavailable."

We'd sat in her kitchen along with Howie for a lot of years. We didn't deserve to get shrugged off like this. "I don't understand. Do you mean Howie's here, but doesn't want to see us? Or has he gone out?"

Miss Denise tensed up and glared at me through the crack of the door. "I mean, Mr. Walker, Howie is unavailable," and she closed the door. We heard her turn the dead bolt from inside.

Devon and I were so astonished we just stood there a moment, trying to process what had happened. "Maybe there's a logical explanation for this," I said.

"Yeah, and maybe I'll win the lottery when I never buy a ticket," Devon snapped. "Shut up and get real."

I guess I deserved that. I was more or less yapping, with no idea what to think.

That night my dad said that typically the entire family would be in shock after such a succession of violent acts, so we should be patient and give them time to heal. Devon's parents said the same thing, but in medical language that required a dictionary and with a lot of numbers floating around.

Waiting was hard on us because it didn't make sense to keep him isolated. Howie probably needed us more than ever now. We gave the family two days. We hoped every day that Miss Denise would call one of us. She didn't. On the third day we planned to go to his house and demand to see him. Stage a sit-in, if we had to.

We were standing at our lockers after school discussing strategy for the Bessamer household when the school secretary approached us. Apparently the principal wanted to see us. Devon and I were still honor roll types, despite everything going on in our lives, so a meeting with the school principal held no particular alarm. We U-turned back into the office hoping he'd make it quick so we could get over to the Bessamers.

The principal was standing in the doorway waiting for us, and invited us to sit down. He started on a little small talk, which I find quite annoying. I don't see why adults think it's the way to go at something. You should choose the right words, say what you have to say, sit down, and shut up. I absolutely couldn't chitchat with him.

But Devon was doing it for both of us. He was brilliant. It gave me time to really watch the principal. All of a sudden I knew what he was going to tell us. Down to the bottom of my toes, I knew. It was going to hurt. His face said it all. The chitchat was like one of those little Mardi Gras masks that hardly covers up a thing. Finally he got down to it. "You're friends of Howard Bessamer, right?" The principal already knew we were. I hate questions like that, but Devon was nodding agreeably, so I tried to follow suit. "Would you say you are his best friends?"

"Probably." For sure I wasn't going to add Allen Mac or Merle-the-line-backer to the list.

"We received a statement from Howard's family," the principal said, and picked up a sheet of paper already open on his desk. He read it aloud. "We regret to inform you Howard Bessamer has been involved in a fatal accident. Please inform his friends."

I don't know what else the principal said after that. I couldn't hear a thing. His voice sounded far away, as though sound was coming through a pond of water around my ears.

Out on the front steps I asked Devon if he got any more information out of him, and he said he couldn't hear anything for a while either. Neither one of us wept. I remember making a decision not to. It felt like I was taking a big chunk of grief and placing it where I wouldn't have to examine it unless I chose to. My palms were sweating and my neck muscles were stiff. I know Devon was hurting, too. He doubled over for a few minutes like he had a gut-ache. "Do you think it's the right thing to go over there?"

"Yes. Offer a few words of condolence to his parents."

As we walked along from the school to Howie's house, we tried to figure out what the phrase *words of condolence* actually meant. Do we say, *Howie was a great guy, best friend in the world?* Do we say, *Howie was so smart he could beat the heck out of all of us at chess and get straight As without breaking a sweat?* Do we say, *You did all you could. Don't feel bad, you were wonderful parents?* What kinds of lies were we expected to participate in?

We still hadn't figured out what was both honest and kind, what we were actually going to say, but Miss Denise answered the door right away. She took one look at our faces and said, "You know."

We said, "Yes. The school told us. We've come to see his parents. To offer our help."

She shook her head. "They aren't receiving visitors." She stood there like a mountain keeping us out.

I said, "I think they'll see us. We're Howie's two best friends ever since grade school. But you know that." I was so angry with her that I almost spat the last few words out of my mouth.

She didn't move. Didn't invite us in. Just looked at our unwelcome feet standing on a mat that said, 'Welcome.'

Devon said, "Would you please tell his parents we're here?"

She shook her head again. "I'm sorry, boys. They gave me strict instructions they were not to be disturbed."

We turned away and slowly walked home. Didn't really know what to do with ourselves. I was angry. We deserved to know what had happened to Howie. The second attack was destructive emotionally, but not physically. So what had gone wrong? Over the years, Devon and I had spent more time with Howie than any other two people in his life and we deserved to be told how he had died.

We went back to Howie's house again the next day. We felt like we were becoming the pests of the century, but we had to know. We didn't even say anything when Miss Denise opened the door. We just looked at her in silence with questions all over our faces that she had to have been able to read. She just said, "Sorry, boys. Now isn't a good time."

On the way back home I told Devon, "I think she seemed a little nicer today. Not so cold." He agreed with me.

The next day was Saturday, so Miss Denise would be off-duty today for sure. Devon and I were determined to talk to Howie's parents. It had become an obsession with us to know what had happened. You can't be with a person day in and day out for eight years and make no response when you're told the person has died. You want to know what happened. Why it happened. You want to make sure people care about his life the same way you care. We didn't even know when the funeral was going to be held.

We rang the bell and waited, like all the other times. Finally Miss Denise opened the door, which startled me since I had expected to see Howie's mother. We asked to see Mr. and Mrs. Bessamer. Once again she was formal. "I'm sorry. They aren't available."

I felt angry and it showed when I said, "When will they be available? We'll come back."

Devon cut me off. He said, "Miss Denise, this has been really hard on you, hasn't it?" She was still standing with one hand on the doorknob, but I saw her shoulders slump a little. Devon went on, approaching her reality. "Of all of us, you've probably cared for Howie the very most." She ducked her head so we couldn't see her eyes. "You've always been there for him, ever since he was just a little kid." Tears trickled down Miss Denise's cheeks. "I'm so sorry. You must feel so sad," Devon ended softly.

She wiped the tears off with her hands and said, "Come in. The Bessamers are out right now and I can give you a few minutes before they get back. Not long, mind." She walked toward the kitchen where we'd drunk all the after-school smoothies with Howie, made by her hand. I almost expected her to reach for a bowl of fresh oranges and the juicing machine. We sat down together at the empty kitchen table.

"Can you tell us when the funeral is going to be held?" I began.

"There isn't going to be one."

Devon was as surprised as I was. "Well, the memorial service, then."

"There isn't going to be one."

"Why not?" I blurted. I couldn't understand what the problem was. Why weren't they going to let us participate in the grieving? If it's formalized, like with Grandma Miriam's funeral, and if you can do it along with other people who cared about the person, it's easier to say a gentle good-bye in your heart. But Howie's parents were shutting the door in our faces.

"Well, I have my own private thoughts about it."

I heard that as a plain signal that she didn't want to keep her private thoughts to herself. She needed to grieve with us as much as we needed to grieve with her.

Devon sensed her reality and said, "Your help to the Bessamer family goes way beyond the terms of your job, doesn't it?"

Denise looked at him carefully, as if making a decision. I could see her features begin to open up with the desire to tell. Gradually she unfolded the story Howie's parents wanted to hide.

Yes, she admitted, for over a week she hadn't gone to her own home at night. She had stayed at the Bessamer house to answer the phone and the door, and to cook meals for Howie's parents. She believed the two of them would have just stopped eating altogether since neither one of them could do anything with food except open a can. They couldn't face going out in public, either. "They've been hit harder than you can imagine," she said.

I tried to dredge up some sympathy for them, but I knew how inept and selfish they'd been, so it was hard. I was also struggling to understand why they wouldn't be generous enough to allow us to grieve with them. And now I had to try to get my mind around a couple that was unfaithful to each other, but so insular that they couldn't turn to friends for help when they were struck with a tragedy.

Devon said, "So you've been here for them, the same as you've been here for Howie all these years."

"Yes, I've stayed to help them for Howie's sweet sake," and Miss Denise began to sob.

It's a good thing Devon was there, because I was totally blown away by the idea of a sweet Howie. I tried to think of anything sweet about him that I could possibly remember. I was working at it really hard while Devon was consoling Miss Denise.

It kind of started coming to me. Friends saw him as prickly, pugnacious, and completely smart. To his parents he was uncommunicative, dour, angry. But Miss Denise had been the one to hear his after-school descriptions of his daily triumphs, to help him ride his first bike, to take him to buy the presents for our birthday parties. Sure, he was *sweet Howie* to her. I could see that.

She said, "In my line of work I'm expected to keep a lot of confidences. I hear things and I see things. I keep them to myself and in a few years the family works it all out in their own way. But I don't like secret things. They scare me. That's why I'm going to tell you boys what Howie's parents want to keep secret.

"I've known plenty of details about goings-on in this house that would raise the hair on the back of your neck. I've always kept them to myself. But this is different. You boys were the only friends I ever heard Howie talk about, the only friends in all those years I ever saw come to the house. You have a right to know. I'm not keeping this to myself one minute longer."

There was something about how she was setting this up that equally intrigued and repulsed me. I didn't want to know and I desperately wanted to know. But Miss Denise had made her decision and there wasn't any deciding left for me to do. She wanted us to know.

She began slowly, "I overheard Howie's parents arguing. I couldn't avoid it because they were screaming at each other. As always. Over the years they've tried to keep a lid on it when Howie was in the house, at least when they can remember where he is. But when he's gone they really let 'er rip. Apparently Howie left a suicide note."

I flinched, visibly, and I know Devon did, too. Suicide.

Neither of us was prepared for that possibility. The Bessamer's letter to the principal had said fatal accident. We'd relied on that being the whole truth and nothing but the truth. I could see in my mind the rope in Howie's backpack last winter and for a few minutes I felt my gorge rise. I was afraid I'd be sick right there on the table. And then the guilt settled over me. Guilt, thick and deep and heavy. I hadn't stopped him. I hadn't done enough. I'd even punched him in the face at the lake house. Drew blood. And now he'd killed himself.

Miss Denise let us absorb this for a few minutes before she went on. "Actually it wasn't the classic suicide note. It was a series of text messages. His mother and father had gone their separate ways again on the weekend the Druj ambushed him in the back yard. Each of his parents had scheduled an out-of-town event with a *client*. They didn't bother to ask me to stay over on the weekend so Howie wouldn't be alone."

Her repressed grief began to spill out in tears. "If you can believe it. Your own baby boy. And you don't want to be with him 24-7 when he needs you the most. Oh, my heart. I think it'll break for my sweet Howie." She wiped her face with tissues. "Well, Howie must have texted his mother a dozen times the first few days she was out of town. He knew she was off on another of her romantic getaways and that his dad was, too, for that matter. Coordinated extramarital affairs! Some people!"

Miss Denise cried some more and Devon handed her more tissues and said quiet soothing things, so nondescript that I can't remember the words so much as the sound of his voice. As much as I wanted to cry along with Miss Denise, I didn't allow myself to let go. If I once let myself start, I wasn't sure there was anything I could grab hold of to make me stop. I was determined to let Miss Denise have her own time of grief with us there to help her through it.

"After the Druj jumped Howie and nearly scared him to death, they took off. Didn't harm his body. But they destroyed him just the same. Once the scene was on the Internet for the world to see, somebody texted Howie telling him to look at the freak he really was.

Miss Denise paused, thinking back. "He texted his dad once, saying, *I'm giving you what you've wanted for a long time.* Later, when the police followed through, Mr. Bessamer told them he didn't answer Howie's text because he was already on his way home. Upon arriving he found the house empty, so he left for the office. "Howie checked himself into a motel and texted his mother one last time. *Where are you?* Then he hung himself."

Miss Denise laid her cheek on the cold table, but no tears were left. Devon and I were silent, trying to comprehend it all. After a few minutes she sat up, very erect. "It doesn't end there. I'm going to tell you all of it. Howie hung himself in the afternoon. Maybe he assumed that housekeeping was finished for the day and he wouldn't be found until the next time the room was rented. But the cleaning staff was running late and called maintenance to get past the deadbolt. They found Howie and called 911. Medics got to Howie before he could die." Miss Denise turned her head away and gazed abstractedly out the window.

Devon and I were stunned, like we'd been hit with another heavy punch in the gut that winded us both for a few minutes. Finally, I collected myself. "Let me get this straight. Howie hung himself, but they got to him in time, so he's not dead. He's alive. He's going to be just fine." Miss Denise turned to look me in the eye and my heart constricted.

"He's alive inside his body, but he's never going to be just fine."

Devon said, "I don't understand, Miss Denise."

"Howie's spinal column is damaged so severely that he's completely paralyzed. He can't speak nor even eat for himself. He's fed through a tube into the GI tract."

She told us that after the hospital staff heroically saved his life, they stabilized him for a few days and then moved him to the state long-term care facility. She reached for her purse and retrieved her address book. I pulled out my phone and recorded all the information.

Miss Denise wiped her eyes and blew her nose, then looked at her watch and stood up. "Boys, it's time for you to be on your way." She walked us to the side door off the kitchen and said, "I've been sworn to secrecy, you know."

"We'll honor that," I said.

At the door Devon paused, then asked the housekeeper we'd known for as long as we'd known Howie, "How can you stand it here?"

"It's probably as hard on the Bessamers having me here, knowing that I know, as the knowing is on me. I've given my two weeks' notice. With my sweet Howie gone, I'm just not interested in the goings-on in this house anymore. They're better off with somebody new."

As Devon and I closed the door to Howie's house for the last time, we were too choked with our feelings to speak. The sun still shone on our heads, the trees still had new green leaves. Everything was the same, but everything had changed.

Eighteen
New Lives

School ended, but Devon and I had nothing to celebrate. Besides, if we reported to our flagger jobs on Mudd Mountain on time, there'd be just enough time to pack and visit Howie before we left. We tried to prepare ourselves for the visit, but we had no model for what we'd encounter. Was it *good-bye* or *see ya later*? We didn't know what we'd say, really, but we knew we had to see him. Another problem was how to do it without betraying Miss Denise's trust. The truth was, we couldn't live with the promise we'd made to Miss Denise.

As we drove to the state regional center for the mentally and physically disabled, we were deep into a shared silence. We held unspoken worries about what to say to Howie and whether we would handle the visit right. But nothing and nobody could have prepared us for the Howie we saw.

An attendant led us to his room. A body lay on the bed wearing some grey sweat pants and a T-shirt we recognized as Howie's. But it was the shape of the body that shocked us. His arms were bent at the elbow and cramped up tight against his body, his hands severely bent down at the wrists. His legs were rigid and straight, his feet cramped inward and his toes bent under. His eyes could open and shut, but he couldn't move anything else on his body.

Devon touched his arm gently. "Howie, we're here. Bill and I are here for you."

Howie's eyes blinked but didn't focus on either of us.

I turned to the attendant and said, "Can we talk to you for a minute?" Outside in the hall, I said, "You could have told us. You could have prepared us!"

The attendant apologized and said he hadn't known this was our first visit. What could he do to help us today? I asked him if Howie knew where he was? Did he recognize people? What was left of his brain? The attendant said nobody knew for sure. The doctors were still doing evaluative tests on him and would have more answers as the months went by.

Devon was near tears. "Months! You're talking months?"

The attendant was very calm and matter-of-fact. He said Howie would never regain more of his motor skills and would never speak. He could possibly gain a little more in his range of facial expressions. Right now he was going through the trauma of adjusting to such drastic life circumstances. He would never be able to swallow well enough to take more than a tiny sip of water, so his nutrients went straight into his gastro-intestinal tract through what they called a g-tube. He'd wear a diaper for the rest of his life.

It was hard for Devon and me to come to terms with the concept of no recovery. Howie would be on that bed, his limbs cramped up and rigid for the rest of his life. I wanted to know how long the life expectancy was for a person in this condition.

The attendant identified it as LIS, Locked-in Syndrome, and said sometimes they lived to be old men. Infection was the problem, both around the g-tube and from bedsores. The programming for his daily routines was just now being worked out. They'd have a better idea in a few months how best to keep him comfortable.

I couldn't imagine a life more dismal. My mind had nowhere to go for comfort, for hope. I needed to talk to my dad. My old dad. The dad before the New Year's Eve dance, before Collette.

But the visit wasn't over, yet. I hadn't spoken to Howie and I knew I had to do that. I told the attendant we needed a few more minutes, so we all went back into the room. I went up to Howie and took his arm like I'd seen Devon do. "Howie, I don't know if you can hear me or understand what I'm saying. I know your soul is somewhere, and I'm going to talk to that soul of yours because I love you like my brother. You are my brother. I'm not handling this first visit very well. Neither is Devon. So we're going to leave now. We'll come back soon. You can count on us." I squeezed his arm a little and we left the building, wordless, spent, the tears lurking in the rims of our eyeballs.

Out in the parking lot, we saw Mr. Bessamer get out of his car. I didn't know what to say to him, but in a situation like that you can't pretend you don't see somebody. I nodded my head in his direction and continued walking toward our car.

He shouted, "Hey, you two!" and began trotting toward us.

Devon and I were surprised. His dad hadn't wanted anything to do with us before, so there was no way to anticipate what kind of connection he wanted now, given the circumstances. It took Mr. Bessamer about two seconds to weave around the cars and stand full in our face, way too close. If any grief was in him it was well covered up. What I saw was a face full of anger. He shouted at me, "Did you see him?"

"Yes."

"Did you like what you saw?"

How do you answer a stupid question like that? I glanced at Devon and he wasn't coming up with anything, either. Mr. Bessamer was practically standing on my toes, which anchored me there, but Devon slipped quickly to the side of the car, which put the hood between them.

Mr. Bessamer shouted in my face, "You are not welcome here. Have you got that?" He turned to Devon: "Do. Not. EVER. Come. Back!"

Devon spoke to him across the car. "We're his friends, Mr. Bessamer. We wanted to see if we could help."

At that Mr. Bessamer brought his fist down with such force that it dented the hood of the car. "Don't you give me any of that! And don't you come here again! Do you understand?"

I backed up fast, out of the range of his fists. "No, I don't understand. Why not?"

"So you can gloat? Is that it?" Mr. Bessamer started after me, swaggering his head a little side to side in a motion I'd seen Howie use. I hated it when Howie did it, but I was terrified when his father did it. I darted around the back of the car as Mr. Bessamer advanced, "So you can show us all how smart you are? So you can lord it over me and my son? You stay away from this place or I'll have the cops after you."

Devon had slid into the driver's seat and opened the back door enough on his side that I could slip in and lock it. He started the motor and we tore out of that parking lot, Mr. Bessamer's eyes boring holes in our retreat. No cops picked us up for speeding, and we parked in front of my house. I couldn't find words at first.

"He's gotta be sick in the head," Devon finally said.

"Crazy."

"Maybe he'll get over it. Heal with time."

I couldn't be that generous. It seemed to me that Mr. Bessamer was pretty well set in the patterns of who he was.

But no matter how you think you've hit a dead end and the world has stopped, in the morning when you wake up, it's still turning. So, Devon and I left for the mountain and our construction job the next day. As we drove, we wished that Howie had agreed to come with us. Maybe things would have turned out differently. Again, all those awful what-ifs. Gradually, the scene around us changed, until the road wound through a beautiful forest. Despite everything, somewhere inside us the excitement of life opened up.

We found the office, got our bunkhouse assignment, and slid our duffle bags under the bunks on the side of the room that didn't look occupied. Two splashed and curling pieces of paper hung over the washbasin area at the far end of the room. The toothpaste spattered weekly schedule was posted beside a battered monthly projection sheet at eye level where you'd expect the mirror to hang. The mirror was actually eight inches to the right of the basin and so small that you could either look at one eyebrow or half your chin, but not both. That was fine with me. I could do without seeing my face for a few months.

That's when I decided to keep the beard. I hadn't shaved during exam week, as much to annoy my mother as anything. But looking at half my chin in the tiny toothpaste frosted mirror, I decided this would be the summer I'd see what kind of facial hair I could produce. Right from the start I thought of it as camouflage. Devon jumped on the challenge, but a blonde beard looks like peach fuzz a lot longer than a black one. He started shaving again after a few weeks.

Seeing Howie the first time had been hard on us, but as we talked over the situation in the sunshine on the top of a mountain, we decided the generous thing to do was to ignore what Mr. Bessamer had done and said in a moment of anguish. Obviously he had been temporarily insane. We pledged to go back to visit Howie every time we had a day off for the rest of our lives.

The first week of work involved a lot of new things—the bunkhouse, the food, the other men on the crew, and especially how to do our jobs. We were exhausted every night when it was all over for the day. But it was easy compared to what we anticipated having to go through in a lifetime of visits with Howie.

The next week as we drove down the mountain in Devon's old junker car with the new dent in the hood, we worried about how to reach out to Howie and how to avoid his father. When we reached the Regional Center, we circled the parking lot looking for cars belonging to the Bessamers. Couldn't see anything expensive enough to belong to them, so we braved walking up the sidewalk into the front doors and announced to the attendant at the front desk that we were there to see Howard Bessamer.

The attendant's face closed up and he said, "Sorry, Howard Bessamer is not allowed to have visitors."

I didn't comprehend his meaning at first and said, "We'll just let ourselves into his room. We know right where it is. Down the hall to the right."

The attendant was a big man and it surprised me how quickly he was able to move out from behind the desk to block me. "Orders for Howard Bessamer clearly exclude all visitors. I have to follow them."

"What?" I still wasn't processing the information.

"I'm sorry. We have to follow the orders in place."

All of a sudden I realized the truth. Howie must have taken a turn for the worst. "I'm sorry Howie's not doing well today. Last week he seemed . . ."

"No, that's not what I'm saying."

Devon wasn't getting it either. He smiled and extended his hand to the attendant, "We understand. We'll call first before we come next time. Save us both the inconvenience."

The attendant did not shake the proffered hand. "I'm sorry, boys. That's not how it works. His parents establish the visiting orders."

I was stunned. "Like what can they establish?"

"Just about everything. What he wears, what visitors are allowed, what holidays he can observe."

"Holidays? Howie's seventeen years old. He's been making those kinds of decisions for the last fourteen years!"

"I apologize. I know this must be difficult for you. But the orders are written right here. Howard Bessamer is not allowed to celebrate Valentine's Day, Easter, Thanksgiving, Christmas, New Year, or his birthday. And he is not allowed to have any visitors."

"Ever?" I simply couldn't process what I was hearing.

Devon kind of mumbled the list to himself. It was ridiculous. I felt the anger bubble up. The attendant was very patient with us. He told us over and over again that parents have all the rights to limit a disabled child's world and could determine every facet of their lives, whether the disabled person was under age or of legal age. Howie would have no visitors until he was an old man and his parents died, if that's what his parents decided. No board of appeal. Final decision.

Finally Devon and I absorbed the information and left. That's not what you call closure. That's not what you call humane. How could it be legal?

When I got back up the mountain, I called Dad at his office. He said it was legal. I wanted to talk to him about Howie, but the chasm was there. I had wanted a chasm and I had gotten one. My dad and I could hardly speak across it.

The chasms I could see from my job on the Mudd Mountain road crew, however, were beautiful in the distance. I told Devon we were going to explore those mountains and every valley between them. Over a whole summer, we'd have time.

Once you get the hang of being a flagger, the job is pretty easy. Some employees find the empty road time in the early morning and the late evening to be the hardest part. They sit down, wander off, start playing around with the company audio equipment. Devon and I didn't do that. We had our own technology if we needed to say something, but usually I just wanted to be bored and alone. I liked it. I liked the spaces between people and things. I wanted to be able to stare off into the mountain ranges hundreds of miles away and not think about anything.

Our bunkhouse had one creature comfort that mattered. When you're hot and sweaty, itching from the dust, coughing with diesel fumes, and you step into a tepid shower, it's bliss. Some days I'd linger over the pleasure. The towels in the bunkhouse are a coarse-textured cotton that practically yank the water off your skin. Love it. Totally different feeling from the towels my mother buys that are very pretty, but non-absorbent. The shower became a sort of transition from the nothing of the job to the intensity of my desire to connect with Collette in French, a language my parents don't speak.

I was the focus of a lot of dumb jokes in the bunkhouse about the French movies I watched on my lap top computer instead of the kind the other guys liked—westerns, horror, adventure—all with sound tracks I couldn't hear over my French audio materials. Ear buds and audio books made me a very tolerant roommate.

Eventually the other men in the bunkhouse more or less left Devon and me alone. It's not like we went out of our way to ignore each other or anything, but they had their connections with each other already made. Devon and I alternated bunk beds every week since there are advantages and disadvantages to both the lower and the upper bunks (to which the other guys on the road crew were apparently oblivious) and they had their own ways of living together figured out. Besides, they knew from the get-go that Devon and I were temporaries, still in high school, and weren't going to finish out this job much less move on to the next one with the crew.

I have to confess a big part of me didn't believe Collette had really eloped with that boy from her hometown. She couldn't have. We meant too much to each other. I believed my dad could have misunderstood the message about Collette's elopement, or exaggerated it in order to make me stop thinking about her. But if he had, the ruse had failed. I couldn't stop loving her. Not without more evidence than a secondhand phone call. I loved Collette and I had every reason to believe she felt the same way about me.

So, despite the evidence about Collette, everything French became a passion with me that summer on the mountain. I bought the illustrated classic, *Le Petit Prince*, and practically memorized it through so many readings. I found an Online collection of short stories with a recording of a woman reading them aloud in French. I listened to the recordings over and over again for vocal pitches, the pronunciation, the vocabulary, and every nuance I could intuit. I now know how to take a taxi to the Louvre, how much to tip the driver, where to hang my umbrella and my over-coat, and on the third floor by the north-east archway how far to the left to move the potted fern in order to discover the stolen Egyptian scarab.

French was in full bloom on my side of the bunkhouse. My study program didn't involve Devon, who finds languages easy to pick up. I don't. I have to really study them. I'd never been exposed to a French immersion program in my school, and until Collette came along I'd never taken my French classes all that seriously. I had just memorized the vocabulary and handed in the assigned worksheets. But being able to speak French to Collette the next time we met had become my impossible obsession. I needed French to tell Collette that her skin smelled wonderful, the line of her nose was divine, and I would love her always, throughout my life and into the eternities.

Nineteen
Rethinking Love

S *ometimes life is awful,* then there's a little bit of wonderful thrown in to keep you going, and sometimes it's surprising. What happened to Howie was awful. When Collette came along it had been wonderful for me. But what happened next to Devon was surprising.

A girl who looked just like the temporary courier from my dad's law office, Brooke Walton, came driving up the mountain. Devon thought he was seeing things. He called me on the other side of the slow-down zone to look for a dark green car coming through with a girl that could be Brooke's double. When I saw her, I called him back. "Think she's a twin?" I was just goofing off, but he took it seriously.

"No. It's her. I'm sure of it. Female identical twin births account for only about 3% of all recorded births. Consequently, the likelihood of a striking similarity between two beautiful girls actually indicating twinning is statistically possible, but improbable. Compared to getting struck by lightning, however, which is a one-in-a-million chance in a given year, but dropping to one in ten thousand over an 80-year life-time . . ."

"Shut up, Devon." He was starting to sound like his dad.

"Yeah, okay, so what's the lovely Brooke doing on our mountain?"

When our shift ended we were men on a mission. On foot, a mountain is vast, but in a car, the number of roads is limited. We guessed that Brooke was probably heading for the resort, but Devon's car is so stupid we were probably better off on foot. Wherever we drove it, we had to find a completely flat parking spot since his hand brake hadn't been known to function since the used car lot. In the city it didn't matter much. There were lots of options. But if Devon's car rolled down the mountainside in our absence it might prove awkward. Devon wanted no handicaps in his pursuit of love and beauty.

We stood in front of the resort hotel and watched a few guests straggle in and out. Went inside and lounged around the lobby for half an hour. No Brooke. Our stomachs started a rumble that did not sound like romance and felt worse, so we agreed on an interim activity of a civilized, non-bunkhouse supper at one of the little pubs. We'd be more efficient sleuths on a full stomach.

Our after-supper dispositions took our feet on a complete tour of the resort. After nosing around here and there, we finally spotted a dark form standing on a balcony of the resort hotel. She had one hand on the railing, looking over the valley. But her hair was the dead give-away—long and dark and curly—quite a bit like mine, actually. The wind would have to be blowing a gale to make my hair move and hers was the same way. She was wearing this silvery grey outfit and for a moment I had the impression that she was no more than a shadow on the balcony. We studied the figure quietly for a few minutes until we were sure.

Devon was so excited I thought he was going to levitate on the joy juice his hormones were producing. He called her name a couple of times. Finally she seemed to sort of wake up and waved back. That's when I realized she was truly corporeal. Devon invited her to come down so we could take her for a soda somewhere. In my view Brooke seemed a little preoccupied, a little distant, like part of her wasn't really with us. But Devon didn't see any of that. He was completely blissed-out.

We were sitting at a little round table and Devon was smiling and gazing at Brooke. I decided to get some information out of her to sort of square things up. "Did you know we began a Find Brooke campaign after you disappeared from my dad's law offices?"

"Disappear? But the job was over. I had to leave."

"But we didn't get to celebrate your birthday," Devon objected.

"Birthday?" Brooke looked puzzled. "How would you know about my birthday?"

"Well, everybody has one," Devon said, trying to make her smile. "So we went to find you at the motel. You weren't there. No trace of you."

"Did you get a DNA sample from the pillows and towels?"

Devon didn't hear the joke and soberly answered, "No, I didn't think of that." Then he looked at her face and realized she was teasing him. "So where did you go, Brooke?"

"To visit some long lost relatives."

"Sounds mysterious," I said.

"Do you enjoy mystery?"

Devon said, "Only yours."

But I answered silently, *No, I don't like mystery. I want facts.*

Devon and I had the early shift, so we didn't have much time to visit with her that night, but Devon got her to promise to a hiking date the next day.

When we woke up the next morning, the world was new. We made stupid jokes, and goofed around like we'd never grieved a second in our lives. I said, "If you fall off the mountain like that tree over there, you'll never see her again."

Devon gave me a shove and said, "Keep your eyes on the yellow Hummer! Your name isn't Stanley and flat is not attractive to girls." I shoved him back. But it was all good in the mountain sunshine (until the deer flies came out).

Devon was so in love with Brooke that I expected them to become a tight little couple. Maybe it was listening to them talking together that caused me to realize I'd never really talked to Collette. We had laughed together, we'd flirted, we'd hidden, we'd kissed—yeah, a lot of that—but I didn't have any idea what she liked to do in her free time. I didn't know what her favorite food was, or even her best subject in school. I just knew how I felt when I was near her.

Devon and I had already negotiated our days-off schedule to be the same and when we invited Brooke to be part of our mountain hikes, she arranged her shifts with the restaurant so she could be with us. They asked me to go with them on every hike. After a few weeks of being a three-some, I told Devon that I had plenty to do if he wanted to spend time alone with Brooke. But the weird thing was that Devon still wasn't dying to be alone with her. So I asked him what was going on.

We were walking back from a shift on a rough section of road where that pine tree was half falling off the side of the mountain, and he said, "Remember when I punched Allen Mac at chess club? Well, that night my dad recognized the kind of abrasions on my hands as being the marks of a fistfight. Asked me what it was about. So I told him how Allen Mac had said Brooke was a hottie and how I had lost it. They'd been working with me about pornography, you know."

"Working with you? How do you work on a topic like that?" I was trying to imagine that kind of a conversation with my parents. It wasn't coming to me.

"We were talking a lot about what to do with troubling thoughts that seem to come out of nowhere."

"What do you do with them?" I still had flashes of fury at my dad for how he'd handled certain things in my life that always made me feel kind of sick and stupid. Guess they'd qualify for 'troubling thoughts.'

"When you get hit by an image you don't want, you deliberately substitute another thought. I change what I'm doing. Like, if I'm studying and all of a sudden my mind has gone places I don't want it to go, then I get up and do something physically active. You practically can't avoid pornography. It's everywhere. What I have to do is try not to see it. I know I can recognize it all over the place if I want to, but I'm learning how to see selectively."

"So diversion helps."

"Yeah. Doesn't matter when or why it starts up, I change what I'm doing as drastically as possible, and concentrate on something else."

"Does it work?"

"Mostly. I'm getting better at it. But sometimes the contradictions in our culture make me feel paralyzed. That's what I worry about. Maybe nobody really knows anything. Like, in AP English we read Shakespeare and learned about the purity of true love. Then we went to Witch Hazel Porn's class and learned the base aspects of sex. If ideas don't match up, then one of them isn't true. Right?"

"So you're saying, if love is pure, then sex has to be pure."

"Right. Because if sex is base, then love has to be base. And if you believe that, then the whole world turns putrid."

"So what did your mum and dad say?"

"That I need to build a holding place in my mind, a place where I can store all the ideas that don't match up, the true things that seem to be contradictory, the evidence that doesn't make sense. All the paradoxes and oxymorons. My parents say that sometimes they will get an answer to a dilemma years later."

"What do they do while they're waiting for the answers to turn up?"

"They're not exactly sitting around, Bill."

I thought about this for a few minutes. I guess what his parents were saying is that you have to keep on with life, do what you do every day, and let the contradictions and the stupidities just sit there, since you're not in charge of them anyway. Well, the problem in high school is that cool and stupid aren't very far apart. And half the time they change places. What was stupid ten minutes ago is now very, very cool. What was cool ten minutes ago is now very, very stupid. We started walking toward the bunkhouses. "So, this holding place gives you time?"

"Basically."

The idea of not having to wrestle the universe for immediate answers absorbed all of my brainpower and I stumbled over a root. Nearly fell on top of Devon. "I wish Howie had known how to do it."

"Yeah, me too. Something for the Regrets Tree, eh?"

I didn't need any more regrets. Not after a year like this had been. I had enough regrets to burn up an entire forest.

Devon and I hiked with Brooke nearly every day whether it was sunny, cloudy, or a drenching rain. Throughout the day there is a big temperature difference in the mountains. I love the early morning when the air is cool and wonderful, just enough breeze to stir the smell of the pine trees across the mountainside. Then it's hot and still under the full sun. At last the day mellows into evening with the night breezes carrying a chill across the meadows and streams.

When hiking with a group, the slowest hiker or the person with the shortest stride takes lead position. The three of us were close to the same height and we all turned out to be fairly fit, so we could hike about any speed we chose. Devon liked to keep Brooke between us, so one of us would take a turn leading and the other covering the rear. He told me it was more or less a protective measure and I fell into the pattern because I knew what Devon was trying to do. He had set an interesting task for himself. How to show a girl you love her without putting your hands (or lips) on her. Putting her in the protected middle was one way to show he loved her.

I could feel the love when I was around Devon and Brooke, but it didn't make me want to get away and leave them alone. It included me, surrounded me, so I felt safe within it. Safe enough that Devon and I could talk about everything around her, including Howie. Interesting girl, Brooke. She never asked us for explanations. No questions about what happened to Howie or what we were talking about. She just listened closely until she pretty much had the gist of the story.

On one of our hikes we were scrambling up some loose shale to where we saw the little rock pikas sunning themselves. They'd whistle their alarm to each other and dive for their burrow entrances if we came too close. I can see why the bears love to catch them. It would be kind of a fun game. The three of us had to think green really hard in order to resist trying our own luck at catching rock pikas. We sat down on the sharp broken edges of the grey-blue shale and sort of wiggled our butts until we had enough of a dish to relax in. We pulled off our visors and leaned back on the rocky outcropping, our faces to the sun, curious pikas popping up from their holes all around us, and basked in the heat for a little while. I hoped one would pop up close enough to me that I could see into his little eyes, sort of get to know him up-close and personal. Dumb idea, I know. But with the warm sun in my face and the gentleness of the love all around, I felt peace in my bones.

Devon said slowly in the drowsiness of the warmth, "I need to see Howie again before I go to England."

"Me, too."

"I wonder if he's gotten any better."

"They said there wasn't any chance he would."

"Yeah, but the hope is killin' me."

"Me, too."

We were both silent, deep into memories of Howie. And Brooke didn't butt in, a thing I really admire about that girl. She let Devon and me take our minds anywhere we needed to go, didn't ever try to control how we were thinking. Having her around felt good.

"It's nice to know he won't have to live in a body like that forever."

I knew Devon was talking about our belief in an after-life with a perfect body free from pain. "But the rest of his earth life seems like a long jail sentence."

"Maybe it doesn't seem that way to him."

"How wouldn't it?"

"If his mind doesn't register his reality, then he wouldn't be in any psychic pain. Right?"

I was working with the concept and didn't respond.

"I want to know if that's true for him before I leave for England."

"Me, too." I was starting to feel the rocks pressing into my back and got up. Brooke stuck out her hand and I gave her a pull, and then she pulled up Devon. I wonder sometimes if the rhythm we had established amongst ourselves was part of the peace I felt up there at nine thousand feet. The harmony in our bodies tuned by the same pulse beat connecting our minds, all the gaps filled with hope and love.

One night when Devon's mother called, she told him that Howie's parents were divorcing. No surprise. Word was they'd sold the house. She was going her way. He was going his. The neighborhood would see moving vans in front of the house any day.

What if they'd done it last year instead? Given Howie . . . what? What would their divorcing have given Howie? My thoughts weren't coming together on this, but my mind wouldn't turn off. What if they'd done it five years ago instead of having affairs? What if they'd married somebody else in the first place? What if? What if? What if? All the useless what ifs!

Sitting on our bunks, Devon and I wrote letters to Mr. and Mrs. Bessamer, a separate copy from each of us to each of them. Mine said,

> *Dear Mrs. Bessamer:*
>
> *As you know, I have been best friends with Howie since I moved to the neighborhood eight years ago. I admired Howie for being smart and loyal. I wanted to be his friend because we played chess together — he was brilliant — and because we did homework together — he was brilliant — and especially because he was different from the other kids. Howie was honest. Howie didn't make up ways to be that were false. I will miss Howie the rest of my life and I will honor him in my heart. Maybe nobody knows what Howie's needs are yet, maybe nobody will ever know what's in his heart now, but if he could talk, I know he'd say,* Please let Bill and Devon visit me. *I know he would, Mrs. Bessamer. Please change the orders and let us visit him sometimes.*
>
> *Sincerely,*
>
> *William Walker, Jr.*

Devon's letter was even better. He can use words to charm away the savage in the hardest of hearts. We mailed the letters a few days apart so maybe the Bessamers wouldn't throw them away in a bunch, like junk mail. Maybe one of the four letters would get through to one of them.

It's been weeks since we mailed the last one and we haven't heard a word back. Did we expect to? Yes! Because there's no point in keeping us from seeing Howie. Even if he does have to wear a diaper for the rest of his life, it doesn't mean he won't be our friend for the rest of his life. Longer. The part of the soul that's eternal will find friendship and love into eternities. That's what I told Howie over and over again! Was that what he was looking for with the rope in his hand?

Longing for a different outcome, one that was easy to imagine, is a peculiarly painful experience. Like how things might have been if Howie had taken a job on the road crew this summer, or if my Grandma Miriam's mind had stayed whole. And Collette. Beautiful Collette that I had loved. I knew I couldn't dwell on any of this grief or I'd start to sink. Feeling the love between Devon and Brooke had more than a recreational aspect to it. I could feel myself healing when I was with them.

Twenty
Fire on the Mountain

*O**ne morning Devon announced*** he was thinking of something extra he could do to show Brooke how he felt about her. He wanted to say good-bye to her in a way she'd always remember.

"So, you're finally telling me you need some time alone with Brooke."

"No, I want you there because you've always been part of my relationship with Brooke. But I want just enough actual time alone with her to . . ."

"To what?"

"I can feel inside me how I want it to be. But I can't see what to do to get there, yet."

I didn't know how to make a useful suggestion based on that kind of a description, so I told him I'd take whatever signals he gave me. We were on different shifts that day, so he nodded and loped out the door.

The day of the hike Devon left the bunkhouse hours before we planned on meeting Brooke. He hadn't told me any of his plans, so I rolled over and turned on one of my French stories. Before he returned, I had learned how to rent a car, chase burglars from Paris to The Hague, and properly order a light lunch.

"So am I your mule for the occasion?" I asked him when he got back. Really, I wouldn't have minded hauling up the mountain whatever supplies Devon had ordered for the good-bye hike. I expected him to have a forty-pound pack on his back, but not so. Devon showered quickly and we both legged it over to the chalet.

Without packs, the three of us seemed to drift up the mountain on the up-drafts. We began in the crisp air of early morning, the sun shining between light clouds. We were friends hiking together for what our heads knew was the last time, but what our hearts understood to be an unbroken continuum of connection. I don't know how else to say it, except that everything felt perfect. Like the only measurable calamity in creation would be to never have another day exactly like that one. I had a glimpse of a new kind of adulthood, then, a way of continuing the lightness inside of me as I grew older that I hadn't imagined possible. Maybe joining the adult world was not the good-byes, one by one, as I had thought.

Devon told us our destination was Flower Point, which had been our first hike together and was one of the shorter on the mountain. There had been no flowers there when we first hiked it, just snow banks, black-edged and icy. But today was far different. I looked across a meadow thick with flowers, the purple-dark mountains rising layer upon layer, the hues ranging through a veritable rainbow, the bees buzzing in a frenzy. We sat down under a lone pine tree near the over-look and felt the timelessness of being young. The valley before us was steep and green, the mountains in the distance unclimbed and terrible. We wanted nothing more, nothing better. We felt the joy of being alive, of existing. We were at the top of a mountain world we'd come to love.

After a while, Brooke said, "Have you ever played Fortunately/ Unfortunately?"

I knew the game because my sisters used to make me play it with them on family road trips. I hated taking the Unfortunately turn where everything had to crumble into a disaster. Howie, on the other hand, was a genius of Unfortunately. Once when he was along on a family trip to the lake house and my sisters discovered that his Unfortunately events were spectacular, they tried to rig the story by changing seats so that he got all the Unfortunately turns.

Today the sun soaked away all my will and all my ideas. I was gazing at the world from the top of a mountain on a perfect day with my two best friends. How many times would that happen in one lifetime?

Brooke began rather biographically, "One day there were three friends out hiking in the mountains. The day was glorious. The sun was shining, flowers blooming everywhere, in nooks and crannies of rocks, in the lush Alpine meadow. They sat down in a meadow near a tall pine tree on the edge of a cliff and dreamed of unchanging beauty surrounding them all of their lives. Unfortunately . . ." She drew out the last word and turned to Devon. "Okay, your turn. You get to think of an unfortunate event that happens to them."

Devon was the master of fantasy disaster, and invented a segment ending in a huge rainstorm complete with wind and lightning. "Fortunately . . ." and Devon drew out the last word, turning to me with a grin.

I squinted back at him in disbelief. Usually I like fixing things, makes me feel good. But he hands me a lightning strike and I'm supposed to turn it into a fortunate event? Okay, I could do this. "Fortunately," I began lazily, "when the lightning bolt struck the near-by tree, the friends were not electrocuted as you might expect.

Curiously, had the friends known it—and not even the forest service had any notion of it—the tree, standing on the brink of the chasm as it did, had absorbed every sad or bad deed of every hiker who had sat beneath it. The friends quickly scooted away from this remarkable tree, now smoldering on the edge of a cliff, and watched in awe as the immense pine gradually transformed into a vast blazing torch. The friends stepped back and back, further and further, as the fire whipped up tremendous gusts of wind, fanning the flames higher and higher. Beauty and terror combined to rid the mountaintop of evil. Unfortunately . . ." and I turned to Brooke.

But she was taking big gasping breaths, her chin to the sky, and trying to drop her shoulders. The girl was trying her hardest not to cry.

Devon laid his arm across her shoulders. "Tell me about it, Brooke."

"That's a Regrets Tree. My uncle told me about the Regrets Tree his family burned at the New Year, that's all."

I was truly surprised. I don't know where I got the idea that the Regrets Tree was exclusive to my family.

Devon gently encircled her shoulders with his arm. "You miss him, don't you?"

She nodded vigorously, but didn't say anything more.

"Fortunately for them all . . . ," he proclaimed with a flourish. Then he scrambled to his feet, rustled in the near-by bushes, and extracted a large backpack. He presented it to Brooke as though it contained the entire wealth of his kingdom, which it probably did, come to think of it. Brooke lifted out each item deliberately, delighted with each new treat. I don't know how Devon charmed that kind of a lunch out of the bunkhouse cook, but it was first-class.

When we'd eaten every last crumb, Devon shook out the tablecloth and rolled it up to make a little pillow for Brooke's neck in the shade of the intact pine tree, still standing in its pristine glory near the edge of the cliff. I assumed they would want to talk privately, so I said I was going to pick some daisies. Devon and I had arranged the term with Brooke on the first hike we ever took together as meaning a private pee-break, and we had all used it since then, as necessary. So, I took myself off, found another flat place on the other side of a rocky out-cropping, and laid down to doze.

When I asked Devon afterward what he said to Brooke, he just smiled. It looked like he wasn't going to tell me. I wanted to know so bad I was seriously thinking of beating it out of him. "So, did you kiss her, man?"

"Once. At the end."

"Why only once?"

"Because I wanted her to think about the kiss for the whole time we were alone."

"Did she?"

"Yes."

"How do you know?"

"I watched her." He smiled at me. "I could see she was imagining how it would taste."

"Oh, you could not."

"No, it's true. I swear, William Walker the Second, if I had kissed her right away and kept on kissing her non-stop like I wanted to, I know that when I got finished I would have felt frustrated and cloyed."

"Cloyed?"

"You know, like Keats."

"No, I don't know."

"We read 'Ode on a Grecian Urn' in AP English last year. Weren't you paying attention?"

"Maybe not to the same things you did. Don't patronize me. I got an A in English, too, you know."

"Keats talks about how the dancers carved on the urn are always yearning for the delights of their lovers, but never attain them. That means they don't ever have to feel their hearts *high sorrowful and cloyed* with the excess of passion." Devon seems to have an inside gauge to the female heart, so I was paying attention. "See?" he said, "That's one of the best reasons I know of to listen in English class. You get all kinds of information about how to romance a girl."

"Okay, okay. What else did you do?"

"I told her what I liked about her."

"What did you say?"

"Same stuff we say about her . . . only I said it way nicer."

"Poetry by Devon."

"Pretty much," he said, and punched me on the arm.

I punched him back and that was the end of it. He must have gotten it right, though, because the next time Brooke was with us, she looked at him constantly. It was like they were memorizing each other, every move, every word, every smile.

That story about the tree torch on the mountaintop had reminded me of one more necessary good-bye for Devon before he left for England. It didn't really involve Brooke, but I wouldn't mind if she was there. I found a little piece of dried-out down-wood, stuck it in a #10 can from the trash barrel, and there it was—the ugliest Regrets Tree you ever saw.

I had it all set up after Devon's last shift on the mountain. The three of us sat down on the battered old picnic table where I had laid out slips of white paper, pieces of string, and pens. I wrote three regrets.

1. *I regret not adopting Howie and protecting him 24/7. I know I could have talked my parents into it.*

2. *I regret not talking to Collette so that I knew what she was thinking.*

3. *I regret my anger at my parents. They deserved it, but it was stupid and useless.*

Brooke wrote about eighteen regrets, but Devon could only think of one. When Brooke and I teased him about it, he said he'd write the same one half a dozen times if it would make us feel any better. Devon and I offered to help Brooke hang hers, but she thought we'd cheat and read them (which was probably true), so she didn't let us.

When the regrets were hung, I said, "Devon, you have offered me the entire sum of your life savings every year for the last six years if I'd let you light the Regrets Tree." I explained to Brooke, "I always refused because I knew there was no money in his account." She laughed, and I went on. "But tonight, Devon, you may have the honor of lighting the Regrets Tree. You may ask *why?* I will tell you. Any man who has only one regret is either as sensitive as an anvil, or else he's the best person I've ever known. Which is it, Brooke?"

She turned to Devon with mock solemnity. "You are the prince of sweet, the best person Bill and I have ever known." Devon started to tickle her and she tried to get him back. I loved hearing them both laugh.

"The moment for fire has come," I intoned, handing Devon a book of matches I'd 'borrowed' from the pub on top of the mountain.

"Stand back and prepare to be amazed," he said, and then had to strike practically the whole book of matches before he could get enough of them to light in order to actually burn up the tree.

We stood together, Brooke in the middle, and watched the flames rise, the smoke ascending. All our regrets drifting away on the night breeze.

Twenty-one
Protection for Sale

he day Devon left the summer job as a flagger, I drove down the mountain with him because we had an appointment with Officer Patron. We wanted him to tell us that school would be safe for students in the fall (even though both of us would be in London), that no one would be forced to buy personal security, that Supreme Maelstrom's Internet business was finished. Finally and absolutely. Case closed.

Officer Patron greeted us, "How are things on the mountain?"

"Good, thanks. How are things with Supreme Maelstrom?" I said, getting straight to the point. Devon would have started the conversation in a more neutral place, but I didn't want to waste one second on chitchat.

"We're doing our best to combat the recruitment on a local level." Officer Patron was shuffling papers and avoiding eye contact. Something about it brought out my prosecuting attorney genes and I said, "Officer Patron, describe the money trail. Tell us who is behind the extortion ring."

He stood up and walked to the window. Brusquely answered a phone call. Sat down. Went to the window again. Devon and I waited, silent. The tension in the room was claustrophobic. Finally Officer Patron said, "I need a coffee. Come on," and we followed him out of the police station. I thought maybe the walk would get him talking, but after a couple of blocks he still hadn't said anything. I knew we weren't heading to a coffee shop.

Finally Devon said, "Officer Patron, my family is moving to London in a few days, so I'll be out of the situation. But before I leave, I want to know that my friends are going to be safe. What can you tell us?"

"That's just it. You're not going to be out of the situation."

"That's London, England, Sir."

"And this is Supreme Maelstrom, Devon," he snapped back, mimicking what he took to be Devon's patronizing tone.

Devon and I glanced at each other in surprise. Officer Patron kept on walking, but I felt like something had changed inside him, as though he had startled himself by showing us that much anger. Devon let the sarcasm pass. "Are you telling us that Supreme Maelstrom's reach is international?"

Officer Patron stopped on the street and looked hard at each of us. Deciding, I guess. "Yes, I am. This has turned into a high priority case, boys. If you, or anybody you know, runs to the press, we could have an even worse stinking mess on our hands. You have to keep what I say to your selves. Can you do it?" His voice was so harsh that for a minute I couldn't think what to say. "Do I have your word I'm not going to see either of you—or your dads or your moms or your cousins or your friends—on the nightly news?"

I was shocked and I guess I must have looked it.

He softened a little. "No, I guess that isn't your style. But I've got to hear you say it. Both of you. I've got to have your word."

We gave it.

"Tell me what you already know," he said, "and I'll fill in what I can."

We told him our theory that *smiling* was a code word for any person who pays for protection, and that Howie had been forced through food restriction and threats of violence to pay for protection at Soldier Ridge Academy. "We think the Nix and the Druj are a cover-up for something bigger. What do you think?" Devon asked.

"Is there some big money behind this?" I asked.

Officer Patron hesitated, so Devon chimed in. "What's the bottom line, here? Who gets rich off it?"

The officer took a deep breath. "Okay, you're right about the Druj and the Nix. They are window-dressing. A mean, nasty operation, but one designed to keep law enforcement busy on the small stuff. They are a vital link, though, in connecting organized crime with social networking."

"Organized crime? The Mafia?"

"Among other syndicates," Officer Patron muttered. "Cyber-bullying has moved into the hands of the old crime families."

I could hardly process what I was hearing. "Since when?"

"Since they figured out that protection is the next big thing if they can bring it down to the little guy. B-Twelve, for example, was a fairly low-level recruit who had started out as a Druj. He had a natural talent for terrorizing high school students. But Howard Bessamer turned out to be braver and more stubborn than most. B-Twelve got the word from higher up the command chain that they intended to make an example of Howie. They used him to test the mettle of any Druj, and offered a sizable reward for whoever could break him, force him to *smile*, to pay up."

We walked along, slower now, because I was having difficulty breathing. My heart was pounding like I'd been running. Devon was having a hard time with the information, too. "Let me understand what this means," he said. "If organized crime links up with social networking, it will put urban crime on an entirely new level."

Officer Patron nodded. "A little money changes hands up front when a wannabe Nix pays to become a somebody, when a Druj terrorizes a kid and gets paid. But the roots are deep in established crime families. A beat-up high school kid here and there is just a tiny tip of an enormous ice-berg."

I began slowly, feeling my way through what was opening up as a new social order. "So if you make people afraid to go to school, afraid to go to the grocery store, afraid to walk down the street to work, then people will pay whatever they have to for protection."

"You got it. It's a *join the family and your safe* kind of an organization. They want to make protection an accepted part of daily life for the middle and working classes. Taking it down to the common man is how to make it into a universal condition, a way of life. They want to embed it in the culture."

The idea was awful. I began to imagine the ways it would change everything I knew. "So can they deliver? If Howie had paid B-Twelve the money, would he have been safe?"

"Maybe for a while. But the price of protection always goes up. Sometimes every month. Sometimes every week. But always the price goes higher. People end up losing everything they have."

"Holy shit! That could destabilize an entire country," I blurted out.

"Yeah, that's what it looks like," Officer Patron admitted. "The IT detectives think that's the goal."

Devon and I stood there on the sidewalk, stunned, trying to comprehend the massive paradigm shift our world had taken.

"The schools have been alerted in every region of the country where law enforcement has seen activity. We've got plain-clothes officers ready to walk the halls in every high school in the state when school begins this fall, but it means we have to pull forces off the streets to do it. We're debating how to organize the parents to make up in numbers what the police force lacks in manpower. But the problem with that option is the whole thing could go vigilante if it's dropped in the lap of the community."

Officer Patron stood beside us, letting us absorb it all in silence. Finally I muttered, "Fusion of organized crime with social networking . . . selling protection . . . yeah . . . I'm starting to see . . . but it makes me burn."

"I'm not asking you to put out the fires of indignation and outrage, Bill. But burning up the world isn't the way to win this."

Devon shot back, "You got a plan?"

"Give us a try first, boys. Some good people are working on this."

"Last spring you said it was up to high school students to protect each other with kindness." I spit out his former advice with as much heat as I could dredge out of my heart. His words now seemed so useless, so puny, so condescending. I wanted to punch somebody.

Officer Patron looked up into the trees lining the street, the sunshine glinting off the oils in his eyelid creases. Suddenly, he looked about the same age as Allen Mac, not a middle-aged police officer trying to hold together an unraveling world. "I did, Bill. How else do you fight something like this? How else except one person at a time? One person who is willing to make the change. One person who will stop competing for blood and glory. One person who is genuinely kind."

We stood there for a while, not saying anything. Each immersed in the prospects of a fight that would take the rest of our lives. Wordlessly he turned to us and shook our hands goodbye. He walked in the direction of the police station and we watched his back as far as we could see him.

When we got to Devon's house, his dad had left the signed transfer document for me to buy Devon's old junker car on the counter beside the 'fridge. Guess he knew that's the for-sure place we'd find it. I handed him five bucks, the asking price, and signed the document. Told him I'd probably sell the car to Allen Mac at the end of the summer when I left for London. We talked a little about the faulty hand brake and whether or not we could get the engine over the speed of seventy—for passing purposes only, of course—but what we were really thinking about was what came next in our lives.

Devon began telling me about the flat his parents had bought near High Street Kensington. "We can walk to a lot of good stuff right from home! Kensington Palace, a lot of the foreign embassies, Royal Albert Hall, Imperial College, a lot of huge museums. When do you think you'll come?"

"I'll work here for a few more weeks. That way your parents can settle in a bit before I move in on top of the family."

"Have you told your parents, yet?"

I didn't want to even think about that conversation. "No, but I'm going to. Right away."

"Hey, I'll send the school registration links as soon as I get there. Let me know what flight you're coming on."

"Will do." I needed to get back up the mountain before it got pitch dark, so I said, "Hey, no good-byes, man. See you in a few weeks!"

"Next month in London!"

Twenty-two
Hero of Middle School

A couple of days later I was headed out for a hot August afternoon shift in my steel-toed shoes, my hard hat hung with a wet bandana, when I got a text from my dad. Mother and he were thinking of driving up for a night on the mountain, and he asked if they could visit me while they were up there. It seemed strange to be asked. I wrote back that it was fine, of course. But the truth is I didn't feel ready for them.

My parents had called once a week like clockwork. Sometimes I'd answer, but when I didn't they'd leave a short message. I didn't want to hurt my parents, but I needed the space and the distance to re-think the family I'm part of. The best choice for everybody was for me to live with Devon's family in England in the fall and finish high school there. Honestly, I couldn't see myself ever living under the same roof as my parents again. It's like I was on information overload where they were concerned.

I walked outside under the full sun and couldn't even smell the pine trees because the dust was so heavy in the air. Soon the other flagger's line of vehicles was coming through on their way up the mountain. I stood to the side and felt the breeze of the vehicle movement whip into my clothes, dust flying up into my face. I was sweating and sticky. Good. A little red car I'd been seeing lately was idling in the next group. Driver might be about my age. Pretty girl. Wondered what brought her up the mountain all different times of the day. If there was a pattern to it, I hadn't figured it out yet. She always slowed down to take a look at me, which was kind of fun.

One thing that really irritates me is when a vehicle doesn't start slowing down when I first start my hand pumping in the slow-down-to-stop signal. I'm talking about the guy in this enormous yellow Hummer who acts like it's my body that's the stop line. When he's in the front of the line-up, his bumper comes so close to my toes I want to kick it with my steel-toed boots. On the other hand, I wanted to keep this job.

I love making the cars stop. I know it sounds stupid. But when you're a kid on a bike, you know the cars are your enemy, your death warrant. You're nine and you aren't scared of a whole lot except for cars. And thunder. Then you're twelve and you're not scared of thunder, but you know that lightning and cars can kill you in one swipe. Then you're seventeen and you get to stop a whole line of cars by just holding up a little red sign. Way cool.

A few cars immediately began to form a line in front of me again. No yellow Hummer, which was good. About twenty more cars had stopped, which was fairly heavy traffic for that time of day. Must be the sunny weather that had called everybody to the resort at the top of the mountain. Then I saw a sleek sports car pull up at the very end of the pack. Black. Clean lines. Pretty low slung for a mountain road with construction. I thought it might be Italian. Gorgeous car. Somebody who liked wearing his money! Whoever owned it should be plenty worried about driving a car like that onto unpaved sections of a weather-damaged mountain road. The driver would probably be the kind who didn't like waiting in a construction line-up.

I checked with the flagger on the other end, but couldn't let the whole line through. There were just too many cars. I counted them through and, as bad luck would have it, the black sports car was in front position when I had to cut off the flow. The driver might be annoyed, but I was glad for a chance to look the car over. A man was driving it, a woman in the passenger seat, and I hoped he wasn't the kind to be steaming from both ears with the double wait. The car had a glossy finish that I wanted to reach out and stroke. Hardly any dust clung to that polish.

Then he honked at me. My heart started to pound. What did that jerk expect me to do for him? Cars were streaming from the other side and I couldn't stop them to give him special consideration. He honked at me again and I started to get mad. I took a real close look at the driver. See what kind of a jerk I was dealing with.

What?

Dad! Mother! They got a new car! Wow! Picked it out without me. Grrrr! They were smiling at me. Glad to see me. I stepped forward and Dad rolled down his window.

"Hey!" I said. My heart rate was still up there.

"How's it going, Son?"

"Good. Nice car."

"Picked it up last night. Take you for a drive later."

Mother leaned around him to smile and say hello. I guess she hadn't remembered my beard. Her mouth slammed shut in a straight little line right on top of the words, "Hello, Bill."

"Hello, Mother." I was more than pleased the summer had produced a good stand of Walker-male facial hair. "Staying at the chalet tonight?" I asked. Dad nodded and I gave directions he already knew. "Parking lot for the chalet is another mile or two up the road. Top of the mountain."

"If you're going to be off work soon, we'll wait for you," he offered.

"The bunk house is the next right turn." Then I changed my mind. "No, go on up to the hotel and settle in. I'll shower and come up when I'm presentable."

I could hear Mother telling my dad that was the better plan.

It's not so much that my parents would hate the bunkhouse, which they would, as what their visit would do to my bunkmates. If I ever have a lot of money, I'm going to hide it. Nobody is going to know. I'll just go around doing secret good things. A lot of astonished people in my trail. Wouldn't that be just about the most fun thing to do in the world! Even better than being a flagger on a road crew. Almost as good as kissing Collette.

I expected my parents to leave the mountain *bright and early in the morning*, as Dad says. But they found the cool air so lovely and their room so nicely sited, they decided to make it a long weekend. Dad took to long walks in sturdy shoes with a packed lunch and Mother had a stack of magazines, a gallon of high SPF sunscreen, and a pool she never intended to wet her swimsuit in, so I guess they were both content.

Dad asked me to hike with him the first day, but I was very glad to say I had to work. The next day he didn't ask, he just showed up about the time my shift ended. I was hot and dusty and thought a shower was about the only pleasure in life I could count on. But my dad patted his backpack and said the hotel chef had filled it with a gourmet lunch for two. Besides, he'd appreciate it if I'd show him Black Feather Trail.

I knew very well that it had excellent signage, so he didn't need me along. I thought of saying that. In fact, I rolled the unspoken words around in my mouth for a few moments. But honestly, I hate the way I feel when I'm boiling mad at him. The differences between us were still there, but my anger was starting to feel like an edge of poison inside me, so I agreed to go. As we began the hike, I suspected Dad might bring up the topic of Collette, so I silently worked on responses until I felt my resistance was ready. I didn't want to talk about her with him. Ever. But I couldn't exactly tape his mouth shut.

On the way up the mountain Dad told me some of the intricacies of a legal case he was working on. No names, of course, but some of the interpersonal complications that make sorting out the legal issues a morass of ethical dilemmas. I began to see my dad as a lawyer whose work was more important than long-winded briefs and bluster in the courtroom. It was good to see his work through his own eyes.

We ate our lunch sitting on a half-rotten log, the ants going crazy around our feet taking care of the crumbs from our foot-long sandwiches. It was nice to see ants doing the job they were made for. Memories of Devon and Howie welled up inside me, of how we tried to rule the ants of the world with fire. Dad was still talking the ethics of his legal world, but I was thinking the ethics of the tragically handicapped world. What was Howie thinking inside his comatose body?

I had been thinking about Howie so intently that I hadn't noticed that my dad had gone silent as we gnawed on our apples together. All of a sudden the silence made me apprehensive that he was still winding up to the topic of Collette as a lunch-hour discourse. We were at the cookies end of the lunch by the time he got himself sorted out to make the speech he'd been planning. I expected he'd give an over-view of the history of the case, outline the aspects of our disagreement, and give me his summary as to why his point of view was the correct one, the one I should adopt.

I was kind of surprised when he began hesitantly, "About Collette, William . . . uh . . . .." That wasn't a particularly impressive opening for any jury to hear, but I had absolutely no intentions of helping him along. When he realized I wasn't going to try to cut him off, wasn't going to yell at him, wasn't going to walk off, that he had the floor all to himself, he started to more or less pick his way through the mine-field he'd laid down in our relationship. This is what he managed to get out. "You're well out of that one, Son," he said. "She had high maintenance written all over her."

"What does that have to do with anything?"

"It changes everything for a man. What his scope can be."

"Scope of what?" I was feeling my temperature rise.

"What he can hope to accomplish."

"That is based entirely on a man's ability and hard work. I quote your own words on the subject."

"True, but incomplete. The woman a man loves can lower the lid on his potential or open it up wide."

I was angry. This kind of hypothetical criticism wasn't the way to mend our relationship. "You don't even know Collette," I said. "You never even had a conversation with her."

As I left him, I hit my doubled-up fist on the nearest tree as hard as I could. So hard I've had severe bruising and it's been beastly painful to hold my STOP sign using that hand. I gave that tree all I had.

The afternoon before my parents left the resort, a gentle rain fell, clearing the air of construction dust and enabling the pine forest to scent the world afresh. They had invited me to join them for dinner that evening in the chalet restaurant where Brooke worked. I finished out my shift with soaking wet shoulders, and as I stood there in the mountain silence, my thoughts began to burrow into places I didn't want them to go. I remembered the family council in the great room of the lake-house last winter after Grandma Miriam's funeral. I remembered my dad's lawyer voice, his words—how the family didn't have enough money to help Aunt Amy. I thought of the beautiful new car and began to wonder how Dad's finances had turned around that fast. It wasn't too hard to guess how much that new Italian sports car must have cost. And then I started wondering who wanted it so bad. Was it my dad or my mom? As I recalled everything that had happened in my family last winter, a kind of rage began to boil up inside me.

I tried breathing deep and holding my breath while I showered and dressed. When my lungs were ready to burst, I'd squeeze the air out of them and hold my diaphragm muscles tight. Over and over again. Devon's dad said it triggered the parasympathetic nervous system and worked to calm the body. I needed to get my pulse rate down.

The evening air felt fresh and cool with a mist hanging over the tops of the peaks surrounding me as I walked up the mountain to the expensive restaurant. We'd just finished ordering when Mother rubbed her hands over her slender arms a little and my father said, "You need a sweater, Lana. I'll run up and get it."

She took his arm quickly and started to say, "No . . ." but my dad added persuasively, "You stay and visit with your son." He turned to me with a smile. "The mountain air up here is a little brisk for us city folk!"

Mother pressed his arm decisively and said, "No, Marc. You're always so sweet to me, but I'll need to find the little jacket that goes with this dress myself. You stay here and have a nice visit with Bill, dear."

The thought whipped through my brain that neither one of them wanted to have a visit with me. But if that was the case, what were they doing up on the mountain where I worked? Or maybe they'd had a conversation in which each of them had told the other to be sure to have a nice visit with Bill. Whatever.

As Dad reseated himself after helping mother with her chair, I sat straight up in mine. I wanted every inch of summer height—facial hair included—to show in the conversation I had in mind. "Nice car, Dad." I said it with a flat tone so he couldn't pretend it was a compliment.

"It sure is. It's been on my bucket list for a few years, now." He hadn't heard my tone.

"She's a beauty." I studied the dessert menu. "Takes pretty deep pockets, a car like that."

"Sort of a man's dream come true." Maybe in some other context his kind of half-dreamy look out the restaurant window at the mountains would have made me back off. Not tonight.

"Pretty nice tax write-off for the firm."

Suddenly my dad was paying attention. "No, the firm's money wasn't involved in this purchase, Bill."

"I see. So your portfolio had a sudden bulge after these last couple of months, and the family budget quadrupled." I looked across the table to see if he knew where I was going with this. He had his 'bluff the jury' face on, so I let him have it. "Pretty convenient, there, Dad. Say no to the debts of your extended family because, after all, you've got an unfulfilled wish on an imaginary bucket list." He hadn't interrupted me, yet, like I expected, so I sailed on. "Not that there's any urgency. You look pretty healthy to me."

When my dad wants to make a point to a smaller, less knowledgeable person his voice takes on a certain teaching tone. The only time the thought of decking my dad crosses my mind is when he uses it on me. He started with it. "There's one thing you've got to learn, Bill . . . a man has to separate his money. The parts of his life can't cross over. My law practice has its own structure and cash flow. The family accounts are a totally different thing. When one particular account is empty, it would be disaster to grab money from another account and shove it in to stop a leak. Bad financial practice, Son."

"Faulty logic, Dad. Maybe a jury would fall for it, but I know a *non sequitur* when I smell one." Mother was going to reappear any minute. I had to make my point fast. "Your personal bank accounts were far from empty when Aunt Amy needed family money to keep her business going. You could have taken money from our personal family account as a loan to the extended family account. No business connections needed whatsoever."

"There are things here that you don't understand, Bill," he began, but we both stopped when we saw Mother enter the dining room. Everyone saw Mother when she entered a room. She was that kind of a woman, even in middle age.

My dad didn't let on about our conversation and chatted with my mother about this and that, so I didn't have to do anything except eat. And think. My father hadn't used any of his traditional tactics to shut me down. Hadn't raised his voice to try to intimidate me. Hadn't used any swagger or sarcasm. I wish it meant he'd felt a little respect toward my opinions, but it was only his signal that he didn't intend to escalate our differences into warfare in a public place. I tried to decide if this was a relief or a disappointment. But then, if you win against a family member, you've already lost.

When we'd finished our dinner and were waiting for the dessert to arrive, well, Dad and I were—Mother never eats sweets unless it's smooth, dark chocolate—Dad pulled a postcard out of his pocket and handed it to me. "This came in the mail for you a few days ago. We thought we'd hand-deliver it."

The problem with a post card is the totally public aspect. The person who hands it to you already knows what it says, so there's no point in putting it in your pocket and waiting for some privacy to read a private message. Everything's already out there. I saw my name and address on the right hand side and found the signature at the bottom left. Collette. My breathing stopped. I became a little light-headed.

She wrote, *Hey, there. David and I had such a wonderful time on our honeymoon here that we decided to stay on when they offered us jobs. It's gorgeous. So is he. Come and visit when you can. Collette.* There was no return address.

I couldn't look at my parents. They'd have seen way too much in my face and I was close to humiliating myself with tears. I kept my head down. Didn't touch the dessert.

Mother asked me to come up to their suite for a few minutes, to see how pretty the chalet was from inside, so I pushed my emotions down deep inside me and followed my parents up the polished curving stair-case from the dining room to the rooms above. While Dad was rummaging in his camera bag for his night lens, Mother and I were left alone, standing out on the little balcony. She began speaking softly. "Being able to love is the thing, William."

I didn't want to hear her talk about Collette or the New Year's Eve party or any of it, so I didn't respond.

"It's your capacity for love that matters most," she went on. "If it was getting all our decisions right that mattered, life would be one constant misery because we'd all fail all the time."

I'd more or less written off my mother as an unreliable adult, so I had a big pile of reserve to cross to even meet her half-way in this conversation. I couldn't both listen and contribute ideas to it, so I decided to let her carry the burden of wherever she wanted to take it.

"Perfectionism can be a curse, William. It's a terrible taskmaster. It can drive you out of your mind if you don't control it. You have to let it go, sometimes."

What did that have to do with Collette or me? Sounded more like she was trying to explain away her own faults.

Dad appeared, specialty camera assembled, and started to arrange Mother and me into the poses he saw in his mind, underneath the stars and moonlit night. It took Dad about an hour to take all the shots he wanted. Sometimes he'd have us remain motionless for the longest time as he waited for the clouds to shift across the moon. Other times he'd use the tripod, set the timer, and join us in the shot. It was a classic German model that still used film. Dad thinks a digital camera is a toy, fit only for light recreational use.

When he left the balcony to put the camera away, Mother said, "It doesn't help how you feel right now for me to say there are many wonderful girls out there in this wide world. So I won't say it. But I want you to remember this. Being able to love like you loved Collette is the thing. It's the thing every woman wants." Mother turned her face to look me directly in the eyes. "Remember that, William."

I didn't acknowledge what she had said. I was still too raw. But I have remembered it. It's been a bridge between us, actually, but she doesn't know that. Dad walked back outside to join us on the balcony and wrapped his arms around my mother. They both looked out into the moonlit night, their sight line trained at the same angle.

Truthfully, I was having trouble knowing what to say to them. The idea of ridding myself of the problems at home by finishing high school in London with Devon glowed in my mind as hypnotically as the most beautiful Regrets Tree ever.

The night was quiet and my parents were motionless. It would have been the perfect time to explain it all to them, cement my plans to leave home early. I wanted to say exactly what had been on my mind all summer. I anticipated that the satisfaction I'd feel would be as evocative of freedom as the scent of ascending smoke.

I looked at my father against the night sky, holding my mother close and smiling at me. Maybe he couldn't be the hero I had set him up to be in middle school, but for the first time since New Year's Eve day when I met Collette, I relaxed my grip against him and took a very deep breath. And right then, a strange thing happened. As quickly as the impulse to speak my mind came, the words I'd planned to say more or less evaporated off my tongue. This happened again and again. I'd begin to speak, but my mouth didn't work, or something.

After they left the mountain the next day, my bruised hand ached for a couple of weeks. When the purple swelling finally went away, it left behind a field of gross green with a yellow tinge creeping around the edges. But as the bruise has healed, so have I.

That evening on Black Feather Trail, Dad had been telling me about himself. He was warning me against his own biggest mistake. No, not mistake. His own biggest burden. A burden he'd chosen. One he adores. My mother.

Twenty-three
Reality Check

fter Devon left, Brooke and I still hiked together. She's cool and we got along great, but it was just a little anti-climactic for both of us without him. When I'd get back to the bunkhouse I didn't have much to do, so sometimes I'd listen to an old recording of Jacques Brel. It's so retro. Those guys in the bunkhouse would have just croaked if they had known what I was listening to. But the French sound, that flat, knowing kind of growl they use for cabaret music, gets to me. It makes me want to whisper love words to Collette, words I might even be pronouncing correctly. I feel half ridiculous to admit I still thought of Collette this way, that I'd given her a gift of loyalty that I didn't know how to take back. How you think is based a lot on habit, I guess. Most of the time I didn't believe she had really married David. It was just a postcard. Maybe she hadn't even written it.

One day when I fell onto the bottom bunk, I moved my shoulders around trying for a more comfortable position, and realized the itchy place by my neck was mail that I hadn't noticed when I sat down to put my ear buds in. I pulled the letter out from under me and looked it over. A letter with no return address. That's never fair. It means the letter comes from somebody who doesn't want to hear what you have to say in return. I felt cautious before I even opened it.

Mrs. Bessamer. She had scribbled a note at the bottom of the letter I had sent her. *You may visit.*

The news kind of winded me. Then I was flooded with relief and fear at the same time. Relief she had finally done the right thing by Howie. Fear because I didn't know how I'd handle the visit without Devon. I wondered what it had cost her. Had she consulted with Mr. Bessamer about it? What if two divorced people could make different rules about a dependent child in a long-term care facility? I'd have to ask my dad if that was even possible.

I needed to tell Devon. Outside, the day had cooled off, but evening breezes were still only a promise. I entered his number. Nothing happened for way too long and I was beginning to think Devon had his phone turned off. But finally he picked up, and I was so relieved I felt tears in the back of my throat. I know that sounds dorky, but you have to remember Devon knows stuff about me that nobody else does.

"Hey, Devon. It's me, Bill."

"Hey."

"So how's it going?"

"How should I know?"

"What?"

"You crock-witted scramble-brained fettercock. It's 2 AM in London."

"Sorry."

"What's up? Better be important."

"Mrs. Bessamer gave permission to visit Howie."

"This is good, Bill. When are you going?"

"In a couple of days."

"Tell him *hi* for me."

"Okay, I will. Devon . . ." I began slowly. I'd never told him about the postcard from Collette. I'm not sure why, exactly. Maybe it was because I didn't want to let go of my French studies and all my love of her. "Devon?" I started again.

"Yeah, I'm still me," he said.

"I got a postcard from Collette."

"And?"

I read it to him.

"Well, if there's no return address, how does she expect you to come and visit her?"

"And what would she do with David while I was there?"

"Sleep with him, you fuzzy-eared horn-swogger."

That hurt. "Do you think they're really married?"

"Well, traditionally a honeymoon comes after the wedding, so I'd say yes."

"Maybe not. It could mean they're just living together for a while."

"Same difference."

"No, it's not."

"Yes, it is. She's in his bed, not yours, Walker!"

"Hey!"

"I don't know what's in your head, Bill, but we can't call it brains."

I didn't want to hear that from my best friend. "Devon, listen to me. You've got to understand how it is for me. Ever since I saw her with snow and sunshine on her skin, laughing, with all the little cousins running after her, her hair flying all around her head, I've loved her, Devon. How do you stop loving somebody because she does something stupid like eloping?"

"She sure was pretty. But she sure wasn't laughing."

"What do you mean?"

"I don't know what kind of a fantasy you've got going there, Walker, but Collette was not the laughing type. Especially not around a bunch of little kids."

I could feel the anger starting to flame my neck. "Yes, she was. She was an excellent nanny."

"C'mon, Bill. I saw her running in the backyard from upstairs in the lake house. I had check-mated Allen Mac for the sixth time in ten minutes that morning, and you and Howie were locked in one of those slow, silent-death matches where neither one of you had the grace to say *okay, it's your turn to win*, so we were looking at taking out Social Security for you by the end of the match, and . . ."

"Stay on the subject."

"Right . . . ah . . . chess, Howie, Allen, small window, ah . . ." Devon sorted backward in his sleep-deprived brain.

"Collette, you frog-breathed spotted eel-face!"

"Good insult, there, Bill. Yeah, Collette was running away from all the kids she was supposed to be tutoring. She was crying out by the tree."

"That's absurd."

"That's the truth, Bill."

"If you think she was crying and I think she was laughing, how are you going to prove me wrong?"

"Go get your picture of her."

"It's in the bunk house."

"Get it!"

"Okay, okay. Hold on a minute." I slipped into the bunkhouse, retrieved the photo from the big Larousse dictionary, and was outside before any of my bunk mates could burp and say, "Hey, it's you."

"Are you still there?" Devon sounded impatient.

"I've got it."

"Look at it real careful, you tootle-brained kidney bean."

"Okay, okay, okay, I'm looking at it. There's sunshine coming from behind her through the snow shower."

"Extraordinary lighting, yes. Which is why your aunt raced out and took the picture. And what else?"

"Nothing else."

"I'm going to leap across the Atlantic and paste you in your stupid face."

"Some of the snowflakes are sparkling on her face."

"Either that or tears. Right?"

I couldn't speak. Melting snowflakes or tears streaking down her cheeks? Which was it, anyway? How could I tell, even with this picture in my hand?

Devon was intrepid. "The reason I know those were tears, Bill, is because I asked her. While you guys were locked in your chess match, I went outside to meet her. I asked her why she was crying. She said she had just broken up with her boyfriend, she hated the cold, and she was going to go crazy if she had to spend one more minute with people under the age of sixteen who expected her to teach them French."

This new way of looking at things had me paralyzed. There was a long, expensive silence as I moved the picture around to catch the light in various ways.

"Well?" Devon was relentless when he had a point to prove.

"I'm looking straight at the picture in my hand, you snoggle-faced root hog."

"Getting inventive. Good for you." Devon waited for me to say something more, but it was like my brain was going half speed. I had to check out so many details of my memories against the new facts surrounding this photograph that I felt like my brain had short-circuited.

"If it was daylight I'd be pleased to hold this phone to my ear and let you use up your flagger wages on dead air while you restructure your past love life. But it's 2:30 in the morning, Bill. Good night."

"'Night."

"Are you okay?"

"Yeah, basically." I hung up. I couldn't sort through my whole relationship with Collette any further than Devon had taken me. Not tonight, anyway. What was real about the girl? I had loved her. That was all. What I had felt was the only bedrock I had purchased with my adoration. And now I knew it wasn't nearly enough.

A few days later I drove down the mountain to take care of some other unfinished business. Howie. He would always be unfinished business. As I entered the Regional Center parking lot I missed Devon like half of me was gone. The front desk clerk recognized me, I think, and called for someone to escort me back to Howie's room. This attendant was experienced and firm, somebody I could talk to without feeling like I was going to crack open and cry. As we walked down the halls, she told me about the tests they'd done on Howie. Recently they had tracked eye movement to check for mental acuity. She wanted me to know that Howie was still a thinking person inside his body. Tests showed he was as smart as ever and heard everything that was said. He simply had no way to respond to the world except through eye movements.

I guess I must have looked as disbelieving as I felt, because she said, "Guess we'll just have to let Howie prove it to you."

When we got to the room, he was lying in exactly the same position as the last time I'd seen him months ago, cramped limbs and immobile face. But his eyes were alive. I went up to the bed and put my hand on his shoulder. "Howie, it's great to see you again. There's not a day goes by when I don't think of you. I want you to know that."

Maybe the attendant thought I was coming on too heavy, because she intervened. "Howie, would you like to play a game with Bill?"

I involuntarily started, then glanced from her to Howie. I watched him look straight at her and blink twice.

"I thought you would. Okay, Bill, you're on! Let's get you boys hooked up."

With the sweep of his eyes Howie dragged open a game menu. When I saw the title, Chess, I admit I felt a moment of awkwardness. How can you feel good beating the heck out of a guy whose biggest effect on the world is through the blinking of his eyelids?

I got over it fast. Within three moves he had me in check and I had to scramble from then on to merely stay alive—no semblance of strategy on my end. Compared to Howie's game, I'd lost all my instincts for aggressive play. I did my best, but he beat me in three minutes.

All of this was completely outside of my expectations. I guess I had thought he would still be lying on the bed more or less comatose, that I would stand at his bedside for ten minutes self-consciously stuttering *I still care about you* kinds of things, and then would guiltily haul my healthy body out of the facility and back to my productive life. When I left, I didn't feel guilty about who I was, just lonesome for the way Howie had been. I felt a general sadness flood over me about the limitations that happen to us all. My parents, me, everyone has them. One way or another.

After a little while, though, that idea seemed wrong. Limitations aren't equal. Some show more than others, and some are infinitely more wrenching than others. I felt that ugly feeling of burning outrage creeping up on me.

I phoned Devon and told him about my visit with Howie. This is what he said, "That's brilliant. He's going to have a real life now."

I was stunned. "What do you mean, *a real life*? Trapped in a non-responsive body? If that happened to me, I'd rather be dead."

"I wouldn't. Any life is better than no life."

"That is so absolutely not true." Devon's cheerfulness grated on me.

"Howie's out of pain, he has friends, he's secure in who he is and where he is. What's so bad about that?"

Sometimes I wish Devon were right next to me so I could punch him. "You have no evidence any of that is true."

"You have no evidence that it isn't."

I pulled my strong feelings back inside and said, "Okay, Devon, I'll think about it, but right now it seems like you're pouring syrup down the drain."

Before he said good-bye he made me go over our pact from last spring. No matter what bad happens to us, we will never, never, never, make the same choice Howie did.

Twenty-four
The Rule of Three

My last day of work this summer, an early morning shift. I can't see the sun yet, but the glaciers and the wisps of cloud above them show pink from its rising, the promise that it's coming. I guess you could say that summer on the mountain with a stop sign in my hand, has helped me put my life into perspective.

I still grieve for Collette and Howie and my grandma. Always will. But you can live with grief. You can't live with anger—it eats you up. But giving up the anger costs me. I'm never quite sure of the ballast I have on hand, which means I have to re-think the weights and balances of a lot of things. That's hard. I wonder if this is what Devon had to go through when he was struggling to get rid of pornographic thoughts. Maybe I'll ask him this fall.

He called a few days ago, sounded a little lonesome. I tell him not to do anything exciting without me. He tells me I'm too late. The first thing he did when he got to England was go to the Tower of London to see all the old guns and swords and armor. In a couple of days I get a post card with a picture of Henry VIII's armor and a note on the back that says, *You think I had a fixation with the P.S. part of a man's life? Look at this dude! A battering ram. He didn't know when to quit and he wanted everybody in both armies to know about it!*

I text him back, *Do you think Witch Hazel Porn knows about Henry VIII? Try asking her!*

No way!

Chicken!

How are you doing over there with all those alluring accents? British girls, Irish girls, Scottish girls, and Welsh girls.

Looking at their pretty faces and wishing one was Brooke.

His parents do a lot of cultural things with the family, and after they all went to the Globe Theatre to see a play by Shakespeare, Devon phoned to tell me about it. They saw, would you believe it, *Romeo & Juliet*. He described the sword fight scenes as encompassing the entire theatre, the actors running through the groundlings. (Those are the people who have cheap, standing-room-only tickets right in front of the stage.) The fight scenes were acrobatic sometimes and dance-like at other times, totally energized. He wanted to be up there doing it with them. He'd have joined Mercutio's gang in a heartbeat. A couple of times he thought the audience was going to get skewered like a bunch of bulgy kabobs. Tybalt was completely charismatic despite being this cold and calculating feline character—everything Romeo wasn't. "Juliet was the most beautiful, delicate little thing I've ever seen. I'm in love . . ."

"Unrequited love isn't all that healthy," I said, trying not to see Collette's face.

" . . . in love with Brooke!"

"What do you hear from her?"

"Good stuff."

I think Devon's lucky. Or maybe he just did things right with Brooke. I think about that as the sun heats up the mountain air and the cars stack up in front of my stop sign. Too long a wait and tempers start to simmer. I signal them through. Hey, there's that pretty girl in the little red car, the one who has smiled and waved to me all summer. I wonder who she is. I've tried to be professional and courteous because I want to keep my bosses happy with my work. Who knows, I might want to come back next year.

A few weeks ago she held up a sign that said, *HARD HATS ARE FOR SOFT HEADS.* Since then I've smiled and given her the thumbs-up every time she's driven by. Last week I noticed her car was covered in dust from top to bottom with a splatter of mud up the sides a good nine inches. What kind of roads does that girl drive, anyway? On second thought, I guess a diet of Mudd Mountain roads would about do it. So when she was stopped right in front of my sign, I wrote on the front of her car in the dust: *WASH ME!* Yeah, not too original. I'm sure it violates the terms of my contract with the construction company in some way. But, oh, well, I figured she wasn't going to make a complaint about me if she's smiling her face off at me all the time. The next day she had another sign for me: *I'M WEARING A MUDD MOUNTAIN MUD PACK.* I like her sense of humor.

The one regular commuter I still dread seeing drives the yellow Hummer. The first day I was on the job I thought he was going to run me over. He drove right up to my toes and I knew there was nothing to prevent him from going right on over top of me. He kept doing the same fool trick all summer and for a while I figured he was a total dork who didn't know how to drive any better than that. I still dread seeing the yellow Hummer coming toward me, but now I chalk it up to poor eyesight. He needs glasses. He can't judge distances and it has nothing, absolutely nothing, to do with me. That's one lesson that's getting whacked into my head. Things happen all over the place that I can't even imagine much less control. And that includes what friends do. Howie. Collette.

Yesterday I realized I was actually watching for the girl in the little red car, hoping she'd have something to say to me. When I saw her car approaching in the lineup I started to tell myself I didn't care, but then she held up another sign, *MY NAME IS SONYA*. Good. I've wanted to know that. I gave her the thumbs up like I've been doing, but she rolled down her window to talk. I walked over and tried to say, nice and casual-like, but still professional (it's a hard mix), "Hello, Sonya."

"Hey, what's your name?"

I had to think for a moment. Am I Bill or William? And would it make a difference? All of this thinking flashed by and yet I only had time to smile at her before I said, "My name is William."

"Nice to meet you, William."

"You, too." I tried for my most engaging smile, but got the signal to let the cars through then and couldn't take any more time with her. Before I walked out into the middle of the road to make sure the cars pulling up further down realized there was a flagger controlling things up here, I looked straight into her eyes. They were smiling.

I'm nearly finished my last day as a flagger. Not much traffic right now and I don't have anything specific to think about. Whenever that happens my mind starts in with a kind of hunt and peck routine like this: *Thirty-seven minutes left . . . pick up my final paycheck . . . tell Brooke everything's cool . . . throw my bags in my old junker car . . . head on down the mountain . . . Mother will have an agenda, I can count on that . . . but I've got a year coming up that will be free from her agendas . . . haven't shaved off my beard yet . . . I'll let Mother fret about it*

until the day of my flight . . . then I'll startle everybody at breakfast with my
bare face . . . twenty-one minutes left as a flagger . . .

Hey, here comes Sonya's little red car. She slows way down as
she approaches me even though I'm waving hard at her to keep an
even speed so all the cars can get through. She stops smack in front
of me with her window down. What's she doing that for! She hands
me a note. I have to take it even if it doesn't look very professional
for a flagger to be accepting a note from a girl. I can't just let it drop
on the ground for somebody else to pick up and read. I slip it in my
pocket. The car behind her honks, so she guns her motor and takes
off fast in the Go Slow zone. Good grief, Sonya!

The cars have all passed, so I take out the note. Her phone
number. Hey! Sonja has happy eyes and the vivid kind of skin that
makes you think of sunshine and fresh air.

Back in the bunkhouse, I pack up my things. Stuff my duffle with
my clothes and my backpack with my French books and recordings.
I'm about to slide my two Collette artifacts, the postcard and
the picture, into a side pocket, but instead I study them for a few
minutes. The more I look at the message on the postcard, the more
it seems like one of those generic greetings that sometimes come
through the mail at Christmas time from people my family hasn't
seen in a long while. The hand-written *Thinking of you with kind*
regards this Holiday Season kind of sentiment, so general it could be the
printed and sold part of the card. Definitely not the *I was blinded by*
love, you'll live in my memory forever kind of message that describes the
feelings I had toward Collette.

The photograph on the postcard is all about illusion. And the
viewer isn't allowed to invent just any story. The handsome couple
is emerging from a little palm-leaf cabana after a night of ecstasy in
each other's arms, but everybody knows they're only models posed

for the shot. The message of glamour and sex on a warm sandy beach is the story of the postcard. Namable, common, tawdry. A very specific Witch Hazel story to sell.

In contrast, the story of the photograph of Collette is almost too delicate to tell. The sunshine filtering through the falling snow, the glistening on Collette's cheeks, the tears of a displaced, lonely girl. A real girl I had loved in a real moment of time.

As I drive down the mountain, I think about Howie sitting at our kitchen table teaching Lanny about the Rule of Three. I have three co-ordinates for my perspective on Howie. I know the dimensions according to the regional center attendant and Devon, and now Mrs. Bessamer. Maybe I'll be able to come to an accurate evaluation of my own pretty soon.

I've also been given three perspectives on Collette—my mother's and father's to begin with, and now that I have Devon's, maybe I have enough information to assess the dilemma of Collette, and make an accurate fourth measurement of who she is in my life. I slip both pictures into the side pocket and zip it shut. I might not need to look at either one of them again for a long time.

One perspective I don't have yet is about my dad. But I'm pretty sure what will give it to me. A one-way ticket to London. Distance. Time and distance should do it. I have my summer wages in the bank. I'm set. Tomorrow I'll buy the ticket and tell my parents. I can't imagine going back to the same high school without Devon and Howie. I can't imagine having to live with the fear of what the Druj could do to me. I need to leave. In so many, many ways.

But here's what happened. On my first day home I get a call from Officer Patron, who wants me to drop by the station for a chat. I don't want to, but it's hard to say no to a cop (and probably not very smart). I finish that call, and immediately Allen Mac phones to let me know the chess club is counting on him and me to do a demonstration match to raise enthusiasm amongst the incoming freshman so they will join the club. I tell him I can't. He starts to yell at me, so I hang up. Grab the keys, and I head off to the police station.

Officer Patron is waiting for me. Says the Druj are targeting an offensive at certain areas of the country, and the police have reason to believe our city is one of them. I tell him that I'm out of all this. I'm leaving for England. Not my problem.

"Who's problem is it, Bill?"

That stops me cold. I sit there trying to think of an answer. I'd give about anything if Devon's fast mouth could answer for me. Finally, I say, "Let me talk to my dad about this, okay?" And that gets me out of the frying pan. The fire's waiting at home, of course, but I have no intention of talking to him about it.

That night I hear my mother ringing this little silver bell she has. Dinnertime. The thought of food makes me sick. I don't leave my room. A few minutes later when Lanny comes charging down the stairs, I tell her I'm not hungry. Go ahead without me.

An hour later, I can hear footsteps coming. Hope it isn't Lanny again. She can be so annoying. There's a knock on my door and my dad's standing there. He sits down in a chair and says, "So what's going on, Bill?"

No words will come. The enemy is out there and has flattened Howie. I open my mouth a few times, trying to frame what I feel, but I have no words for any of it. My dad doesn't say anything more, but he doesn't leave either.

We sit in my bedroom a long time. Finally, I start sneaking looks at him. I know it sounds weird, but in the time he's been sitting here in the dusk of my bedroom, it occurs to me that I need an ally. What if he's my best option? Sure isn't going to be Allen Mac.

He sits there staring at the floor. I wonder what's going on in his head. An idea startles me. What if my dad thinks of himself as my champion? I mean, why else is he still sitting there? And then another idea captures my pitiful brain. What if my dad and I could figure out an approach from both sides of the chasm? Seems like a wild notion at first. I think about it until the idea seems a little tamer. Sort of massage it from my left brain to my right brain and back.

I can feel the telling roll up out of my belly toward my tongue. That desperate need to be known.

And then I tell him. All of it.

I expect him to bluster and fume, but he is grave and mostly silent. He doesn't pretend to have the answers, and in one way that's a relief. But his silence is also the realization of my worst fears. A world without answers is not a safe place. Is it possible to create a large enough holding bin in my mind to contain all of my unanswered questions?

Suddenly I have the strangest sensation. It's like a wash of warmth throughout my body. Compared to the fear I felt when I was telling my dad about this terrible, dangerous world we have to live in, this feeling is a deep calm. I wish I could stay like this always.

The feeling only lasted a few minutes. But I know it was real, the calm I felt. And then the understanding came to me that I would be living at home for one last year. Important things need to happen in my family.

I slept well during the night, and I'm just barely awake when I pick up this text from Devon's mum. She asks when my flight is and says they are willing to adopt me to get Devon off their hands. They didn't know what a pest he was until I was no longer around.

I realize I'm late in doing some important communicating, so I send Devon a text. *I can't believe I'm going to say this, but I need to stay here for school. Sorry. I've got to work things out with my dad.*

He wrote back, *What's up?*

Some things I have to do here.

Half an hour later he said, *Mum is asking if you can come for semester break in the middle of October?*

Sounds fun. I might have to miss some school, but that's okay. Tell her thanks.

Devon fires back, *Tell her yourself.* So I do.

Meanwhile, Allen Mac keeps texting me. He sure doesn't give up easy. He's been on me for a week about this stupid chess demonstration for the incoming freshmen, so finally I cave. I say I'll do it.

It wasn't so bad, I guess, once I got into it. Strange thing, though, my dad showed up. I looked up and there he was, watching me. I was determined to beat Allen Mac, so I nodded in Dad's direction and tried not to feel like the heat was on.

I won. Felt kind of good.

I just took a shower and I'm dressing for one of mother's family dinners. Gotta handle the whole ritual of it just right— make her happy.

There's a knock on my door and my dad steps in. I expect him to say, *Not a bad game, Bill, but you might consider doing this and such next time.* I brace for it and hang up my wet towel. Pull on a clean shirt and start buttoning it. In a few minutes he still hasn't said anything, so next I expect him to say, *Time for supper. Now remember your manners for your mother.* But he doesn't say that either. I pull on my socks and shoes, waiting for whatever is coming. And he's still standing there.

Finally he says, "I love watching you play chess, Bill."

That's all. Nothing more. In the silence I feel the old anger empty out of me. Without it I feel like I'm going to tip over. Into him.

He puts both arms around me and presses me in a wordless embrace I will remember until I'm an old man. For that moment in time there is no ego in either one of us. It feels like our DNA is one strand emerging from the depths, events ancient and new, connecting us in an interminable string of shared knowledge.

Regrets Tree on Fire

Jean Stringam

Re -grets Tree on fire! _____ Re -grets Tree on fire! _____

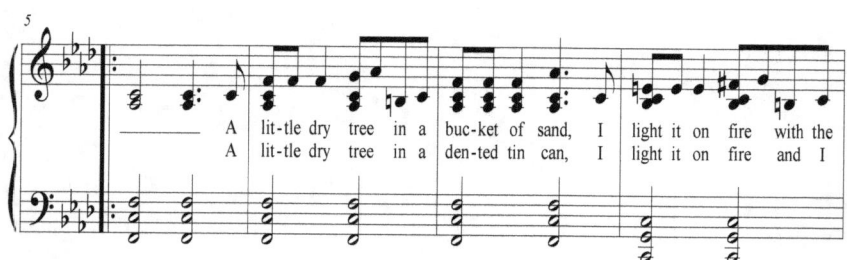

A lit-tle dry tree in a buc-ket of sand, I light it on fire with the
A lit-tle dry tree in a den-ted tin can, I light it on fire and I

stea - di - est hand, Things that I said, ___ things that I did, ___
feel like a man, Some-thing I did, ___ Some-thing I did - n't,

Peo - ple I hurt, _____ times I was curt, ___ All hung on the tree, those
Some - thing I should-'ve, Some-thing I could-'ve, I take my re - grets and

There's no more to say, Re - grets blown a - way! _____ Re-
subito p

grets Tree on fire! _____ Re - grets Tree on fire! _____ Re-
pp _____ *ppp*

grets Tree on fire! _____

About the Author

Jean Stringam has worn many hats, from piano teacher to English professor and from member of SAG to member of SCBWI. Born and raised in Alberta, Canada, she has lived in half a dozen US states, plus England, France, and China.

Her definition of home is wherever the people she loves happen to live. She thinks stories are wonderful because you can live everywhere you can imagine and be anyone you can envision.

You'll love *How Not to Cry in Public & Other Victories*, the next volume in the Cousin Cycle.

Join her in the new holiday series, Christmas Far Away. You'll want to start with *Gathering the Wise Men* for a journey that could have been, should have been, and can't be proven not to have been. Then discover *Beyond the Polar Sea* for an unusual Christmas journey that takes the ancient Greek historians at their word.

Discover the magic of her Calgary Stampede Adventure series. Begin with *Solstice Magic*, then follow the characters to new heights in *Riding on a Wish*.

Available in paper and eBook at Amazon.com, B&N, and your favorite bookseller.

For more information, please go to http://JeanStringam.com.

How Not To Cry In Public & Other Victories

The Cousin Cycle, Book 4

Coming soon in paper, eBook, and audiobook.
Available at Amazon.com and your favorite bookseller.
For exciting updates, see the author's web site at
http://JeanStringam.com.

One
The Tip-list

Brenna called over her shoulder as she walked to the car, "Sorry I can't offer you a ride, Bobbi. We're celebrating." Douglas pulled away from the school and Brenna watched in the rear-view mirror as Bobbi's mother drove up. She was nice, in a limited sort of way, and Brenna had learned loud and clear what the limits were way back in fifth grade.

Douglas had assured her things would change as everyone matured. She wanted to ask Douglas whether maturing meant your perspectives became broader, or if your preconceived opinions just got deeper. But then, it might make him go vague, which she hated.

She needed an alert and attentive Uncle Douglas to hear her brilliant plan for their life.

"Was that a fond farewell with Bobbi on the last day of school?" he asked, with half a smile.

"It appears she's tipped me onto the friend list."

"What does she want?"

"Me to be a counselor at Camp Green Link with her. Ginny's mother won't let her."

"Are you going to?"

"I told her I'd let her know tomorrow."

"How will one more day change your first impression?"

"I thought I should run the plan past my dear Uncle Douglas, since he's so highly opinionated about my life."

"But so accommodating to your every wish."

"Yes, he is. And so handsome and clever that he should have found himself a wife by now."

"Don't start. I'm on my lunch hour. How about Fast Fall on the corner by my office?"

"With the ambience of a pogo stick in a thunder storm."

"But their sushi is good."

"Okay, let's do Fast Fall, but I'll always hate the name. I mean, who in their right mind would choose that name for a restaurant situated in the middle of the financial district of a world capital?"

"Sort of like the title "A Boy Named Sue" for a cowboy tune. Johnny Cash made a fortune on that song and I suspect Fast Fall turns a healthy profit."

"A dangerously uncool name in America's saloons." The song was one of her uncle's favorites from some prehistoric era. Sometimes on a road trip she'd find it on a golden oldies station and he'd always sing along. He was singing it now in a furry baritone, the words drifting away into the air.

"Where did you learn it?"

Maybe it was the gentle breeze wafting around his neck. Maybe it was the liberating effect of the sunshine of May on his face after a long, dark winter in a big city. Maybe it was a way to leap the chasm. Whatever it was, he said, "My dad used to sing it to us."

Every nerve in Brenna's body went on alert. Her uncle would never talk about his family. Ever since she had come to live with Douglas she had questioned, prodded, coerced, cajoled, stormed, sulked, pleaded, and begged—all at varying levels of sophistication depending on whether she was five or fifteen—but as soon as she began, he'd go blank. Vacant. His mind would leave the room. Yet here he was, actually volunteering what his father's favorite song was. Brenna knew she was pressing her luck, but despite the thumping of her heart she managed to ask the next question rather smoothly. "Where did your dad grow up?"

"The West."

Brenna had filed away every bit of information about her relatives ever since the day her mother deposited her on her uncle's door step, a sign around her four-year-old shoulders, a small suitcase on the pavement beside her, and clutching a worn teddy bear in both arms. Today's item might not seem much to a casual observer, but Douglas had just admitted to having a father who had a favorite cowboy song and had sung it to a plural number of children. Of course, that could mean Douglas and his sister, Brenna's mother. But it didn't rule out other siblings, aunts and uncles. Cousins!

Douglas skirted traffic that had double-parked illegally in front of the restaurant. Apparently her uncle's brief lapse into nostalgia was over. "Give it up," she said. "There's never on-street parking at noon. Why not use your reserved stall?"

"What?" he asked absently, but nosed the convertible into the correct lane, as though entering the parking complex was a brand new concept and not an action he did on a daily basis.

Brenna thought this was strange behavior. "Which explains why you were circling the block instead of automatically entering your stall at the bank?" Her uncle was preoccupied, halfway between vague and angry, which was an unusual mix for him. He didn't usually do the angry bit. But she couldn't quite identify what was going on in his middle-aged mind.

His voice hoarse with tension, he said, "As soon as I park in the corporate slot, I have to be the corporate man. I have to think corporate! Eat corporate! Sleep corporate! Die corporate, if they tell me to!" His knuckles whitened with an intense grip on the steering wheel and the big vein bulged in the side of his neck.

Down the elevator and onto the street, Brenna weighed Douglas's anger and wondered at the short transition from singing the dumb cowboy song to being an angry international investment banker. They slid onto stools at the chrome bar and Brenna glanced from wall to wall, checking the iconic photos of freefalling humans: a motorcyclist flinging himself across 14 buses, a lean and long ski jumper in an Olympic uniform, a couple embracing in the free fall before their parachutes opened, and her favorite—a cliff diver from Acapulco at night with a torch in each fist. The décor of the restaurant was engineered to look like various kinds of metal, even if it was really plain old plastic.

Weirdest of all, the music was an eclectic mix of every possible taste in the world. They played European symphonies, golden oldies, indie rock, Broadway tunes, Italian street songs, reggae, Strauss waltzes, gangsta rap, Chinese folk instruments, Native American drumming, hard rock, German lieder, all mixed together. If you stayed long enough, you got an earful of every cultural group in the world. It was dislocating.

Brenna studied the menu hand-written on white boards between the over-sized photos and grumbled, "It's impossible to position yourself with any accuracy in this place."

"How does anybody figure out how to position himself in this world? We're all inaccurate all of the time."

"But you know exactly where you are at a burger store, or at the bagel stand, or at a fish and chip shop. At Free Fall you don't even know what country you're in because the music is in 41 languages. The menu changes absolutely every day, so you can't come in and order *the usual*. Nothing is ever usual here."

They sat in silence, as they tasted their crab bisque. "The photos are meant to be so enticing," Brenna went on. "Like jumping out of a plane into a free fall toward earth at 120 mph is something we all want to do."

"But you don't?" Douglas asked.

"I object that I'm supposed to want to when I walk in here. The truth of a free fall is smashed bones and a brain turned to jelly."

"Only if your parachute doesn't open."

"That's my point."

"Maybe Free Fall is a metaphoric reminder to the banking district to protect the hopes of all people everywhere."

"Does anybody but you get it?"

"Well, I am quite remarkable," he said, and laughed dismissively.

"I'm trying to wrap my mind around a banking district sensitive to metaphor."

"We're immersed in irony all day long. Why not salt it with a little metaphor?"

Douglas ate his lunch with the same intensity he would have used on the corporate earnings statement and Brenna decided now might not be the best time to open up a whole new set of plans. She liked meeting him for lunch at any place he suggested, even the Free Fall. They didn't ever do a lot of chitchat, so his silence over lunch evoked no sense of foreboding.